SAVE BUDDY HOLLY
BLUE DAYS BLACK NIGHTS

TRAGEDY IN IOWA

INFORMATION · WORLD · BUSINESS · FINANCE · LIFESTYLE · TRAVEL · SPORT

Plane Crash Kills 3 Rock 'n' Roll Idols

3rd Feb 1959, Buddy Holly, J.P. Richardson (a.k.a The Big Bopper), and Ritchie Valens, die in a plane crash shortly after takeoff from Clear Lake, Iowa. They had been traveling across the Midwest on their "Winter Dance Party" tour.

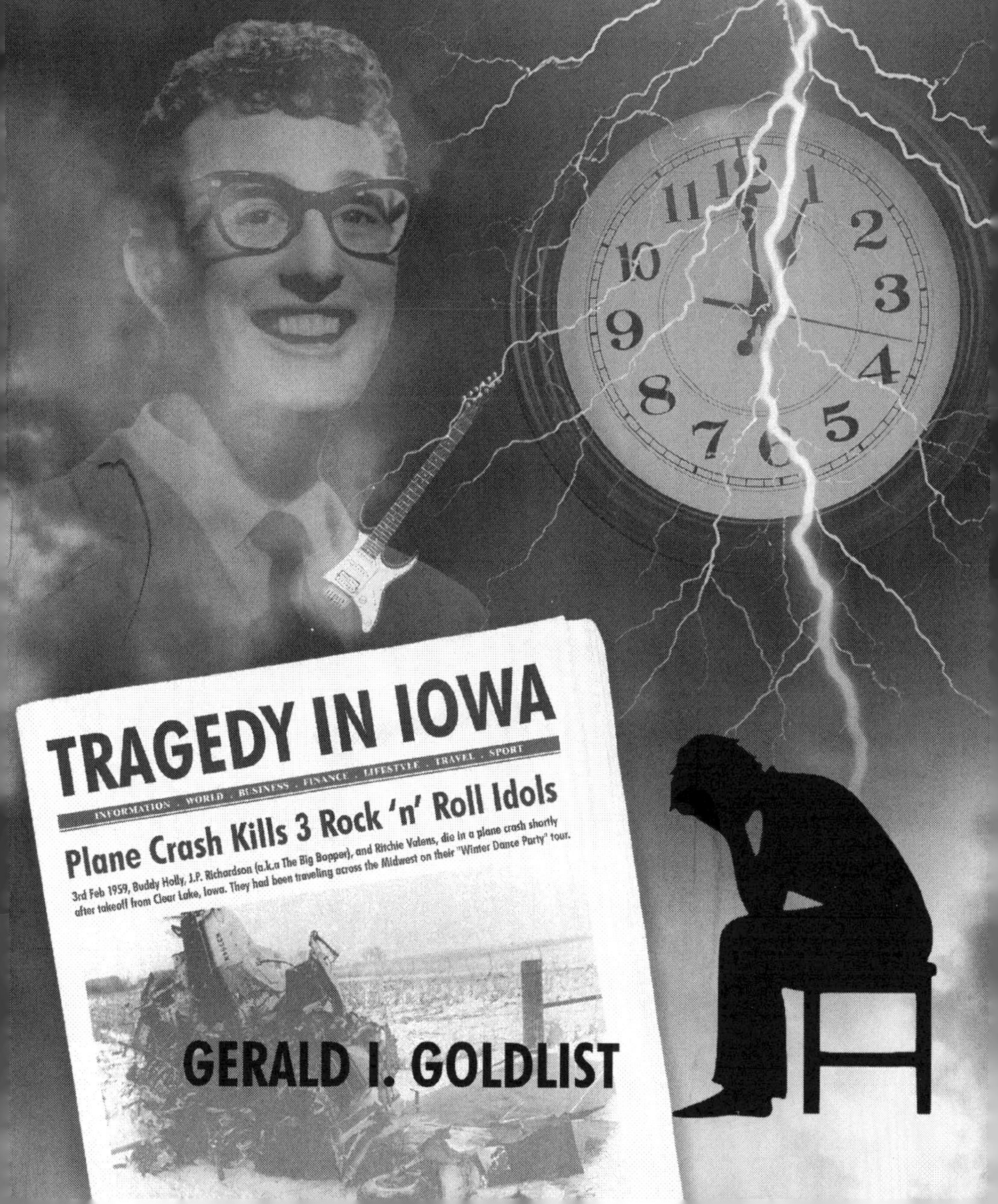

GERALD I. GOLDLIST

Saving Buddy Holly
Blue Days Black Nights

Copyright © 2023 by Gerald I. Goldlist

All rights reserved.

No part of this publication may be reproduced, distributed, or transmitted in any form or by any means, including photocopying, recording, or other electronic or mechanical methods, without the prior written permission of the publisher, except as permitted. For permission requests, contact gerry-1@rogers.com.

Book Cover Art and Interior Layout by Bibliofic Designs

Buddy Holly Cover Photograph:
https://commons.wikimedia.org/wiki/File:Buddy_Holly_cropped_(cropped).JPG

Paperback ISBN: 978-1-7381873-1-7
Hardcover ISBN: 978-1-7381873-0-0
Ebook ISBN: 978-1-7381873-2-4

DEDICATION

This book is dedicated to the two great women in my life. To my mother Sarah Ita Goldlist, who encouraged me in everything that I did since I was a baby and throughout her life. In our family she was the power behind the throne: the power behind my father, my brother and me; the one who pushed her men to succeed.

And then I found the love of my life (not kidding). Leza's strength has gotten me through some very difficult times. Although I am not a particularly great man, let me paraphrase the classical saying: without Leza, the great woman behind me, I would not have been able to accomplish what I did with my life. Leza bought me a guitar to propel me into my mid-life crisis. Then she followed me to Iowa during a record cold February. And followed me again to Texas to pursue my Buddy Holly hobby.

Thanks to Leza (who thinks that every bad thing I say about her is what I believe and every good thing I say about her is sarcasm) for encouraging me in this endeavor and reading my drafts as they progressed while suggesting improvements gently so as not to bruise my fragile ego. Leza, thanks for being the source of so much happiness in my life, as well as the inspiration for some of the funniest parts of this book. What is real, what is exaggerated and what is totally made up will forever be our secret.

And of course, this book is dedicated to Buddy Holly: the music, the man and his fans.

Rave on!

THE WINTER DANCE PARTY DREAM

He had dreamed of going to Clear Lake for the Winter Dance Party Tribute. The trip was amazing. He had shaken hands with The Crickets. He had met Buddy Holly fans from all over the world. He had danced on the dance floor of the Surf Ballroom as the Crickets were aplayin' Buddy's songs.

Afterwards, he could never tell what had been dream and what had been actuality, as the dream and the reality had become the same. It was a dream come true and so could remain a dream forever.

Another Buddy Holly Tribute Song
Vocals, Guitar and Composed by:
Gerald I. Goldlist

It was another era;
It was another time.
I wish that I could tell him,
He was a friend of mine

His time has long since come and gone
As soon I guess will mine.
But through my life he was a light
That helped me carry on.

His music kept me going
When I was feeling low.
I wish that I could thank him.
He was way too young to go.

I sometimes saw his picture
Hanging on my wall
It gave me strength to carry on,
So I didn't chuck it all.

A gentler kinder fellow
You'll probably never find.
He left a legacy of friends
And he lives within their minds.

I dreamt about the crash site.
I nearly froze my hand.
I danced into the Ballroom
And I listened to his band.

I flew on down to Texas.
I talked with Peggy Sue.
She told me to his memory,
She'd always be true.

I never got to meet him.
It really is a shame.
He never even dreamt of me,
But he often called my name.

His time has long since come and gone
As soon I guess will mine.
But through my life he was a light
That helped me carry on.

It was another era; It was another time.
I wish that I could tell him,
What a friend he was of mine.

Listen on YouTube: https://youtu.be/eZX_r4PBW08?si=C5KuLMKqTgEWVWuU

ACT III SCENE 1 HAMLET
WILLIAM SHAKESPEARE

To be, or not to be: that is the question:
Whether 'tis nobler in the mind to suffer
The slings and arrows of outrageous fortune,
Or to take arms against a sea of troubles,
And by opposing end them? To die: to sleep;
No more; and by a sleep to say we end
The heart-ache and the thousand natural shocks
That flesh is heir to, 'tis a consummation
Devoutly to be wish'd. To die, to sleep;
To sleep: perchance to dream: ay, there's the rub;
For in that sleep of death what dreams may come
When we have shuffled off this mortal coil,
Must give us pause: there's the respect
That makes calamity of so long life;
For who would bear the whips and scorns of time ...
But that the dread of something after death.

ACKNOWLEDGMENTS

My daughter Susie and my son Mikie, who encouraged me and made suggestions when this novel was barely in its embryonic stage.

All those, including my family, friends, office staff and patients, who suffered in silence, and not so silently, through my ravings about Buddy Holly trivia.

Dr. Brian Hoffman, who helped me and told me that he liked the idea of a historical science fiction. I wish that he had been able to read this.

The people who helped with editing this book: my sister-in-law, Marcia Goldlist, my niece-in-law, Daphne Hoffenberg-Szweras, and my neighbor, Lauren Lindberg, whose detailed suggestions led me to make significant changes in punctuation and phraseology.

The friendly people at the Surf Ballroom in Clear Lake, Iowa, who made Leza and me feel so welcome at the Buddy Holly Tribute Dances that we attended there. The British Buddy Holly Society, who took me into their circle of friends when we got to the Surf Ballroom. Among them were Paul and Dot King, Clive Harvey and Dave Williams. It was a picture of Paul in a magazine that inspired me to go to Iowa and meet all the Buddy Holly fans there.

C.J. Schoenrock, the Texas lady that I met online in a Buddy Holly chat room, who encouraged me to come to Lubbock, Texas and then introduced Leza and me to Peggy Sue. After I had shlepped my guitar and amp with me from Toronto, Peggy Sue graciously allowed me to sing the song that was written about her to Peggy Sue herself. What a thrill that was. I have never seen a picture of Peggy Sue do her justice: her smile made the room light up.

Dr. J. Davis Armistead, Buddy's eye doctor, who prescribed those famous glasses, and who treated Leza and me like family when we were in Lubbock.

Buddy's family and friends, including Sherry Holley, the daughter of Buddy's oldest brother Larry, and Buddy's other brother, Travis, who came out to meet me and later made me an acoustic guitar.

Shawn Nagy, who arranged for me to sing in a small Texas bar just outside Lubbock. The patrons of the bar mercifully did not throw beer bottles at me.

I only mention the world-famous science fiction writer, Robert J. Sawyer, because he acknowledged me in his trilogy, "Wake", "Watch" and "Wonder". I also would like to thank Rob for his encouragement and advice as the book got closer to completion. He even took the time to help me convert my WordPerfect version of this book into Word.

Rob also introduced me to Avery Olive of Bibliofic Designs, who created the layout and drawings for this book and, after my repeated pestering for changes, created the exquisite cover for this novel.

Those people on Twitter who, over the years, answered my grammar questions, including Lorrie Goldstein, a newspaper editor and columnist for several Toronto newspapers. I especially want to thank Media Critic @TalkCritic, the professional writer that I met on Twitter, who advised me on punctuation, manuscripts and for years, urged me to keep on writing.

Sam Laufer, my beloved and oldest friend. I have known Sam since we were pre-teens in the 1950's. I know very well that he is a tough judge of everything and everybody. He is, in fact, my harshest critic and the only person rude enough to have walked out on me as I was demonstrating my newly acquired guitar-playing skills. When I began this book in 1994, I wanted his opinion and so I read Sam the few pages that I had written. When he said: "It's good. Write it," I knew it would be worth trying to write this novel.

PROLOGUE

The days were blue, the nights were black, but the mornings were the worst.

He would wake up in the early morning hours, 4 and 5 o'clock. He would lie awake waiting for the alarm. He would lie awake, curling into the fetal position, trying to get comfortable, trying to fall asleep again, hoping to pass the time more quickly in slumber rather than lying awake sweating, fearful of the coming day.

What was it he feared when he awoke frightened in the early mornings? Everything. He was afraid of everything, even when he had nothing to fear. It was an absurd fear. He was afraid of making a mistake at work. He was afraid of making decisions: they might be wrong. He was afraid of being criticized. He was afraid of being ignored. He was afraid. The essence of his being was insecurity.

Just before the alarm was to go off, he would become nauseated with fear. After forcing himself out of bed and to the bathroom, just the movement of the toothbrush in his mouth could make him retch. Some days it was only dry retching, but on other days his stomach would heave out its contents until there was nothing. His doctor called it anticipatory anxiety. Whatever it was called, it was agonizing.

CHAPTER 1

A pattern of depressive mood swings had started while Charlie was in late high school. Every few months, he would experience episodes of depression during which he would be tired and worry inappropriately. It got worse in university. Then after finishing university, with the excitement of being a graduate, an engineer, a responsible adult, there was a decrease in frequency and depth of his depressive episodes.

Years later, after Charlie had reached a position of senior responsibility, his mood swings came back. His down cycles, the blue days and black nights, would return for a few days or a few weeks. Sometimes the downswing would only last for hours.

The early mornings were fearful. His fear was illogical: he had always been competent, or even better, at whatever he did. There was nothing for him to fear but fear itself. He was afraid to go to work, but he always went. Duty trumped his fear. He was like a good soldier, who was cowering and panicking inwardly from dread of death, maiming and pain, but nevertheless followed orders and charged into battle. Courage is not the absence of fear, but the ability to carry on in the face of fear.

When he was extremely depressed and anxious, Charlie would work like an automaton, by rote, putting his mind into autopilot, shunting the fear and anxiety aside, so that he could perform his job.

Saving Buddy Holly Blue Days Black Nights

Charlie's genius shone through on the days when his mind flipped into high gear. On those days, decisions came easily. Ideas became crystal clear. He whizzed through paperwork, solved difficult problems, got outstanding ideas and achieved the types of things that got him to where he had climbed in the work force and scientific community. Although much of the time his mind was filled with turmoil, those around him only noticed that Charlie was a moody fellow. They were unaware of his inner tremblings and pain.

CHAPTER 2

Charles Harding was a few years away from 40. He had been born in a large city in the northern United States. His mother and father had been loving and kind middle class parents. They had learned about child-rearing in books and had taken courses. His mother had stayed home to raise him, only returning to the workplace when Charlie began attending high school. She had helped him with his schoolwork when he was little. He soon outgrew the need for her help so she would only provide encouragement and praise. It worked. He had learned at an early age that success earned praise. He craved praise. He had always worked diligently at his schoolwork. Charlie had strived hard, not because he had to, but because he enjoyed it. He liked to see the word "excellent" on his assignments, tests and report cards. It made him feel good. It exhilarated him. Charles Harding had always been extremely bright, and he very much enjoyed learning.

He had been adored by his teachers. Only helping a struggling student who finally succeeded, could give a teacher more satisfaction than dealing with students like Charlie. Charlie had been polite and obedient. He had learned quickly and easily. He had always loved school, just as school had loved him. He had been a teacher's pet. He cleaned the chalkboard because it was fun but the thank-yous felt good too. First he made large oval circles with the brush, then vertical strokes from top to bottom and finally a few horizontal strokes to tidy up the board. He was organized and he was a perfectionist. These traits would go on to serve him well throughout his life.

He was intense at play as well, always playing hard and striving to win, but acquiring knowledge was paramount. Acquiring the skills and using the logic of mathematics and the physical sciences were his strengths. Although he could admire art, he was unable to create it. He was drawn to things that he was good at and so after he had grown to manhood it was only natural that he quickly learned to despise golf.

As a child he had developed a clique of friends who were also bright and academically inclined. They did their homework with ease and fun. They did their projects with the care and perseverance of someone older and more mature. At the age of ten Charlie was excelling as a brilliant student. His friends were of a similar mettle. Even in primary school there was competition among this small group of pals. Their rivalry drove each of them to work harder in their academic pursuits. Outside of school, they would play games together: board games, sports games, card games. Eventually, this group of geniuses would spawn several card playing experts: poker geniuses and a world-class bridge player. Genius can be misused but no corruption emerged from this group. They all had solid moral values.

As they grew into their teens most of the group hung together. They went to high school at Northern Collegiate, a school known for its exceptionally high academic standards. Charlie and his friends continued to excel in their schoolwork. They were involved in many extracurricular activities that included the school newspaper and chess club.

Their physical abilities did not allow them to play school sports, but they were avid fans. They watched every school football, basketball and baseball game. They especially enjoyed the games between their high school and the nearby rival school, Eastern Tech. Like many teens, when they played on weekends they emulated their professional heroes, but only in their imaginations. There was no lack of intensity but their skills were far removed from their imaginations.

In their last year of high school, three members of Charlie's clique, Charles Harding, Art Simmons and Jim Rich, held down three of the top ten positions on the school's honor roll. Each of them settled on a career in engineering.

Charlie remained close to these two boyhood pals. After attaining his engineering degree, Jim travelled for two years and then settled down in England where he married a young English lady. Every other summer Jim would return to America to visit his family. He made a point of seeing his old mates too.

Charlie and Art both became experts in the mathematics and physics of space exploration. They found it easy to remain tight friends as they proceeded through their lives at similar paces and even shared rooms in university. They both married girls that they had met at university, and they had their first child within a year of each other, both boys. Art and his wife went on to have another child, but Charlie and his wife Sue stopped at one. Charlie had insisted on this.

Charlie's depression caused him to be tired much of the time; he often felt fatigued, even after a good night's sleep. The disruption of a crying child, combined with his underlying depression, left him feeling so exhausted that he had to consume vast amounts of coffee to keep him going through the day. Unfortunately, when he became extremely sleep-deprived, the coffee could make him nauseous. This would be a problem when he was with other people.

Charlie had nagged Sue continually about his disrupted sleep patterns and about not having another baby. When she finally relented to having no more children, she refused to have the operation. "You want surgical birth control, Charlie, you have your tubes tied." So Charlie had a vasectomy.

♪♫♪♫

Not only did Charlie and Art have glowing references from their professors but they had both published superb research papers that were at the cutting edge of space-age physics and mathematics. Charlie and Art were rocket scientists, both literally and figuratively. As postgrad students, the quality and content of their work had caught the attention of elite rocket scientists. They were both highly sought after and had the choice of several good jobs. After finishing their formal education both Charlie Harding and Art Simmons were grabbed up by the rocket industry. Their careers brought Charlie, Art and their families to Florida.

Art Simmons and Charlie Harding were not only friends, but also co-workers. They worked at Space Navigation Incorporated. They were doing rocket research and so worked closely with the National Aeronautics and Space Administration, better known as NASA. The two buddies did well in Florida. They contributed to the space program and especially to the advancement of theoretical space exploration.

Charlie had always enjoyed learning new things. He relished learning all things. As he grew older, he discovered that much of what he had learned was helpful to him in a practical way, or if not practical, still interesting. He loved to gaze at things around him and relate them to the basic science facts that he had learned in school. How did a fireplace work? Why did the flames rise? Why was snow white, the sky blue and only some sunsets red? Knowledge might be power, but it could also be fun.

He enjoyed watching sports. He was particularly enamored with the finer points of sports, the strategies, and statistics. While watching baseball games on TV, he would calculate batting and pitching averages just for his own amusement. He did much of it in his head. It was easy to remember that two hits in 7 at bats was a .286 batting average but knowing that 14/49 and 32/112 were also a .286 batting average, now that was cool.

He collected baseball cards and sports memorabilia. There had been pictures of his favorite baseball players taped inside his school locker. He would smile as he thought back to the time that his high school vice-principal had walked by his locker and did a double take as he realized that Charlie's pinups were baseball players and not suggestive pictures of scantily clad females.

As he was one of the youngest and smallest pupils in the school, it had been difficult for Charlie to earn good grades in physical education; nevertheless, he put out his best efforts just as he did in all subjects. His physical education marks had always been moderate but inauspicious when compared to his academic grades. It embarrassed him to think back to the time his mother had actually had the audacity to berate his gym teacher for giving Charlie marks that pulled down his overall grade average. Charlie always wondered if his phys ed performance in the next term had really improved that much, or if his mother had something to do with the fact that his marks improved.

13-year-old Charlie had been humiliated when, in order to teach ballroom dancing, the teacher had chosen him to be her dancing partner. She demonstrated the tango and the waltz. One, two, three, four. One, two, three, four. If someone looked carefully at Charlie dancing to rock 'n' roll, the earlier influences of ballroom dancing could be discerned as he had incorporated some of those steps into his dance moves.

CHAPTER 3

Early in his university days while he was working on his undergraduate degree, Charlie had an abnormal gloomy spell. Charlie had been getting straight A's at the time and his chums could not understand what was happening to him. Charlie was having doubts about his chances of succeeding in his courses. They kept encouraging him and pointing out the absurdity of the anxiety he was feeling. He ultimately snapped out of his pessimistic depressed mood and got A's in all his courses.

His mood swings became more intense and frequent. There had been minor mood problems when he was younger, but they had had little impact on his functioning. As a pre-teen his mother had teased him about his mood swings. She used to say that his temperament could cycle like the hormones of a girl. She would mock him playfully by asking him if he was retaining fluid or having cramps. The mood peculiarities never lasted longer than a few days.

In his later teens, Charlie began to experience even more significant mood swings. Every few weeks he would feel energized, need less sleep, and seem to do everything quickly. After doing all his studying, pleasure reading and playing, he would be on the constant lookout for more and more interesting things to do. This high energy level and up mood would peter out over the course of a week or two. At other times he would feel so tired that he would have trouble waking up. The tired episodes never interfered with his schoolwork. Duty trumped fatigue. His alarm always got him out of bed, he always completed assignments on time, and he was always able to be on top of his game for a seminar, test or exam. Charlie discovered how invigorating the boost delivered by a cup of coffee could be. He used the weekends to recover by sleeping until noon or even later.

After college and into university his mood swings became more noticeable. Acquaintances began to call him moody. This was not considered an abnormality but just an element of Charlie's personality. His coping mechanisms allowed him to stay on top of his work. Even when he was severely depressed, he would barely get behind in his studies. Somehow Charlie learned to manipulate his mood swings. By sleeping in, drinking coffee, self-hypnosis and whatever else he could harness to control the ups and downs, his life and mood were almost invariably in an upswing for exam time. He would look back later and wonder how he was able to be depressed for weeks before exams and then come out of the down mood and into a high in time to ramp up his studying and do extremely well.

He could tell when he was becoming unbearably complaining and pessimistic. At these times he would try to avoid his friends as much as possible so as not to alienate them and lose their friendships. When he was in a mild down swing, his friends would be a source of humor and recreation. For Charlie, laughter was the best medicine. The camaraderie and joking with his chums would often be enough to lift his spirits and end the down cycle in his mood.

He had to conform to schedules imposed by others. Attending classes and lectures had been a battle, a battle between his depression and his willpower. His responsibilities always won. Duty trumped depression. Once he got to working on his master's and doctorate degrees, his agenda and time were more under his own control and so the mood swings were much less of a hindrance. During his depressive states he would sleep a lot but at other times he was able to accomplish enormous amounts of work. Regardless of his moods, he always did his tasks carefully and extremely well.

Charlie realized that something strange was going on in his mind. After some reading, he had concluded that what often gave him the strength and ability to get massive amounts of work done were periods of mania or hypomania. After psychotherapy he came to understand that what he considered mania was actually the normal state for most people. Charlie ultimately came to the eerie realization that most other human beings did not repeatedly feel depressed for no obvious reason. Other people had a zest and drive to stay alive. Eventually Charlie felt that most of the time he did not have this zest and drive for life. It had been lost. When did he lose his drive to live? When did he start feeling that he had stopped living and was just existing?

As his life progressed, the depressions got worse. The peaks were not as high, and the valleys were deeper. As he reached positions of more authority, he was able to delegate more and control his work environment. It was thus easier for him to cope with his moods as he got his work done adequately, in fact, more than adequately. He would get large amounts of work done when he was feeling up and he would work with less intensity when he was feeling down.

The amount of effort required to get things done varied with his mental state. He frequently felt extremely fatigued. Although it had its origin in his brain, the fatigue was both mental and physical.

Over his life he had developed mechanisms to cope with his depression. When he was depressed, he was extremely careful, double- and triplechecking his work. The quantity of work he accomplished decreased but even when he was depressed the quality of his work did not suffer.

His extremely bright mind, along with a perfectionist desire to do everything well, had got him through school. When he got into the work force, they were also able to carry him through the difficult times. He was diligent and methodical in times of depression. He was extraordinarily swift in everything he did when he was "up".

CHAPTER 4

Charlie was head of the division of a company called Space Navigation Incorporated. Space Navigation Incorporated was a mouthful, so it was called SNI. SNI was a successful semi-private company. It had initially been a private company but because of its many government contracts there came to be a significant degree of government influence. Much of its basic research had come to be intertwined with the nearby university. It was an unusual hybrid that had developed after years of cooperation, threats, loss of grants, new grants, public money and commercial money.

The corporate activities of SNI could be very confusing but it was a useful conglomerate for all concerned. Its money came from various sources: from government, the university and private business. The government got what it needed. The university got quality research. Commercial enterprises made a profit from the spinoffs of the research. SNI's creations were sought after in both public and commercial sectors. SNI was an innovative company and generated excellent products. Its mainstay was the rocket industry: rocket fuels, materials for rockets and military operations. When it was not a security risk, its inventions and patents were sold to other governments and companies all over the world.

Its head office was located at the outskirts of the city on the same site where its research and other activities were done. Someone had had the foresight to find a location with lots of undeveloped land and so the SNI site had expanded as it branched out in whatever direction its products and research took it. The only nearby structures of consequence belonged to the university.

SNI performed well because its employees were there for more than money. There was a lot of latitude in which direction they could take their work and so people had more freedom to pursue their individual scientific interests. Many were drawn to SNI by the basic research encouraged by its university connection. The people working at SNI did not take many days off. Coming in on weekends to finish an experiment was common. They loved their jobs and did not have to drag themselves in to work. Except Charlie, when his depression weighed him down.

As head of his division, Charlie had his hand in many things. His preference was to pursue the theoretical details and possibilities of new projects. An individual would come to him with an idea. Charlie would analyze the theoretical aspects and pragmatic possibilities. Among his responsibilities was to supervise and check the work done by others prior to their being presented to other departments, potential collaborators and prospective purchasers of their products.

As each other's best and longest-standing friend, Charlie and Art and their wives would socialize frequently. Occasionally Charlie and Art would collaborate on projects. More importantly, they met for coffee and had lunch together almost every day.

Early in life Charlie had developed an intense interest in time travel. It had become a serious hobby and side project for him. The fact that his job at SNI gave him access to what he needed for his time travel pastime was a bonus.

CHAPTER 5

Charlie's favorite baseball team was the Braves. He was a diehard fan and watched them on TV, listened to the games on the radio and studied major league baseball in newspapers and magazine articles. He was a mathematician and devoured baseball stats. He knew the stats of the Braves and the stars on other teams. He was even a fan of baseball history and had read books and watched all the movies.

Like many other baseball zealots, Charlie had organized his summers and falls so that he could watch the Braves during baseball season. He had tried to arrange meetings, doctor appointments and social engagements to keep his baseball watching agenda clear. For baseball zealots, it was almost a religion. How else could one explain a movie in which a Senators' fan was willing to sell his soul to the Devil so that his Senators could beat those "Damn Yankees"?

His cherished Braves were in first place and the playoffs were coming. It should have been an exciting and glorious autumn for him, but Charlie realized that something was amiss. The Braves were in a pennant race, but Charlie was not ecstatic and exhilarated. Even though this passion of his was going so well, he found himself generally feeling joyless, ill at ease and discouraged. Instead of excitedly asking fellow Braves fans: "Did you see the game last night?" "Did you see that fork ball to end the game?" he found himself too quiet and uncommunicative. This was out of character for Charlie the baseball fanatic. He would respond appropriately to questions, but his answers were curt. He did not initiate baseball conversations. His friends and coworkers knew that he was a moody fellow and so did not think much of it. But Charlie knew that something was wrong.

He felt fatigued and tired. He lacked energy even after a good night's sleep. Inexplicably even early in the day when he should have felt refreshed, Charlie felt fatigued. He would put his head on his desk and shut his eyes. A thick dark cloud had moved above him and blocked the sunlight from his life. He was in a deep depression.

When his parents had died unexpectedly in a car accident, Charlie had reacted normally with grief. The grief remained for months but the physical symptoms began to lift after two weeks. This was as his parents would have wanted it. That had been a reactive depression, a reaction to a bad event. This depression was not the same. Things were good. It came from inside Charlie. It was an endogenous depression not a reactive depression.

Charlie explained his illness to Art. "You can't will yourself out of depression. You can't 'snap out of it', just as you can't snap out of diabetes. Even if you can't understand how, what, and why I feel it, at least believe me when I say that I feel terrible and that I feel helpless."

At Charlie's worst moments, just knowing that Art was around or available was comforting. He came to trust Art to not judge his illness as anything more than an illness. There was a stigma to mental disease. People did not understand that one could not will himself out of depression. A depressed person does not concern himself with the fact that his life is full of fabulous people and that he has a physically comfortable life.

Alongside his depression he began to feel tiny jabs of anxiety. It surprised him when he was shopping and experienced slight bursts of anxiety in his gut. He did not even understand what he was anxious about. Was it the fear of overpaying or buying the wrong thing? As his depression worsened, he began to second-guess himself about things he bought. What if he did not like it when he got home? What if it was defective or did not work as he expected? Maybe he would have to bring it back to the store. There might be a confrontation. He was afraid of confrontation. He never haggled when he bought things as he felt that the other person needed the money more than he did. Then he noticed something even worse. He had developed generalized guilt. He felt as if he did not deserve to have money. He felt that his life was a sham, and he was not, nor had he ever been, as talented and competent as people thought him to be. He felt that he did not deserve to get paid for a job that was easy, and that so many people could do his job better than he did.

Whatever he bought, Charlie obsessively kept the warranties, but he absolutely hated to make use of them. When something malfunctioned, he would find the warranty in his meticulously organized filing system. He found himself hoping that the warranty had expired. He wanted to feel that he had already got his money's worth, and that there would be no need for confrontation, no need for anxiety and the guilt that accompanied his anxiety.

Charlie found himself yawning when he was not tired. His tiredness was not normal. His fatigue could not be satiated by sleep. He was waking up early in the morning and lying in bed worrying. He would worry about the day ahead of him. Would he be too tired to work? Would he be able to function properly? He awakened with his teeth grinding together, his teeth clenched with fear and anxiety. He was smiling less. He was weepy. He did not cry but felt tears in his eyes. His fatigue gave him a sensation of being pushed back relentlessly by rolling waves of seawater or walking against a strong steady wind.

He realized that he was sick. He talked to his doctor, but the depression endured and so his family doctor referred him to a psychiatrist.

CHAPTER 6

With the benefit of an excellent health plan, over the years, Charlie had been able to see umpteen psychiatrists. Many of them had the typical air of a psychiatrist with that Freudian beard and "go on" speech. Those with the affectation of holding a pipe in their mouths usually had the decency not to light it in his presence. He playfully asked himself why psychiatrists never smoked a corncob pipe. Had the doctors looked carefully, they would have discerned a hint of the smile that Charlie was holding back. He didn't want them to think he was crazy.

He agreed with what psychiatrists had repeatedly told him: depression was like carrying a sack of flour around. When the depression lifted the sack was gone and there was a feeling of increased energy. The load had been so burdensome that as it lifted Charlie thought that he must be euphoric and getting manicky. His doctors had reassured him that he was just feeling as normal people do.

Charlie's depression was right out of a textbook. When his depression lifted, he could accomplish so much more, both physically and mentally, with what felt like the expenditure of less physical and mental effort. He was more comfortable with and could cope with the stresses of ordinary life, the kind of stresses that others did not even consider to be stresses, like deciding what to eat for dinner. The most trivial decision was a burden when the weight of depression was on his shoulders. Even deciding which to do first in the morning, shaving or brushing his teeth, was formidable.

When his depression lifted, work was fun. It was easy. He caught up with reading, writing, planning, and whatever else needed to be done. Difficult decisions became a breeze. Complex problems unraveled. Work was worth doing and life was worth living.

But when he carried the weight of depression, any tiny problem felt like the proverbial straw that broke the camel's back. Notwithstanding the routine use of modern antibiotics to treat infections, Charlie would worry that a simple ear infection could spread and cause meningitis of his brain. He worried that a headache could be the sign of an impending stroke.

Wherever and whatever he was doing, Charlie felt teary-eyed and on the verge of crying. When he was depressed and alone, he could let the facade of normalcy fall away. He could sit at home immobile and unsmiling. He would weep. Life was so sad. He would sleep inordinate amounts in an attempt to replenish his energy for the next struggle in his life. Was sleep a way to hide from life itself?

When depression hit hard, he was disconsolate about all manner of things. He would feel discouraged by his work, despondent during leisure, defeated by life. He would feel weary, tired, fatigued, exhausted. Weariness was a facet of depression that people did not understand. Depression was not just a feeling of extreme sadness: it bore down upon the whole body and caused a feeling of enormous exhaustion. He could feel the depression in his brain, his eyes, his heart, his arms, his legs, his fingers and his knees. His speech, his walking, his sitting, his thinking, all slowed.

Depression affected his guts. He would suffer nausea, diarrhea and cramps. He would become anorexic, lose his appetite, and then lose weight. He would become disinterested in sex. But the mental anguish was even worse, at times almost unbearable. He would find linear scabs on his arms where he had been tearing at his skin hoping to distract himself from his psychic pain.

Saving Buddy Holly Blue Days Black Nights

One doctor told Charlie that his depression was of moderate severity. With moderate depression he was profoundly aware of his intense mental anguish. Charlie thought about this and after doing some reading came to the following conclusions. With very severe depression he might have been institutionalized. He might have become catatonic and unable to move after total collapse of his mind from the inability to cope with life. He might have been lying destitute in the corner of a room, curled up like a ball as he had seen in pictures of medieval insane asylums, with his mind blank and aware of nothing, unaware of the psychic pain. But that's not how it was. His doctors had encouraged him to continue working no matter how difficult it was as this gave order and routine to his life. Feeling that he must go to work forced Charlie up from lying in bed with exhausted gloominess. Having always been disciplined, Charle followed doctors' orders and continued to work no matter how tired and weighed down he felt. He imagined himself pushing a giant boulder up a hill. He knew he would feel guilty if he were to stop work and collect disability insurance. And so he continued to work, toil at times, and contend with living his life while grappling with his disease. He was very conscious of his predicament and felt that he had the most difficult depression to deal with: moderate depression.

CHAPTER 7

SNI's well-outfitted fitness club was a convenient place for Charlie to exercise. On weekends he would jog outside but when the weather was bad he drove to SNI's fitness center and ran on the indoor track. He lifted weights too, but he spent most of his time at the fitness center jogging and in aerobic classes. The aerobic classes incorporated pounding music with driving beats. This was also the kind of music he listened to when he jogged. The music gave him a mental and physical lift.

The aerobic classes consisted of 70% women and 30% men. It was perplexing how many of the women never sweated. Was it something on the second X-chromosome? Did they all jump into a vat of antiperspirant before exercising? It seemed to Charlie that the women who wore the most makeup did the most intense workouts and perspired the least. It must be something on the Y-chromosome, because male eyes and minds instinctively perused the provocative female bodies pulsating to the rhythms. By the end of a class a good number of the women had been visually undressed, some of them more than once. For Charlie, exercising itself, whether in aerobics class, on the running track or running outside, became an important part of his life.

♪♫♪♫

Saving Buddy Holly Blue Days Black Nights

The first 20 minutes of aerobic exercising are the most difficult. After the initial push through those 20 minutes, the body begins to slip into a steady state of fat burning and endorphin production. Endorphins are chemicals present in the brain that relieve pain, reduce emotional stress and cause a feeling of pleasure. They are called "feel-good" chemicals because they cause the perception of well-being and happiness. The name endorphin comes from the words endogenous, which means from inside the body, and morphine, which is a pain reliever. Endorphins interact with the same receptors in the brain as morphine and heroin. They are made in the hypothalamus and pituitary glands of the brain and induce the well-known runners high that is felt after sustained exercise.

There had been a time when Charlie enjoyed playing squash with his friends and colleagues. The games were competitive but good-natured games. As his squash buddies got busier and their schedules less flexible, arranging game times became more difficult so Charlie switched to activities that did not require coordinating timetables. Charlie was religious about exercising three or four times per week. When he was depressed and had to choose between taking a nap and exercising, it could be difficult for Charlie to motivate himself to get moving. Many times, it would have been so much easier to give up, lie down and take a serious nap. Sometimes he did give in and lie down. Once he could force himself to get to the gym or outside to jog, he pushed himself past his personal steady-state endorphin point of eighteen minutes. After that, the rest of the workout became easier and more enjoyable. When he missed one of his workout days due to fatigue, his mood or work, Charlie became annoyed. If he missed a few workouts in a row, Charlie became angry and resentful, sometimes at the circumstances and sometimes at himself. Inwardly redirected anger triggers depression and guilt.

♪♫♪♫

Gerald I. Goldlist

When he was on the rowing machine or pedalling on the exercise bike, Charlie's eyes would close. Working out in a gym with his eyes closed was a lot safer than running outdoors with his eyes shut as there was little danger of smashing into a tree. While on the rowing machine, he imagined himself in the old movie Ben Hur as a galley slave chained below deck.

When exercising alone, boredom was a problem and there was a need for distraction. Aerobics with music was less tedious and more enjoyable than exercising with just his own gloomy thoughts and troubles for company. Music, especially songs with a strong tempo kept him going. He found the rhythm not only gave him a cadence to follow but it gave him an emotional lift as well. Charlie chose upbeat songs from his music collection and made mix tapes to keep him company as he ran, biked or rowed.

It was dusk. Charlie had just finished another jog and was looking westward as the sun set. As the sky darkened, he detected a flicker. He watched the evening star get brighter as the Sun went further below the horizon. The star didn't twinkle. It wasn't a star. It was the planet Venus. As a child Charlie had learned that Venus is closer to the Sun than the Earth. He later learned that in order for us to see Venus we have to look in the direction of the Sun, but not directly at the Sun itself, at dawn or sunset.

Charlie watched the leaves on the trees and saw them turn from sunlit bright green to dark green and then black as the Sun went down. He beheld the pale blue sky merging in the far west with the pink sunset near the horizon. Red sky at night, sailors delight; red sky at morning, sailors take warning. When he was depressed, instead of the majesty and beauty of Nature, he saw frightening images in the trees and pictured a bleak desolate world in a desolate galaxy.

Charlie saw bats darting back and forth catching mosquitoes. He initially got a cold feeling in his neck. Then he thought about how many mosquito bites the bats had saved him from. He smiled to himself as he thought that Dracula and bats weren't really so bad but that they just had dreadful publicists.

Charlie had finished a pleasant weekend afternoon run and was feeling good. He sat down and sipped his water. He stared at the clouds. He saw images of dogs, a bear and lots of women's breasts. On other days he saw witches, scary faces and demons. He could hear what sounded like the buzzing of a large bumblebee nearby. It wasn't a bumblebee: it was a delightful little bird. He knew it would be a cheery day when he saw a hummingbird.

CHAPTER 8

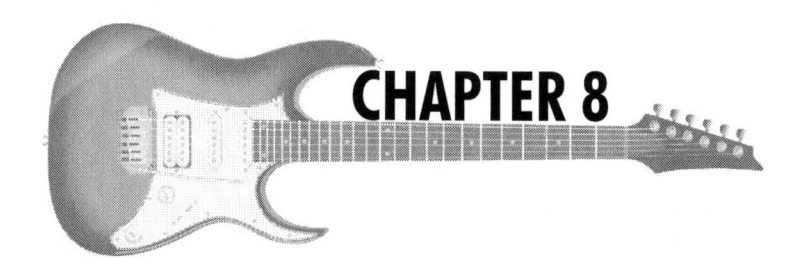

One of Charlie's coworkers, Fred, and his wife Gertie had watched the movie "The Buddy Holly Story". They were fascinated by the plane crash that had killed those early rock stars, Ritchie Valens, the Big Bopper and Buddy Holly. The plane crash had occurred at 1:00 a.m. on February 3, 1959, near Mason City Airport, which was only minutes away from Clear Lake, Iowa where they had finished their last performance just a few hours before. The red and white four-seater V-tailed Beechcraft Bonanza they had been flying in, crashed into a snow-covered cornfield in the middle of a bone-chilling Iowa winter.

Even those with a passing interest in music knew that Buddy Holly was a famous singer, who had died in a plane crash in the 1950's. Buddy Holly was the first young rock 'n' roll star to wear glasses while performing. In fact, his distinctive heavy-rimmed black glasses became part of his performing identity.

Buddy Holly was born in 1936 in Lubbock, Texas. He died at the age of 22 on February 3, 1959. It was the day that was later commemorated in the song "The Day the Music Died". He wrote and recorded 50 songs in a stunningly brief time. His most famous were "Peggy Sue" and "That'll Be the Day".

He was one of the first to write his own songs, play guitar, and sing his own music. He had a lasting impact on music, influencing many rock 'n' roll performers and songwriters. The Beatles and the Rolling Stones were admirers of Buddy Holly. Buddy Holly's band The Crickets was among the first to feature two guitars, a bass and drums. This was the same arrangement that the Beatles and the Rolling Stones later used. The name The Beatles was a spinoff on Buddy Holly's group The Crickets.

The untimely death of this rock star was for many teenagers of that time their first exposure to the death of someone they felt an emotional attachment to. Partly because of his untimely death Buddy Holly left a legacy of worldwide diehard fans, who made his life and music their passion.

It came to pass one day, that Fred was speaking to Charlie about music. He asked Charlie if he liked Buddy Holly.

Charlie's reply was, "He's alright, Fred. I hear his songs on the radio and I remember 'Peggy Sue' was his. And what's the other one? 'That'll Be The Day'. That's the other one I remember."

"'Peggy Sue'", said Fred. "I think a lot of girls were named after 'Peggy Sue' or the girls in other rock 'n' roll songs like 'Suzie Q' and 'Wake up Little Susie'."

Charlie added, "'Susie Darling' and 'Run around Sue'."

"Do you think your Sue could have been named after one of those Sues, Charlie?"

Charlie replied, "I don't think my Sue was named after the girls in those songs but I'm sure a lot of other girls were. Susan used to be a popular name, but I think more kids are named after actors and actresses nowadays."

Art chimed in, "I have a cousin who's a doctor. He told me that when he was an intern, he worked with an obstetrician who lobbied the new mothers to name their kids Bill after him. My cousin is a good guy. Interesting too. If he comes down here for a convention or holiday, I'll introduce him to you guys."

"Any friend of yours, Art, is a friend of mine," said Charlie.

"Sorry," said Art. "I interrupted."

Fred said, "That's okay. Bill the obstetrician is funny. Anyway, Charlie, my wife got me a bunch of Buddy Holly's hit songs on tape. I'll try to make you a copy. Let's see if you like them."

Charlie replied, "Thanks. I'm sure there are lots of other Buddy Holly songs that I don't remember hearing on the radio lately. The stuff I like is the rock 'n' roll from the sixties and seventies. Buddy Holly's stuff was earlier than that."

"That's true," agreed Fred.

Charlie continued, "I'm not really into 50s music. Some of it's okay. I never liked those doo wop songs. I don't even like all of the 60's and 70's rock 'n' roll. Well nobody likes everything. I never liked blues and Motown. My Sue loves Motown music. She has to drag me onto the dance floor when she likes something and I don't. That's only fair because I have to drag her to dance to stuff I like too. Fortunately most of the time our musical tastes overlap. I find that lots of 60s and 70s songs with strong beats are great for jogging. You know, it's got a back beat you can't lose it, right?" Charlie continued, "Do you know whose song that's from?"

"'Back beat you can't lose it'? I think it was someone like Jerry Lee Lewis. It wasn't Buddy Holly. That's for sure."

"Jerry Lee Lewis? Doesn't sound right. Someday I'll look it up and let you know whose line that 'back beat' is."

"It really doesn't matter."

"It does to the guy who wrote it. Maybe I'll hear the song on the radio. One day, I'll have the answer for you, Fred."

"Okay. I think you'll like a lot of my Buddy Holly songs, Charlie. I'll get that copy for you really soon."

A few weeks later Charlie received his tape of Buddy Holly hits. Fred's Buddy Holly tape became a frequent companion on Charlie's long jogs. From then on Charlie experienced numerous runner's highs while jogging with Buddy Holly's music in his ears. It could energize him for the rest of the day.

♪♫♪♫

Saving Buddy Holly Blue Days Black Nights

The endorphins released while jogging eventually created a strong association in Charlie's mind between the runner's highs he experienced and the Buddy Holly tunes themselves. Buddy Holly's songs would lift his spirits and sometimes the exhilaration would propel him to run miles more than he had originally planned.

Charlie's collection of Buddy Holly recordings increased. After listening to so much of his music, Charlie became intrigued with Buddy Holly the person. After reading several Buddy Holly biographies his interest in Buddy Holly deepened and he began making trips to used bookstores, music stores and music memorabilia shows.

Charlie spent a significant chunk of his spare time immersed in his new Buddy Holly hobby. He became obsessed and fanatical. It took years, but Charlie became one of the world experts on all things Buddy Holly.

Over the years he fell in love with so many of his songs: 'Tell Me How', 'Oh Boy', 'Peggy Sue', 'Rave On', 'Brown Eyed Handsome Man', 'Peggy Sue Got Married' and 'Crying, Waiting, Hoping'.

As an adult now, Charlie no longer drove like a teenager: with windows open and music blaring. He did, however, tap his foot on the brake and accelerator pedals to the rock 'n' roll music on the radio. Of all the songs recorded by Buddy Holly, Charlie Harding's most favorite favorite was "Tell Me How". Officially it had been written by Charles Hardin, Jerry Allison and Norman Petty. Jerry Allison was Buddy's drummer and old friend. Norman Petty was his manager. Ironically, Charlie Harding's favorite song had been co-written by Charles Hardin. Charlie Harding knew that because of contract issues Buddy had used the pseudonym "Charles Hardin" for a few of the songs that he had written.

Charlie saw Fred in the elevator. "Hey, Fred, you remember the song 'Brown-Eyed Handsome Man'?"

Fred sighed. "I think so. Oh yeah, Buddy Holly sings it. It's one of the songs I gave you."

At other times Fred would have been more interested in musical trivia but it was the end of a tiring day and Fred's mind had already shifted into a lower gear. He just wanted to go home, eat dinner and lie down in front of the television set.

Realizing the lack of enthusiasm in Fred's voice, Charlie said, "Listen, I'll be quick. Chuck Berry was the one who wrote and sang 'Brown-eyed Handsome Man', and he also wrote and recorded 'Rock and Roll Music'. That's the song that says, 'It's got a back beat, you can't lose it.'" Charlie continued, "You look tired, Fred. Go home."

Then Charlie went on. "Oh wait! The Beatles sang 'Rock and Roll Music' too. And another Chuck Berry song, 'Roll Over Beethoven'. Oh yeah, and the Beatles recorded some of Buddy Holly's tunes too. And the Rolling Stones had a big hit. You remember, 'Not Fade Away'. 'Not Fade Away' was one of the Stones' hits and Buddy Holly wrote it. And he wrote it under the pseudonym 'Charles Hardin'. Cool, isn't it? Charlie Harding loves a Charles Hardin song.

"What were we talking about again, Fred? Oh yeah. Chuck Berry's song 'Brown Eyed Handsome Man'. Chuck Berry wrote it and recorded the song first. Buddy Holly recorded it afterward. Lots of singers do that. Singing another singer's song is called covering it. Buddy Holly recorded a lot of songs that he liked that were not originally written for him. Many of those recording sessions were never even officially released but somehow they are available to Buddy Holly fans who know where to look for them. Many singers have covered Buddy Holly songs. You know who Linda Ronstadt is?"

Fred's eyes were closing and he covered a yawn with his hand. Charlie noticed, "Sorry, Fred. I better let you go."

Fred replied, "Yes, I better go. I'm beat. I'm glad you like the Buddy Holly songs I gave you."

"I sure do. Buddy Holly and the Crickets. See you tomorrow."

"See you."

♪♫♪♫

Fred had given Charlie a tape of Buddy Holly hits. Charlie had listened to the music while he jogged. For Charlie, the pleasant endorphin-induced positive mental experiences and Buddy Holly's music converged in his mind. And thus began Charlie's love for his music and later the man.

As Charlie became more passionate about his Buddy Holly hobby, he read rock 'n' roll books and more biographies about Buddy. He was amazed by the number of books about Buddy Holly that had been written and that were still coming out.

There were no fan clubs left in North America, so he joined the Buddy Holly fan clubs in England. Through these he made pen pals and friends around the world. He met some of them at tribute dances and parties celebrating Buddy Holly's birthday. He visited many of the American ballrooms and arenas where Buddy Holly had entertained his fans. He even visited Maple Leaf Gardens in Toronto where Buddy and The Crickets had played in Canada for the first time. They eventually played in nine Canadian cities, including a couple of small ones in Ontario near Toronto: Peterborough and Kitchener.

He visited the city where Buddy had been born. He visited the site where Buddy Holly had died, and he visited the place where Buddy was buried. And so, Charlie had fallen in love with the music, then the man and finally the fans. Like other fanatical Buddy Holly fans the world over, he had become a "Buddy Hollic".

CHAPTER 9

I remember when rock was young. Me and Susie had so much fun, holding hands and skimming stones. But the biggest kick I ever got was doing a thing called the Crocodile Rock. We were hopping and bopping to the Crocodile Rock. I never knew me a better time and I guess I never will.

–Elton John

♪♫♪♫

Charlie and his future wife Sue were both nineteen when they had been introduced. On their second date, Sue and Charlie went to a bar playing rock 'n' roll music and that also had a dance floor. Dancing to rock 'n' roll music became their favorite date.

After they got married, they went dancing with other couples but if there were no friends available, the two of them would go alone. Dancing was an aerobic workout for Charlie, an unsynchronized freestyle workout. Charlie romped all over the dance floor. Slow tummy rubbing songs were never his cup of tea.

♪♫♪♫

After Sue had said "yes" to his proposal of marriage Charlie said dreamily, "I feel like I just jumped off a cliff."

"That sounds terrible," chided Sue.

"No. I just made a leap into a new part of my life and there's no going back. We are in this for better or for worse. Until death do us part."

Charlie and Sue walked along the street hand-in-hand. When they passed other girls, Charlie would look them over and say to Sue that he had the most beautiful girl in the world beside him. As they passed a hot girl, Charlie would furtively check out her breasts while squeezing Sue's hand. He would whisper, "You're bigger," or "You're better." At first Sue had been a bit annoyed by this. Charlie told her about the time he had been at the mall with Sue's father and her father had been pointing out cute chicks to him. Sue adored her father so she could never bring herself to complain about Charlie's wandering eyes again. It was clear to both of them that leering was one thing but touching other women was a no-no. So Sue tolerated his leering but also got the fringe benefits of it later that night. As Charlie was a breast man, Sue played along and wore provocative low-cut dresses for him, especially at home.

Even in his dreams he was true to Sue, his girlfriend, his fiancée and then his new bride. Charlie had been dreaming about World War II pinup beauty and actress Rita Hayworth. She had seduced him into her bedroom but even in the dream Charlie interrupted and said, "I have to ask Sue if this is okay."

Charlie and Sue had gone out to dance at a new bar. They unexpectedly found themselves listening to country music.

"Did you know that rock 'n' roll had its origins from country & western and the blues?" asked Charlie.

"I don't know much about blues music and I'm not much of a fan of blues or country music."

"Blues and country are the same: sad stories of lost love. The main difference between country music and the blues is the rhythm and the color of the singer."

They watched as others danced but when the music changed to rock 'n' roll Sue and Charlie hopped up to the dance floor. After a stretch of rock 'n' roll songs, a country two-step song started. They were confused for a moment when Charlie suggested, "Do the polka we learned in high school and slow it down a bit."

Before long Charlie smiled and said, "Hey, we're doing the Polish two-step. Look. Some of the crowd are watching us. It looks like they think that we are doing an advanced two-step. I sure hope they don't do line dancing. There is no way I can fake that."

Sue and Charlie both had lots of schoolwork to do and wanted a quiet place to study. Early in the evening they went to the college library together. They sat two desks apart to avoid the temptation to talk. Several times they went outside and grabbed a Coke and junk food while they chatted each other up. They had been there a few hours and the room was emptying out. They packed up their stuff and walked out of the library.

Before the ride home they each went into their respective washrooms. After they both came out Charlie asked playfully, "Have you ever been in the boys' washroom?"

"No," answered Sue. "Why would I? There's no difference anyway."

"You're kidding."

"What do you mean?" said Sue.

"There's a difference between the boys' and the girls' washroom."

"There is not. You're just teasing me," insisted Sue.

"You're serious, aren't you? You don't know there's a difference?"

"What do you mean?"

"Do you want to go in and see for yourself?"

"I can't go in the boys' washroom," Sue replied bashfully. She had never and would never commit that social transgression.

Charlie prodded. "There's no one around. Just go in and take a look for yourself."

"I can't do that."

"Sure you can. I was just there. There's no one in there."

"Are you sure?" Sue said sheepishly.

"Absolutely. There's no one in there."

Charlie held the door open. Blushing, Sue dashed into the boys' washroom and in a flash dashed back out.

"See I told you. There's no difference between the girls' and boys' washroom. But I don't understand why you guys rate foot baths."

SNI was having its annual Christmas party. Charlie wasn't much of a drinker, a cheap drunk. He felt a bit guilty about being tipsy and phoned his young wife at home.

"Hi, Sue. I am so drunk."

"No, you're not. You hardly drink at all."

"That's why I am so drunk. I got taunted into three vodka shots in ten minutes."

"Did you drive?" Sue asked somewhat concerned.

"No. Art warned me and a few of us are splitting a cab to get home. Don't worry. I'm fine. The only problem is I have this giant grin that makes me look like the Cheshire Cat."

Knowing that Charlie was talking to his young wife, a female coworker wickedly snuck up close behind Charlie and said in a loud sultry voice, "Hi, Charlie, honey. What you doing?"

Sue heard this and said sternly, "Charles Harding, remember that being drunk is no excuse for adultery."

♪♫♪♫

Charlie had been extremely pissed at the time, but in retrospect it was funny. Charlie had called Sue at lunch time.

"Don't forget, Sue, you promised me a long sexy evening tonight. Do you want me to pick up pizza or Chinese food?"

"Oh no! I forgot to tell you I'm going out with the girls tonight. We're going to the museum," Sue replied.

"Hey, we had a deal."

"I committed to the girls,"

"You committed to the girls?" Charlie's voice got louder. "You made a commitment to me first."

It's the last night of the King Tut exhibition. It'll be my last chance to see it."

"Tomorrow's my birthday. You promised this evening to me weeks ago."

"We can have sex anytime. But going to the museum, that's something special."

"I don't believe what you just said," Charlie yelled into the phone.

"Pardon me." Sue said derisively.

"Goodbye, Sue." He was about to slam the phone down but contained himself enough to just hang up. Charlie tucked this incident into his memory bank and vowed to get even one day. But how could a male get even with his mate for not having sex with him anyway? Would he withhold sex from Sue in retaliation? That would be the day. It would be against human nature, evolution and the survival of the species. Whenever the opportunity arose, Charlie never did get even.

Charlie and Sue decided to get a second car. They agreed that the new car would be their primary car, the one they would use when they went out together. Charlie had been complaining that he had always driven used cars. As Charlie drove much more than Sue, they agreed that the new car would be his.

Saving Buddy Holly Blue Days Black Nights

"It'll be your car," Sue said. "I don't care about cars, but you do, and so I want you to have the new car." Sue had said numerous times that Charlie could pick his new car and everything about it.

On the way to the dealership Sue said it again, "Charlie, you choose the car. You drive it. It's yours."

Charlie was partial to a gearshift but once they got to the dealership Sue explained that it was easier to drive in the city with automatic transmission. Charlie agreed that, although gearshift was more fun and automatic would use more gas, it would be easier to drive an automatic, especially on the rare occasion that Sue drove the new car. So they went with automatic transmission.

Charlie was thinking of splurging on a fancier trim for his first new car.

Sue said, "I don't think it's worth the extra money. But it's gonna be your car so it's your choice, Charlie."

After further discussion, they went with the basic trim.

They checked out the colors of the automobiles on the showroom floor and on the lot. Charlie had always wanted a bright red car. After checking out the red cars with him, Sue steered him toward a few powder blue cars.

"It's your choice, Charlie lover. Pick whatever color you want."

They got powder blue.

They walked around the showroom checking out the various models. Charlie wanted sporty bucket seats, but Sue convinced him to get the more practical bench seat.

"When we go to drive-in movies, we want to be able to cuddle up without you getting injured. It's still your choice though, Charlie," she purred. "You'll be driving it and so it's okay to spend a few dollars more for bucket seats to make you happy."

So, Charlie chose a powder blue, automatic transmission with bench seats for his first brand-new vehicle. It was going to be his pride and joy.

Sue's car did not have air conditioning, but the new car did. On the first hot day after they picked up the car Sue pleaded, "Charlie honey, it's so hot today. Can I please use 'your' car?" Charlie lent her the new car for the day.

It was hot again the next day. Charlie lent her the new car again.

And finally on the third day, it was hot again. Sue demanded, "It's hot today, Charlie. Please don't use 'my' car."

It was Saturday morning. Sue's alarm went off. She pressed the snooze button, closed her eyes and whispered to herself, "Five more minutes. Five more minutes."

After she was finally awake, Sue rolled over in bed and poked the still sleeping Charlie in the ribs. Sue asked, "How do you spell niece?"

"N-I-E-C-E. Don't you believe in dictionaries?"

Sue cuddled up to Charlie and smiled. "It's easier to ask you. You're so smart. Don't you realize that's why I married you?"

"Not because I look like an Adonis?"

"Nope. It's your mind that attracted me to you and it still does."

Charlie slid his hand across Sue's hips under her pajamas.

"Hey! Wandering hand problem? I'm not just a sex object you know. I have a mind too," Sue mocked.

"I don't understand why women complain when they are treated as sex objects. I don't mind being treated as a sex object. I'd love to be called a trophy husband."

Charlie flipped behind her and love tapped her on her bottom. Sue twisted around and grabbed his wrists. She pushed him over onto his back and held him down. Charlie was pushing his head upward as he puckered his lips when Sue let go and jumped out of the bed.

"Oh my God!" she yelled. "I have to be at a meeting."

"It's Saturday," Charlie reminded her.

"I've got to get up and get ready. I don't have time for sex."

"What are you talking about? We have been having sex."

"What do you mean? I have to get going."

"Don't you know what foreplay is?"

"Oh."

"Sometimes you can be such a sexual cretin," Charlie scowled. Then he smiled. "Sometimes I think you have the sexual insight of an amoeba.".

Sue said, "And sometimes you're so funny. Quick. Give me a kiss."

He did and then Sue asked, "Hey, wait a second. What's a cretin?"

"Don't ask." Charlie tried to look serious. Then he screamed playfully as a pillow hit him in the face. "Don't hit me in the head or you'll make me stupid."

"You are stupid, you uncouth bear." Sue mocked. "After the meeting, I'm planning to spend some time at the flea market with some friends. Do we have enough in the bank for me to take out a couple of hundred dollars?"

"But I gave you your own credit card on our wedding night."

"They don't like credit cards at the flea market. I get better prices for cash."

"What are you thinking of buying?"

"Don't worry, Charlie. It's for a good cause."

"A good cause? And what would that cause be?"

"Me."

"Hey Sue, remember the time that I was at the cafeteria and took out my wallet to pay the cashier? I opened my wallet and a moth flew out."

"Yeah, but I left you a nice note in your wallet that said, 'I love you.' I even drew a heart on it."

Charlie cocked his head to the side and stared at her. Then they both laughed out loud. The most important things to keep a relationship strong were sex and laughter, not necessarily in that order. Charlie always said that his favorite sound was Sue laughing.

CHAPTER 10

Charlie had always been an avid reader. He had a craving to know as much as possible about everything. Sue had always been a great listener. She was good at drawing people to talk about their own interests. This made her an engaging friend and was one of the things that made her so attractive to Charlie. Sue became infatuated with Charlie's ability to discuss and talk on so many topics. She was also adept at feigning interest in topics that she could barely understand. She liked the sound of his voice when Charlie got excited while expounding to her.

After they were married Sue told Charlie that when he explained things to her, she became sexually aroused. Charlie's heart and ego swelled with pride. He became even more motivated to explain things to her. Sue told Charlie that she fell in love with him for his mind and stayed with him for his body.

Charlie smiled and said, "I'm not just a great mind."

Charlie became interested in time travel and time machines as a teenager when he first read H.G. Wells' book "The Time Machine". Sue was one of the first people that Charlie had shared his thoughts about time travel and his multiple time line theory.

"I like to call paths through time 'time lines'. Imagine a highway of time going from point A to a point B. The highway can widen and narrow along the way but ultimately the path tapers down to a single lane that ends at point B. Even if a tortuous path is taken, the highway eventually winds up at point B."

Charlie went on. "Let me explain it again in another way. Envision yourself driving from home on a quiet street to an isolated cottage. Your trip starts out from your driveway. You back onto the road. You have lots of options to get to the highway. When you get to the highway, you get to choose one of the two lanes going in the direction of the cottage. When the highway widens to six lanes, you have three lanes to choose from. Eventually, as you get closer to the cottage, the roads narrow to fewer lanes, so your choice of lanes becomes limited. In the end there is only one choice, the dirt road that takes you right to the cottage.

"As well as the choice of lanes on the roads, there are multiple combinations of roads to take from home to the cottage and there are many possible events that can happen along these paths."

Charlie reiterated, "The beginning of the journey is at home. The end of the journey is always, always at the cottage." Sue put her arms around Charlie, closed her eyes and kissed him voraciously.

CHAPTER 11

Charlie was depressed when he sat down in front of the television and picked up his TV Guide. At that moment Charlie did not know that one day he would become obsessed with Buddy Holly. Being a rock 'n' roll fan, he decided to watch "The Buddy Holly Story". He was watching the final scene of the movie. It was Buddy Holly's last show, a triumphant concert with the singers, the audience and the music filling the screen with exuberant joy. Charlie felt tears welling up in his eyes. It didn't make sense that Charlie was about to cry. And then the movie ended suddenly with the announcement of Buddy Holly's death.

Charlie got up. He found Sue and fell into her arms sobbing uncontrollably. Sue knew that he was moody, emotional and sensitive, but she did know what to make of this. Charlie eventually figured it out. Buddy Holly had died at the peak of his career. He was looking forward to a career of writing, singing, playing and producing records. He was full of confidence. He was happy and should have enjoyed a much longer life. Charlie was also at a splendid point in his life with a successful career blooming and a beautiful young wife. His life was good, but Charlie was feeling sad as he looked forward to a life of more pain.

♪♫♪♫

Sue was worried. "You look and are acting really tense this weekend. You seem very anxious and irritable. Charlie, are you sick?"

"I'm tired and sad but I'll be okay. I'll just lie down again and take a nap."

"But you've hardly gotten up at all today."

"I know," said Charlie lethargically. My mood is very low and I'm so tired. I know it doesn't make sense."

"Are you suicidal? Do you want me to stay home and keep you company or do you want me to go out and leave you alone for a while?"

"You can go out for a bit if you have to, but check in on me once in a while."

"Check on you? Are you suicidal?" Sue was concerned.

"No. I'll be fine. I'll just give in to the exhausted feeling, do nothing and go to sleep."

Charlie had been feeling so sad and so bad that death and suicidal ideas had been percolating through his mind. He told Sue the truth. He said that he had been thinking of suicide but went on to say that he felt sure that he had enough self-control not to do anything radical. Sue had been concerned about Charlie for days and she had asked Charlie over and over again whether he was suicidal. Charlie had told Sue repeatedly that he was thinking about suicide but would not ever carry through with it. All this weekend he had been doing little and had been very low in mood and energy. Sue was rightly concerned that Charlie was suicidal and so she decided to stay home.

As Charlie was waking up from his nap, he saw that Sue was holding her handbag.

Sue noticed him looking at her and said, "I'm going over to see my cousin Sharon. She called and told me about some scary results on her biopsy. I promised I would visit with her for a while. I'll call you from there. I'll be back soon."

"Okay. But don't go too long. I'm feeling like hell. I need you to support me. I need you to hug me. I need hugs."

Sue embraced Charlie and gave him a big reassuring squeeze. Then she left. Just as she was about to close the door she turned back and Charlie saw her anxious face.

"I'll be back in just over an hour. Two hours at the most."

A couple of hours later Sue called and said, "Sharon is very depressed and I'm going to take her out for lunch. I'm hoping that will make her feel better."

"Please come home."

"But Sharon needs me. She's scared and depressed."

For the last few days Sue had been asking Charlie over and over again whether he was suicidal so when Sue said that she was going to take her depressed cousin Sharon out for lunch Charlie became furious.

"You stupid fucking bitch! I cannot believe what you just said." He smashed the phone down. It seemed bizarre to him that after several days of worrying about Charlie's committing suicide, Sue could actually choose to go out with her depressed cousin. She decided to comfort someone else rather than her own husband.

Charlie was still angry when Sue came home later. Charlie confronted her with the bizarreness of what she had done. Sue replied that her cousin was depressed and might be dying and so she wanted to spend time with her to get her mind off her illness. She couldn't fathom Charlie's fury and he could not understand how she had chosen to comfort her depressed cousin rather than her depressed husband. Charlie was so frustrated that he punched the wall repeatedly. His knuckles hurt. After the wall had been repaired and painted, a hint of an indentation remained in the wall to remind Charlie of Sue's choice. Charlie could never accept what Sue had done and she could never understand why he had been so upset.

CHAPTER 12

Their late teens and early 20s were good times for Sue and Charlie: first dating, then their engagement, and then newlyweds. Their lives teemed with good times and happiness. Among their greatest pleasures were dancing and listening to music. Then the cloud of Charlie's depression drifted over their sunny world.

Sue smiled. "Charlie, please help me with the garbage."

Charlie sighed and groaned. "I just can't do any more!"

Sue was surprised. "I didn't ask for much, Charlie."

"I know. I want to do things, but I feel so tired all the time. I can do them if I have to."

Tears welled up in Sue's eyes. "Don't worry, Charlie. It's not a big deal I'll do it myself. No problem."

After Sue left and went outside Charlie put his head down and wept.

Charlie talked to Sue about methods of suicide that he had considered. He told her that if it happened suddenly and unexpectedly, getting hit by a giant truck would be a great way to die. It would be over before he had a chance to feel pain or even feel scared. He told her that he had done research and was confident that the pain centers in the brain would be destroyed before the pain fibers in the body could even get their messages to them.

At first Sue had been compassionate and tried to soothe Charlie. Eventually his suicidal thoughts began smothering her.

Sue screamed, "Charlie, stop talking like that! I've heard that kind of talk too many times from you. Stop it! I don't want to hear it anymore."

Sue worried that one day Charlie would kill their son and her during one of his down cycles. She had read about murder suicides but after talking to Charlie's psychiatrist and a counselor of her own she no longer worried that Charlie would ever kill her or their little Davy.

When Charlie was depressed, he was irritable and sensitive to noise. He was easily startled, and loud sounds felt painful. Even when people spoke to him in a normal tone of voice, he felt as if they were yelling at him. A mild disagreement could feel like a major argument to Charlie.

Charlie had to control his irritability at work and in other places where he had to conform to social niceties and act civil and levelheaded. Having suppressed his sense of being abused and yelled at all day, Charlie finally let down when he got home. Sometimes his frustrations would lash out at his wife.

Charlie was in the kitchen and Sue in another room.

"Charlie," Sue sang out to him from another room in a melodious voice, "Are you there?"

"Stop yelling at me! What do you want?" Charlie barked back.

Sue was taken aback by the outburst. She eventually grasped that his irritability and ill temper were part of his illness. Home may be "the place where, when you have to go there, they have to take you in," but finally Sue refused to put up with the abusive behavior and began avoiding Charlie whenever she could. Divorce was inevitable.

After his outbursts, he would come to Sue and apologize. "I'm sorry," he said in a remorseful voice.

"Oh, you're sorry you yelled at me?"

"Actually, I'm sorry you give me so many excuses to yell at you," Charlie blurted out.

After realizing what he had done, Charlie lamented, "Oh no. I did it again. It's me again. You don't deserve how I treat you. I'm sorry that I yell at you so much."

It was gut-wrenching for Sue to watch Charlie suffering with his mental anguish. She would hear him moaning in his sleep. It hurt her so much to see the love of her life in pain. Charlie's depression was ruining her life as well as his. She worried that it would ruin their son's life too. It was difficult enough for his loving adult wife to live with his suffering and irritability, but what effect was Charlie's illness having on their little boy? What would be worse for Davy: a life with no father in his life or a life with an abusive father?

Sue had gone to a counselor on her own to help her deal with Charlie's depression. Sue told her about the different drugs and therapies Charlie had tried. The counselor had gone into great detail about the drugs and explained that Charlie was about as good as he would get. Having basically tried all of the medications that medical science had to offer, it was unlikely that the mood swings would be better controlled by any available therapies. Lots of research was being done on depression and eventually the situation would change as dramatically new treatments were discovered.

One day Davy asked Sue, "Mommy, why is Daddy so nice to everyone but us?"

In the end, Sue could no longer handle the stress of her predicament. She had been married to Charlie for eight years, but she felt it would be so much better for Davy and her to get out of the situation. She never stopped loving Charlie but after years of enduring the torment of his depression, Sue finally gave up. She still loved Charlie but had become convinced that she had to leave him for her son's sake.

After their divorce Charlie put up little resistance when Sue got a job in another city and moved away. Charlie was never angry at

Sue for leaving. How could he be? She was the love of his life and he alone had driven her away. He was angry at himself.

Years after she had remarried, Sue came to realize that, although her life would never be perfect again, the life with the new devil she had married was better than the life with the old devil she used to know.

Charlie wondered how Sue looked back at their days together. He hoped that she had some fond memories and not just the bad ones. Did she ever think that it had been worth being with him at all? He thought that Sue would mostly remember the trying times that she had endured with the man she had once adored. Did she still remember the man who had treated her like his princess and who she had worshiped as her prince? Theirs had been a marriage created in heaven but when Charlie had gotten sick her marriage and her life had exploded in Sue's face.

CHAPTER 13

Love is a given, but respect is earned.

♪♫♪♫

A parent gives a child love and the essentials of life. A child gives back by just existing. There is the joy of watching your child breathe and sleep, the warm feeling as your baby ceases crying when you pick him up and then seeing him look at you and smiling.

His first steps are sensational. Changing diapers is neat at first and then a pain in the ass. Blowing soap bubbles together is exciting. His going to school for the first time is both thrilling and sad.

Charlie always kept his promises and was very careful when making them. He even told people truthfully that he would keep a promise unless he was in hospital or dead. Charlie broke only one promise in his entire life, to his son.

He had put Davy on his lap and hugged him close as they were about to go down a water slide. He promised not to let go when they hit the water. But the water was deeper than Charlie thought so to keep Davy's head above the water he pushed Davy up and out of the water and held him like that. When they got out of the pool

Davy said, "You broke your promise." The fact that he had broken a promise, especially to his son, bothered Charlie for the rest of his life. Davy forgot about it, but when Charlie saw Davy years later, he shared the story of what had happened and that he was still feeling guilty for breaking his promise.

"Dad, don't be stupid. I mean silly."

Charlie appreciated Davy's words but, nevertheless, felt guilty about it forever.

Davy was invited to a birthday party. Charlie overheard Sue on the phone talking with the mother of a child that had not been invited to the party. The mother was very angry. On the sly, Charlie phoned and warned the birthday boy's mom that if she wanted to keep a friendship with the angry mom, then she should invite the other child too. She shrewdly invited him, and Charlie kept that friendship intact. Charlie craved praise and wanted to tell somebody about what he'd done. He was torn between being altruistic and keeping quiet, and being praised. In the end he was the only one, other than the mother he had warned, who knew about his good deed.

Charlie was reading when young Davy said, "I want a new baseball glove."

Charlie replied, "Your glove fits just fine and it is only one year old. You must learn frugality."

"What's that?"

"It means not wasting. It means saving and showing restraint."

"Dad, my friends just got new gloves and theirs are less than one-year old. Dad, it's not fair. It's not fair."

"When you see kids starving on TV that's not fair."

"Come on, Dad. This is North America. You cannot compare poor people in Africa to us in America."

Saving Buddy Holly Blue Days Black Nights

♪♫♪♫

Charlie worried about there being enough money to raise Davy if anything happened to him. He and Sue bought life insurance. Charlie was torn between the pain of living and his responsibility to stay alive. When he got a life insurance policy, he made a promise to himself not to commit suicide before the two-year restriction in his insurance policy had expired. It read: "If the death of the insured is caused by suicide, while either sane or insane, within two years of the issue date, the death benefit of this policy will not be paid."

Charlie was watching Davy play outside. Davy fell and skinned his knee. He ran inside to his mother. Mom washed it, put antibiotic cream on it and finally covered it with a band-aid. Davy came back outside. Charlie called him over and said, "Mommy really loves you and takes good care of you, so when you're in trouble you can always run to Mom for help. You will always be her baby so remember that when your mom is cold and tells you to put on a coat, don't argue. Just put on a coat. And remember that you can always call on your dad when you are in big trouble and need lawyers, guns, and money."

When he was in high school, Charlie was given the nickname "Mr. Perfect" by other students. Charlie may have been a know-it-all, but his salvation was that he was always willing to help out other students when they needed it. Had he not been assisting them, the bullies would have been all over him. Instead, the high school bullies would approach Charlie for help with their schoolwork and Charlie remained under their protection.

Charlie knew that calling him "Mr. Perfect" was fair. It was difficult for him to let even the smallest error pass. Had Sue not left him, Charlie imagined himself looking at Davy's homework and saying, "You only got very good. Where is the excellent?" Or if Davy got 99 out of 100 on a test, Charlie thought he might have said, "What happened to the other mark?"

CHAPTER 14

Who has not had the nightmare of sitting in a classroom about to take an exam and realizing that they had been studying for the wrong exam?

♪♫♪♫

After he became an adult, Charlie avoided horror movies. He hated to be startled and his life was horrible enough. As a kid, however, Charlie had watched horror movies. The black and white ones were the best, or the worst, depending on how you looked at it. He had seen Frankenstein movies many times and so young Charlie dreamt of Frankenstein's monster. The Frankenstein nightmare occurred regularly. In it, the ungainly grotesque monster marched loudly around his parents' house looking for a victim while Charlie hid in his bedroom closet. Charlie envisioned the monster turning his head from side to side as he walked through the kitchen looking about. He heard the monster tromping up the stairs and into the hallway near his bedroom. As the monster got closer Charlie cowered in the closet fearfully waiting for the door to open and his coming face to face with Frankenstein's monster. As the closet door was opening, he had always startled awake without knowing what happened.

Gerald I. Goldlist

♪♫♪♫

Charlie had dreamt of water rushing toward him as it crashed through a hole in the skin of a mortally wounded submarine. He had dreamt of the landing at Omaha Beach on D-Day. He saw men being torn apart by machine gun fire ripping into their chests, heads and faces. He saw body parts flying through the air and falling onto the beach and onto scrambling troops. He saw arms and legs lying on the beach and floating in the water. He had dreamt of medieval battles with men running towards each other and being impaled on pikes. He saw men on the ground with missing limbs hacked off by swords and axes. As they moaned in pain, unable to move and knowing that their situation was hopeless, they yearned for a merciful enemy to finish them off.

In his dreams, he had fought in the American Civil War. He had fought with the Blue and he had fought with the Gray. At Gettysburg he had charged across in one of Pickett's divisions with canister exploding overhead and shrapnel streaking everywhere. And then after Confederate General Armistead had been wounded, he limped back from The Angle and over Emmitsburg Road. He had also fixed his bayonet beside the Union's Colonel Chamberlain and charged down Little Round Top. The enemy had dropped its weapons, surrendered or run away. In another nightmare, the brave Rebel soldiers charging up Little Round Top did not surrender, and bayonets pierced into them. A Rebel soldier, transfixed by a bayonet, looked up with a fierce hateful grimace while another was lying on the ground severely wounded looking up with pleading eyes. Charlie flinched awake as a bayonet impaled him.

♪♫♪♫

Charlie rolled over in his sleep as another nightmare began. A large transport truck was approaching in the oncoming lane. Hitting a truck that size would demolish his car and he would almost certainly die immediately. The transport passed by and Charlie felt his car being pushed sideways by the surging gust from the truck.

Now there was a car coming toward him. It was weaving along the road and crossed into Charlie's lane. As the nightmare continued Charlie took off his seatbelt. The car was now in front of Charlie coming directly at him at high speed. It was coming closer and closer. The oncoming vehicle was not going to get back into its lane. The two vehicles were racing toward a deadly collision. They were seconds apart. As his brakes screeched, Charlie turned the steering wheel hard to the right and the car veered off the road. Once his car had stopped, he looked behind him and saw the tire ruts dug into the patchy grass. There was not a scratch on the car or on Charlie.

Charlie awoke with a start. Sweating with his heart pounding, it only took seconds for Charlie to realize that he had been dreaming. "Shit!" he said out loud. "Shit! Shit! Shit!" Even in his dream he did not have the guts to kill himself.

CHAPTER 15

Fred asked Charlie, "Do you ever worry about strange dogs chasing you when you're jogging?"

"I carry dog treats, but Art taught me that dogs wear their hearts on their tails. If its tail is wagging, then the dog is happy."

"But that could be because the dog's happy that it's going to bite you."

Art smiled. "I love dogs but I was always afraid of how sad I would be when a pet died. Somebody once told me that the pain you suffer when you lose a dog is the price you pay for having them in your life, but it's worth it. After I lived through it myself, I agree. When we got our first puppy, I took her out for a walk on a hot day. It was soon too much for her and she sat down exhausted and panting. I picked her up, cradled her like a baby and carried her home. Nothing binds us to another living being and creates love and affection more than holding a totally dependent tiny creature in your arms. That's why uncles love and hug their grownup nephews and nieces so tightly."

Charlie preferred to jog on an indoor track. It was more convenient and safer as he did not have to worry about how far he would go before getting tired. He could allow himself to be mesmerized as he looked down at the monotonous track without worrying about running into a tree, person or ferocious beast.

Saving Buddy Holly Blue Days Black Nights

Although he liked the scenery when he was outside, in his mind he measured distance by counting imaginary laps on an imaginary track. Charlie wasn't superstitious, but he did not walk under ladders, and he avoided black cats when he was jogging, just in case. Why tempt fate?

He was jogging outside and ran through a heavily deciduous section of trees after the leaves had begun their yearly change. As he was responding to the runners high caused by his endorphins, a feeling of bliss and contentment came over him. He was enraptured as he ran among pendulous branches covered with deep red, orange, yellow and green leaves. As he rounded a curve Charlie was enveloped in a colored arch and envisioned himself running through a multi-hued tunnel. He wanted to be embraced by the tunnel and run suspended in time and space forever.

Some parts of the road were uneven with potholes and cracks. Charlie recalled the time he had been running outdoors on the university track. It was ironic that after finishing five miles on the well-groomed track, he was walking on the grass when his foot dropped into a shallow depression. As his ankle twisted over, one of the ligaments on the outside of his ankle gave way. The sprain that he suffered required a cast for four weeks.

While moping about his difficulty getting around in his cast, Charlie would think about the jogger that had been running on a city street and had slipped on a small stone. She had fallen off the sidewalk and under the tire of a moving bus and died, cut in half with ropes of her guts and gore holding the crushed halves together. Had it been predestination and merciless fate? Even though he had heard the story years ago, whenever Charlie saw a stone in his path, instead of running around it, he shortened his footsteps and kicked it out of the way.

He found himself stopping and brushing frogs into the woods. He chose to prevent pain, suffering and death when he was able to. He even avoided stepping on ants as he hated to see living creatures die for nothing. Killing someone not only destroys that person but all of his potential offspring and their future generations.

In childhood, other kids would burn ants with the sun's rays and magnifying glasses, but never young Charlie. He watched a couple of times and walked away. Charlie imagined the ant's family waiting for their dear relative to come home for dinner and that the little ants would have no one to tell them bedtime stories.

He wondered if he would ever be able to put an injured animal out of its misery. Would he be able to kill a severely hurt dog that was lying in the street whimpering after it been hit by a car? Yes. He would force himself. They shoot horses, don't they?

Charlie found the exercise bike a good place to ruminate about things. He would figure out project issues and plan budgets. He would do calculations in his head. He would think of places to take his son. He would recall which of his friends and relatives he hadn't seen for a while and what socializing would interest them. He brought a pen and paper to the exercise room so that after he got off the bike he could write ideas down quickly before he forgot them.

He had freefloating anxiety so he would worry while he was exercising. He could worry about anything. He worried about the world's financial system collapsing. He worried about local insurrection, world war and nuclear war. He worried about every worst-case scenario. Weather disasters knocking out power. An epidemic or pandemic. What if he got a sliver in his finger and his body forgot how to heal? While exercising, endorphins masked the discomfort and made worrying less onerous.

There were many songs that especially lifted Charlie's spirits, but in his collection of exercise music there was no other artist that appeared more frequently than Buddy Holly. When he jogged, the pounding of the drums carried Charlie along like a surfer being lifted by a great wave. As he ran, Charlie raised his arms up into the air as bursts of adrenaline and endorphins sustained him onward until exhaustion overtook him. His gait slowed, and then he walked with his head hanging in front of him, gasping for air to replenish the biochemical pathways in his muscle cells with the oxygen that they were owed.

Charlie had barely started an outdoor run when dark clouds began rolling in. With the full moon peeking in and out of the clouds Charlie thought of eerie movies: it was a dark and stormy night. He was thinking of turning back, but he had already put in the effort to get there. He had changed into his jogging pants and a T-shirt. His audio player was already loaded with a Buddy Holly tape. He had already put on two pairs of running socks. (He found that a second pair of socks increased the cushioning and prevented sore feet.) He had tied his laces exactly to the right tension for comfort and support. His running shoes were high quality, and they were 300-miles old. He never used running shoes for more than 500 miles and so after each run he noted the number of miles he had run. When he reached 375 miles, he began a search for new shoes.

After just a few minutes of running, Charlie was loath to waste his efforts to get ready. He heard the sound of distant thunder. He looked in that direction and saw a tiny flickering flash of lightning. This was not a day for outdoor jogging. He heard a thunder roll coming closer. He should go back. He was now running in a light rain. Charlie kept an eye on the flashes in the distance as he felt the refreshing sprinkles of rain coming down.

"Oh, what the hell." He continued jogging but turned away from the storm.

CHAPTER 16

As a five-year-old boy, Charlie had been fascinated by the goldfish that his parents had bought him as a pet. He would gaze into the flat-bottomed round bowl and watch the solitary goldfish swimming. The graceful movement of its tail propelled the little fish through its small watery world. Charlie stared. Goldie stared back. What was Goldie thinking?

The little boy had watched his mother sprinkle food into the fishbowl. The crinkled brownish-gold flakes floated on the water's surface as Goldie swam up and wolfed them down. As the morsels of dehydrated marine life became waterlogged, they floated down to the bottom of the bowl where Goldie continued to suck them in. One afternoon little Charlie watched his fishie's mouth opening and closing. His fish was hungry. Charlie loved Goldie and did not want her to suffer hunger pangs. He had watched his mother feed the fish so often that he was sure he could do it too. He found a box with holes in the top. He had seen his mother sprinkle with this container too. The flakes that came out of the container and sprinkled down into the fishbowl were not exactly the same color as those that came out when his mother fed the fish but to the proud five-year-old they looked like fish food.

A few hours later his mother was gently explaining that the powdered household cleanser was not food for fish. She consoled her crying boy. Charlie Harding never spoke of the murder he had committed, but he never forgave himself.

Saving Buddy Holly Blue Days Black Nights

♪♫♪♫

Depressive people have very harsh consciences and suffer regrets for trivial misdemeanors and mistakes. Maybe it was guilt over killing the goldfish, but Charlie avoided swimming in the ocean and even in lakes. Maybe it was a worry that the animals might exact revenge for the goldfish murder, but he had developed a fear of animals in general. His fear of animals had become amplified by a dog near his school. As he walked by its yard, it had barked to protect its territory. Charlie perspired with terror whenever he walked past the dog. When the dog smelled his fear, it snapped at him even more. He finally chose to walk an extra three blocks to school to avoid the growling demon dog.

After its cage door had been left ajar, a pet mouse at school had escaped into his classroom. The tiny creature had wreaked havoc as it ran along the walls from corner to corner of the room. One brave young lad marched over boasting that he would pick the mouse up. The girls were shrieking and the other boys were cowering behind their desks. Charlie's eyes bugged open as his heart raced. The janitor saved the day by dispatching the creature with a deadly mop. The experience left Charlie with musophobia — a morbid fear of mice.

Charlie's son Davy was with his mother at a kids fair and won two goldfish. Just as every other kid did, Davy had initially promised that he would look after the fish. As his interest waned, the task of looking after the fish ironically fell to Charlie, the one who years ago had murdered their cousin.

Adult Charlie watched the goldfish propelling themselves through the water. When a goldfish came near the glass, it turned. For the fish it was the end of its universe. Charlie imagined he would have a similar experience if he ever reached the end of the Universe. He would not even realize that his direction of movement was limited. The option to go through the edge of the Universe would not even exist. As far as he would be concerned he would be choosing from among all the options he was aware of: to turn left, right, up, down or back.

Did the fish communicate? Were they just rivals for the food that was dropped into their bowl twice daily? One day one of the goldfish began teetering sideways. Charlie watched as its bowl mate swam up beside it and tried to nudge it straight with its own body. There must have been some element of comradeship there. These two swimming creatures had lived together in their clear bowl for over a year. Charlie thought of the goldfish when Sue encouraged him to snap out of his depression. He pictured himself starting to flounder on his side and Sue's trying to straighten him up with her hurtful words of encouragement. As the dull orange fish finally tipped horizontally onto its side, the other goldfish gave up and swam away.

CHAPTER 17

Charlie and Art had been good friends since childhood. They had become even closer friends as they continued through undergrad engineering, getting their PhD's and working together at SNI. Like Sue, Art was a good listener. As Charlie's time travel ideas evolved, Art became an important sounding board for Charlie's time concepts. Charlie had started with basic physics equations that he had learned in high school and early university: $E=mc^2$, $E=hv$, $F=ma$. He loved formulas, symbols and numbers. As Charlie's time travel visions progressed, they incorporated quantum mechanics and theories beyond quantum theory. His formulas became more complex and sophisticated as he refined and expanded his theories.

Art said, "I remember talking to you about going back in time and warning Buddy Holly not to get on that airplane."

"I have thought about it lots of times. Maybe I will go back in time and warn Buddy Holly of his impending fate. I think that if I could get close to him somehow, some of my wisdom ..." Charlie stopped and continued. "Some of my memories and knowledge might pass into Buddy's mind and warn him about what happened after he played at the Surf Ballroom in February 1959."

"What was the exact date of the plane crash?"

"The last show was on Monday, February 2 but the plane crash was after midnight, so Tuesday, February 3, 1959 was the day the music died."

Gerald I. Goldlist

♪ ♫ ♪ ♫

"Quiz time!" Charlie called out to Art as he sat down beside him. "What was the first song released by Buddy Holly?"

Art thought for a second. "'That'll Be the Day'?"

"Nope. That was released as the Crickets' first hit but it wasn't the song first released by Buddy."

Art tried again. "Then 'Peggy Sue'."

Charlie smiled. "Nice try. 'Peggy Sue' was released as a Buddy Holly song even though the Crickets played on it. It was released after 'That'll Be the Day'."

"Was Buddy Holly's first song released before he got famous?"

"Yep. 1956."

"Charlie, give me a break."

"It was recorded in Nashville by Decca Records. It was called 'Blue Days Black Nights'."

"Never heard of it," said Art.

"Most people haven't. It didn't do well. I only know about it because I'm researching Buddy stuff."

Art asked Charlie, "So if you traveled back through time and changed the past, what do you think it would do to the present or to the future? Is history inevitable?"

Charlie replied, "Let's consider a short set of possible time lines that could occur in a walk around the block. First you walk out the door, and then you have the choice of turning left or right. After that you continue to walk on the sidewalk, and you can choose to walk right next to the road or further away from the road. That's two more time line options. Someone is walking toward you. Who makes the first move? To the left or right? Or not at all and you collide. The collision is unlikely but possible. Even if you keep it simple and basic by not crossing the road at intersections, you still have to make five turns after walking out the door. There are options along the way like stopping to look in a window, avoiding walking under a ladder or turning away from a black cat. Even if you only make five right turns from the door or five left turns from the door, there are still slightly different pathways that you can take until you are back at the doorway where you started. So, your starting point and your end point are the same but the paths are different and so the history between the starting points can change. And that's my time lines in a nutshell. There can be time lines that have vastly more complicated pathway choices; these would be much more protracted and widely divergent."

"Like in Isaac Asimov's story 'The End of Eternity', a tiny change made by going back in time didn't alter the ultimate destiny of mankind, but it did make the duration of suffering through a horrid period shorter. The time travelers moving through Eternity didn't change where the world ultimately ended up, but they did cause changes to the future."

Charlie said, "Yes. That's also similar to Asimov's Foundation Trilogy in which Hari Seldon's psychohistory formula predicted the future. Parts of that future were changeable and Seldon tried to make changes in order to decrease suffering too."

Art considered what Charlie had been saying. "So long term trends are inevitable, but the details are not. We know that throughout history every empire ends. There were Portuguese, French, Spanish and Persian empires. The British Empire ended not long ago. Alexander the Great's empire didn't last very long and once he died his empire fell apart. And remember that you and I didn't even study all the Chinese dynasties."

Charlie said, "I think that while people are living through an empire it must seem that the empire will never end. Look at the Soviet Union. It just ended a couple of years ago. Those living in the Soviet hegemony must've felt that it would go on forever. I know I did."

"Yes. It must've felt like forever to those who lived under an empire. The Pax Romana lasted for centuries and now we are wondering how long the Pax Americana will last. But how can there be multiple time lines between the beginning point and endpoint?"

"Multiple universes."

Gerald I. Goldlist

♪♫♪♫

Charlie had confided his depression to Art while they were in school. They were together so much that he had had to. Charlie was having a coffee with Art. "Art, I sometimes find myself asking God to take away my depression, but it makes no sense since I don't believe in God anymore."

"It's ironic that the phrase 'Good Lord!' is used by many atheists. "Here's a better one that's really funny," said Art. "You know that the exclamation 'Jesus Christ!' is not used nearly as much as it used to be. I read that it's now most commonly used by middle-aged Jewish men."

Charlie laughed. "That's pretty funny. Do you think that should offend religious Christians?"

"No more than for anyone else who uses the expression. I don't think you should look at it that way at all. For me, it shows that Jews, just like other ethnic groups, have assimilated into our society and have adopted our country's mannerisms, concepts and expressions. I think it's hilarious."

"Have you ever thought of how words and expressions came into our language? Some words were originally bigoted but as they became used more and more, their bigoted origin was forgotten."

"Give me an example," said Art.

"Look at the expression 'to Jew someone down'. That comes from the antisemitic stereotype of Jews as being swindlers and cheap. There is also the expression 'to gyp someone' that means to cheat someone. It's a 'gyp' means 'it's a rip-off. They come from 'Gypsy'. But even though there is a stereotype of the Scottish being cheap too, I've never heard anyone say 'to Scot someone' or 'to Scot someone down.' I just think that there has been nothing comparable to the centuries old history of antisemitic feelings toward the Scottish."

Art said, "That makes sense."

"I never told you this before but even as an adult I used to be afraid of the dark and slept with a nightlight. Then an older Jewish man told me how he'd survived the Holocaust in Europe in the early 40s. He had lived in a small town in Poland. Like most of Europe, Poland was a horrific place for Jews during the Holocaust. This Jewish man had been hidden in a barn by a Polish family. He was only seventeen years old. At that time in Europe people were very superstitious and it was commonly believed that devils, demons and ghosts were everywhere and would come out at night to kidnap and torment people. He was a teenager who'd been separated from his family and was hiding in a dark barn with no light at all. He spent nights alone trembling in fear of being found by Nazis or ghosts. The old man told me that after two nights alone in the barn, he stopped believing in ghosts as he was sure that if they existed, ghosts and demons would have already torn him to pieces.

"That makes me shudder."

"Yeah. It still gives me goose bumps to tell the story but after I heard it, I immediately lost my fear of the dark. I never slept with a nightlight again."

CHAPTER 18

The SNI cafeteria could hold fifty people. Charlie's lunch group included Art Simmons, Frank Funk, Fred Wilson, Daphne Dombrodski and Marcia Smith. The rows of tables reminded Charlie of his high school cafeteria. For teens, high school could be the best of times and the worst of times. For Charlie, high school had been the best of times: the chess club, the debating club, working on the school yearbook, Friday night dances, cheering on football and basketball teams. He loved learning and he did well in all of his high school subjects. He particularly enjoyed and excelled at the maths and sciences, which would become crucial to his university education and ultimately to his work. He relished these subjects so much that they could have become hobbies. As an adult he had re-read some of his high school textbooks just for fun. Alas, whenever he saw Latin expressions like 'semper fidelis' and 'a mare usque ad mare' he regretted that he had thrown out his Latin textbook.

Charlie and Art were in the cafeteria. Fred joined them and the threesome's conversation turned to movies.
"What's the worst movie you ever saw?"
"I don't remember the name. I purposely blotted it out of my mind. After 30 minutes I stopped watching. It had the plot of a porno movie but without the sex."

"Sometimes I feel that I waste too much time watching TV and movies."

"I used to feel it was a waste of time too, but then I considered that our ancestors spent most of their time trying not to starve and running away from saber-toothed tigers. So watching TV isn't so bad."

Art said, "I used to be leery of movies rated "R" for their violence and not for sex. I find that action movies like the Diehard and Lethal Weapon movies are so impossibly physical and so violent, that I've become immune to the violence. I watch them as stress relievers since they are so far removed from reality that I can think of them as cartoons."

"Like Road Runner."

"Poor Wile E. Coyote."

"Do you know how to spell it?"

"There is no "y" and 'E' is his middle initial."

"I always rooted for the poor coyote trying so hard to catch Road Runner with all that Acme stuff."

"What would Wile E. do if he ever succeeded in catching Road Runner? He'd have no purpose in life anymore."

"Maybe he'd immerse himself in religion."

"Oh stop it," sneered Marcia, who had heard the Road Runner conversation as she was sitting down with the others.

Charlie said, "After watching war movies and reading the graphic details of battles going back to the beginning of civilization, the violence of sports, especially football, seems to be a much healthier outlet for us to deal with our aggressive instincts. Like a platoon of soldiers, football teams bond and become a unit working together to pursue a common goal."

"Have you ever seen the rapport and attachment of soldiers to each other? I've even heard of war reunions that included enemy soldiers."

"It seems strange for enemy soldiers to do that, but opposing teams reminiscing at sports reunions seems much more reasonable."

"I heard about a short truce during World War I during which a group of opposing soldiers celebrated Christmas and then went back to killing each other."

Art said, "At times sports seem silly and violent but when you look at sports from the perspective of aggression, it isn't as bad as soldiers and civilians blown to bits, men charging into the mouths of cannons or prisoners being hacked to pieces."

"Winning a trophy is a lot less gruesome than taking scalps off the vanquished or shrinking their enemies' heads to keep as souvenirs. The violence of wrestling and football is a safer way to get it out of our systems."

Marcia asked, "Do you guys prefer watching and reading fiction or nonfiction?"

Fred said, "After reading nonfiction for work, I like to relax with fictional stories in movies or books."

"I learn stuff from historical fiction. Although I find it difficult to watch some of the horrific images in these movies, it's easier for me to handle the pain and suffering when the movie is not the literal story of an actual person who lived the terrible details shown in the movie. I find it less overwhelming when the story is at least this tiny step back from reality."

"Me too. I refuse to watch an individual's true story like the movies about Anne Frank and Schindler's list. That is a reality that hits me too hard. It makes a real individual's suffering so vivid and makes me think of what I would do in the same situation."

Art was pensive. "Harsh stories make me appreciate how lucky I am to not have gone through anything like that. It's similar to being inside on a cold freezing day looking out at a blizzard and feeling so good to be inside and warm."

Daphne sat down with them.

"Hi, Daphne. Isn't it fascinating how in movies all the chicks are beautiful? They've got stunning figures and perfect lipstick even when they've been walking through the jungle for a week. Perfect smooth skin and even when their hair is messed up it looks sexy. When the chicks wake up from sleep, they look like they were just at a beautician."

"They can even run away from lions in high heeled shoes."

"And if they perspire, which they rarely do, it makes them even more seductive."

Daphne chimed in. "Guys in movies too. By the way I'm going to a specialty spice store on Saturday. Does anyone want me to pick up something for them? Sometimes it upsets my stomach, but I love spicy food. I'm going to get some really hot canine pepper."

"Canine pepper?"

"Daphne, did you get dropped on your head as a baby?"

Art said, "I avoid the really scary stuff, but I do find Stephen King to be a very good storyteller."

"Would you ever write a book, Fred?"

"I wish. If I could write as good as King."

"Well," corrected Charlie.

Frank asked, "Are you obsessive about grammar, Charlie?"

"I like to think of myself as disciplined."

Art smiled. "Mr. Perfect."

Fred smiled too, "Perfectionism is important in brain surgery and rocket science. I wish I could write as well as King. Remember the movie 'Shawshank Redemption'? The book was great and so was the movie. I saw other movies based on King's books that were also great. King must insist on a lot more control over the movies than other authors do."

"When King's books are made into movies, they tend to be long," said Marcia.

"I've noticed that too," said Art, "I think that King doesn't let the directors or producers leave out a lot of stuff that's in his books."

"I've seen lots of movies, not King's, where they leave out important details that are in the book and then some parts of the movie literally make no sense."

"Maybe the directors just figured that King's stories were so good that following the book exactly was the way to go," Charlie suggested.

Charlie, Art, Fred, Marcia and Daphne kept talking.

"Have you ever heard of King's 'Dark Tower' stories?" asked Art.

"Oh yeah. I remember them," Fred answered. "It was a series of books that King wrote over many years. I listened to the last one as an audio book. King was the reader on this audio and at the end he apologized for not finishing the series. He said that he hoped to finish it before he died. He actually snickered. I wonder if he will ever write the end of the 'Dark Tower' series."

"They should make a movie, no, a miniseries based on the 'Dark Tower' books. A miniseries would be much better than a single movie. In a miniseries, the characters can be developed early on so there is more time for events and details in the following episodes."

"A miniseries is like a 6 or 8-hour movie."

"Do you ever notice the little asides that Stephen King puts into his stories? I find the tangents he works in interesting and funny. I can just picture King smiling as he writes cutesy things about the Boston Red Sox."

Art smiled. "Do you remember the hilarious side story in the 'Dark Tower' about the retarded kid who tells a witch that his pecker fell off?"

Charlie feigned outrage. "Art, did you ever hear of the term politically correct?"

"What do you mean?"

"Politically correct means that you don't use insulting words like 'retarded.'"

"But the kid was retarded."

"Now we're supposed to say 'mentally challenged' instead of 'retarded'. The idea is to be polite and not offend people. It's like not calling Black People 'Negroes'."

"Martin Luther King called himself a 'Negro'.

"'Negro' is an insulting word.

"I don't think so. It's descriptive. The way that bigots and racists think of Negroes is what's insulting. It isn't really the word that's insulting. Even the word 'nigger' started as a descriptive term. It comes from the Latin word 'niger', which means the color black. And look at the names of the African countries Niger and Nigeria."

"'Nigger' has had negative connotations for quite a while. It is definitely used as an insulting term."

"I would never say 'nigger'. Never. Earlier in the 20th century, the term 'Negro' became more polite. And now young Blacks do not like that their parents were called 'Negroes' because racism became associated with that word too. It's the racism and negative connotations that are the problem and not the word itself. Changing the word doesn't change what bigots think or do. I consider a racist to be someone whose thoughts and actions are racist."

"So, you think that the term 'Black' will be changed again in a generation or two?"

"I would think so. They're even starting to change the term 'Blacks' to African Americans. I already said that Martin Luther King used the term 'Negroes'. The word itself is not the real problem. If someone doesn't treat or think of the group 'Negroes' or 'Blacks' in a respectful way, then the word itself is not being used respectfully. Once the disrespectful connotations themselves disappear the words themselves shouldn't be a big issue."

"You mean if the term 'mentally challenged' and 'challenged' had been around for 100 years and they had been called 'challenged', then political correctness might now be trying to change it to 'mentally retarded'?"

"Definitely. We then would be encouraged to say 'retarded' instead of 'challenged'."

"I get your point," Charlie continued. "So, we need to change the underlying feelings about the issue more than the words. This would make creating and promoting politically correct terms a waste of time."

Fred interjected. "That sounds interesting and all that, but we were talking about my book. Remember?"

Art said, "You know what we need to get you, Fred? A really crummy book to read. Something that your writing skills can definitely outshine. That would give you the confidence to write your own book."

Fred said, "Great, Art. Maybe I should write a book so I can put you in the acknowledgements."

Art made a stupid face.

Fred smirked back. "I couldn't write a book as a job but maybe as a hobby."

"Writing a novel might be an interesting thing to make a long-term project. Start now. It might take you 30 years."

Charlie whimsically thought about a book's being written in which the premise was that Buddy Holly and the others had been murdered by someone's sabotaging their airplane. It could be a conspiracy theory satire in which the villain was an envious singer, who dies ironically in a plane crash too. He believed that someone could write a book like that, but it wouldn't be Charlie.

I'll read your book too," said Daphne. "I won't snuff you." The others did a double take. "I hate what happened at a school reunion recently when one of the cheerleaders snuffed me. I wouldn't do that to you, Fred."

The guys looked at each other and bit their lips to avoid bursting out laughing.

"What? What did I say?" asked Daphne.

Now the others couldn't hold back their laughter.

When Frank first realized that Daphne was a brunette but could put blondes to shame, he had asked Daphne where her last name was from. "Dombrodski is an interesting name."

My parents are from Eastern Europe and they anglicized it just before they came to the US."

"I wonder what it was before they anglicized it."

As he was laughing Charlie said, "We know that you weren't brought up in our culture and you're such a good sport about it when we catch you in a mistake."

"Good for you, Daffy. We have to laugh at ourselves," said Frank.

"What else can I do?"

CHAPTER 19

It was almost impossible at work, but Charlie needed to space stresses in his life so he could recover from them. When his depression was lurking somewhere in the background waiting for any excuse to latch onto Charlie's mind and body, any stress, no matter how trivial, could be the one to knock him down again.

Although the pervasive feeling of melancholy could be triggered by real-life events, it came from inside him. Charlie suffered. Charlie suffered from the miserable mood disorder called depression. When it blossomed forth it made Charlie unhappy, sad and blue. He felt discouraged and dejected. While he was weighed down with despair and hopelessness, he was also weighed down physically with overwhelming fatigue. Everything was arduous when he was depressed. Even pushing himself to sharpen a pencil became an effort.

When it was in its full splendor, the feeling of despondency was crushing and excruciating. He could be dejected for no obvious reason. His depression was cyclical in nature, coming for days, weeks and months at a time. He had an exaggerated feeling of hopelessness about his life and life in general. Only those who have felt depression's dispiriting destitution truly know the feeling of utter desolation. Sad and blue did not adequately describe the forlorn dejection of depression.

Those around him could tell when Charlie's mood was dark but although his mind was in extraordinary turmoil, he frantically tried to control his internal turmoil so the outside world did not see the profoundness of his distress. Some part of his brain was able to maintain an external facade of normalcy. He might have wanted to shriek out loud, but he was not quite insane enough to allow himself to totally break down in front of others. When he was alone and when no one could hear, Charlie would scream in the shower, hide in a closet or lie down and whimper on the floor.

A major facet of depression is physical fatigue and an exhausted feeling. Charlie had a reclining chair for his private office. He would flatten the chair back, lay still, breathing slowly and deeply as if he were falling asleep. He continued to think and worry. His mind was active, but his physical body was resting. His limbs were flaccid. As his chest moved up and down his breath moved slowly in and slowly out.

After his rest, Charlie lay there and envisioned himself sitting up. Then he willed himself to get up. After bolting upright, he gulped down a cup of coffee. When he opened the door, no one could tell that only minutes before Charlie had been immobile.

Charlie drank coffee to stimulate himself and push through the weakness of depression and fatigue. To keep going at work he downed many cups of coffee. There was a bathroom nearby. He knew that there were caffeine pills that truck drivers took and that he could have used them instead of coffee to boost his mind and body, but he didn't want to use caffeine pills as he hated the idea of using another medication. Sometimes coffee grounds would wind up at the bottom of his mug. In his haste to get the coffee down he swallowed the dregs too.

There were chemicals, neurotransmitters, in his brain that got out of whack. When they were getting back into whack at the end of a down cycle, he sometimes imagined that it was some good news that had precipitated the upturn in his mood. It was not really a good event that got him out of a bad cycle though. As the depression waned and began lifting, he developed the will to feel better. He then listened to music and the music accelerated his mood improvement. But no matter how good his mood would get, it never got beyond fair to good. Fair to good was as good as it got.

Charlie had genes that predisposed him to depression. There was depression in the double helix of his DNA. There were also environmental triggers to cause the genetic predisposition to express itself. Even in identical twins, with identical DNA, it was not uncommon for one sibling to get depression while the other did not. There must have been triggering events, or a combination of events in childhood, in adolescence and in adult life that caused one sibling to suffer the demon of depression while the other did not.

When he was depressed, he tried to think of justifications to make himself happy but the good things in his life were overwhelmed by depressive thoughts. How could he be happy? At any moment someone somewhere was suffering; in fact, thousands, probably millions of people were. The world was a cruel place. He had once heard a scurrying sound coming from a wooded area that was followed by a louder rustling sound. The running noises stopped. He heard whimpering and then a crunching sound and short cry. The whimpering and crunching sound still haunted Charlie.

Animals were being killed. A robin was ripping apart a worm. A carnivore was stalking and killing its prey. A lion had just taken down a zebra that was being eaten while still alive. A hog was being slaughtered. Battles were being fought. Men were being shot, stabbed and executed. People were starving and developing cancer. There was always something somewhere on the planet being tormented. Horrors! What if even vegetables felt pain while they were being cooked and eaten? How could he feel pleasure or happiness while someone else or some living creature was suffering?

When times were good, he would think about the bad times coming back. When times were bad, he felt that the pain would never go away. As if things were not bad enough already, he knew that so many bad things were going to happen in the future. In a hundred years everyone he knew would be dead. His friends and relatives would all die. There would be countless natural disasters. The Sun would eventually go nova and destroy the Earth and everything on it. The Universe would implode. Everything was hopeless. Optimists must be mad.

CHAPTER 20

Her name was Dolores, but she called herself Dolly. They were introduced a few years after Charlie's divorce. Charlie and Dolly began to see each other regularly, then frequently and soon exclusively.

Dolly's children were grown and lived far away. Dolly was a widow. Her husband had been claustrophobic and did not wear seat belts because he was afraid of being trapped and drowning in a car.

Dolly worked part time and had flexible hours, so she could go out in the middle of the week with Charlie when he felt energetic and in the mood. Charlie and Dolly became deeply in love but both of them were afraid to remarry. Dolly was afraid to lose another husband and Charlie did not want to formally inflict himself and his depression on another woman. He had caused his wife Sue so much anguish that he could not bear to do that again to someone else that he cared for.

Dolly was a confident woman and so could chide Charlie for being a rocket scientist. "Ooh, you're so smart."

"Oh, Dolly, I don't care if you love me for my body and not my mind. You can treat me as a sex object any time you want."

As they had both been married, it seemed natural for them to live together. They both were living in houses and so they kept them both. Thus, they shared two homes, going back and forth freely between them.

Dolly had a weak glasses prescription and although she only needed them for driving and movies, she wore them as a fashion accessory and would buy new glasses regularly. At first Charlie thought that Dolly was being frivolous and wasteful. She explained that she wore different clothes and glasses were very noticeable, so she might as well have glasses to match different outfits. Once she explained it that way, it seemed a reasonable thing to do.

Charlie told her that he thought her glasses made her look sexy.

"Why? Do I remind you of Buddy Holly?" She mocked mischievously.

"No," Charlie answered sheepishly.

He had been surprised and taken aback by the question.

Dolly laughed. "Charlie, I was just kidding. Come give me a kiss."

Charlie relaxed and smiled. "I'm sorry. I'm just in a sensitive mood and the crack about Buddy caught me off guard. You know I usually take a joke well and love to be teased."

Dolly smiled and put on her glasses. She walked over and gave Charlie a giant bear hug that was followed by a peck on the cheek. Then their lips met.

Charlie sat back for a moment and stared at Dolly. "You do look sexy in glasses."

Dolly walked in the front door as Charlie was reading the newspaper. "I've been thinking about you all day," he acknowledged.

"Oh really?" she smiled. "Why was that?"

"I was getting coffee this morning and in the bathroom stall someone had written 'For a good time call Dolly.'"

"You bastard!"

"I was thinking about having a good time with you."

"Oh? Were you thinking about taking me out to dinner?"

"No. That's not what I was thinking about. I was thinking about what I was going to do to you."

"Really."

Saving Buddy Holly Blue Days Black Nights

"I was thinking about slowly taking your clothes off."
"Charlie, you're such a romantic."
Dolly grabbed Charlie's crotch.
"Dolly, you're such a flirt."

CHAPTER 21

Charlie used to watch older couples dance to music from previous eras: swing, jive and jitterbug. It finally dawned on him that people's favorite music was the music that they had danced to and listened to in their teens and early 20s. Rock 'n' roll was the music of Charlie's and Dolly's youth. The music of their youth was associated with good memories and fun times.

Charlie explained to Dolly that jogging to music was much like dancing. The beat, the physical exertion and the release of nervous energy left him in a state of well-being.

One time Charlie and Dolly found themselves in a bar filled with a younger crowd.

Dolly lamented, "I'm not comfortable dancing here. The way these kids dance is different, and I'll be embarrassed. I'm already embarrassed just watching and being the oldest ones here."

Charlie coaxed her, "I'm not embarrassed. Why should you be embarrassed? Do you know anyone here?"

"No. But I feel really awkward. I like the beat, but I don't think I'll be dancing right."

"Don't worry," reassured Charlie. "You're probably never going to see these people again. So what do you care? Just look at me and let the rhythm carry you along. Feel the beat. Look me straight in the eye and let the music move you."

Dolly gave in. "Alright Charlie. What have I got to lose?"

"You have nothing to lose. Remember, dancing is just a form of aerobics and self-expression that often leads to sex."

Dolly countered with, "For some people, just waking up in the morning leads to sex. Just bowling leads to sex."

"Are you some kind of nymphomaniac?"

"Don't you wish, Charles Harding."

Charlie shot back, "I doubt it. You always say that chocolate is better than sex. I think that jogging is better than chocolate and better for your health."

"So, you think that jogging is better than chocolate?"

"I'm not hungry for an hour after jogging and a runners high seems to be like a woman's orgasms. So I've heard."

"It isn't."

"I guess you are pretty sure of that. You are very confident of your sexual expertise. A regular Dr. Ruth."

"Charlie, you always turn the conversation to sex. I thought you wanted to dance."

"Same thing." He smiled.

"Thank you, Dr. Ruth."

Charlie never changed being an animated freestyle dancer. Once they had danced a few unfamiliar songs they discovered that their freestyle dancing fit in quite well. They soon realized that dancing did often lead to sex, even on the dance floor. When grinding belt scrapers were played, many of the couples transformed their dancing into what appeared to be mating activities. In the late 50s those parents and preachers were probably right when they called rock 'n' roll the devil's music. But who cared? It was a lot of fun.

Along with the modern devil music there were choreographed group dancing songs. The whole dance floor would pulsate in unison with a combination of hand movements plus steps forward, back, side, together. Charlie and Dolly did a decent job of copying the others, laughing as they made blunders. It took them a while to figure out that the gestures used by the group dancing to YMCA were actually spelling YMCA.

One song in particular interested Charlie. It was about time or time travel. It was called the "Time Warp". The song was popular, and they had watched people in other venues dance to it as well. Dolly feigned mock horror as they attempted to do the pelvic thrust. During one of the breaks Charlie asked the disc jockey about the "Time Warp".

"What's that song with the jump to the left and the step to the right? Time something."

"The 'Time Warp'?"

"Yeah. That's the one. What's it mean?"

"It's a dance from the movie 'The Rocky Horror Picture Show'."

'What's that? I've never heard of it."

"The one the kids go to see over and over again. A cult film with Dr. Frankenfurter and Rocky Horror. The one that the kids throw stuff and yell at the screen."

"I think I may have heard something about it. Who stars in it?"

"I don't know many of the actors but the fellow who played in 'Clue' is in it. He plays one of the stars."

"I know who you mean. I can't remember his name. Who else is in it?" asked Charlie.

"The female lead is ... What's her name? She became really famous. She was an unknown when they made 'Rocky Horror'. Susan something."

"Susan Hayward?" suggested Charlie.

"Who?"

"I guess that was way before your time. Mine too. I think she was actress of the year in 1958."

"Hello. 1958? I wasn't even born yet. My parents were still too young to date."

"Sorry. Bad guess."

"'Time Warp' the song," the DJ said as he thought. "'Rocky Horror' the movie. Susan the actress. Sarandon! Susan Sarandon. She was one of the female leads in the movie."

"Really. Wow! I should see that movie."

"I saw it once. Lots of kids find it really grabs them and they go back to see it over and over. It didn't do well until it caught on with the kids as a cult thing."

"What is it about? Time travel?" asked Charlie.

"Naw. I don't think so. It's not really that good of a movie. There are kids who go regularly and know all the lines, throw stuff and come in costumes. You could sort of call it a musical science fiction I guess. It isn't really about time travel but about space travel. I think a time warp lets people travel through space really fast or something like that."

Dolly tapped him on the shoulder. Charlie took her hand and said, "Just give me another minute and we can go. I'll just finish up quickly. Okay?"

She smiled and nodded.

"So are there any other famous actors or actresses in this play?"

"Umm. Not that I can think of. Wait! Meatloaf. Have you heard of him?"

"I thought Meatloaf was the group that sang 'Paradise By The Dashboard Light'. Is that the group you are talking about?"

"That's him, but Meatloaf isn't a group. Meatloaf is just one singer. He has a part in the movie and he even sings a solo in the movie. Actually, even though the story is kind of dumb, the songs in it are pretty good."

Charlie thanked the DJ for the information about the song and the movie. "Someday we have to go see that movie. We had a great time here tonight and we'll be back. Maybe you'll slip in some good old rock 'n' roll songs for us. Some Buddy Holly stuff like 'Peggy Sue' and 'Rave On'."

When they got outside Dolly asked Charlie, "Who's Susan Hayward?"

"I always mix up Susan Hayward and Rita Hayworth. They were both actresses in the 40s and 50s."

"I've never heard of either of them."

"They were sex symbols of that era. Rita Hayworth was the most famous pinup girl during the Second World War."

CHAPTER 22

"Dolly, look how one choice affects the future. Say you're thinking about feeding the ducks. First you decide whether you should throw stale bread into the garbage or go to the lake and throw it to the ducks hanging out there. After they eat your bread, the ducks eat less of other things and so some plants, fish or frogs survive another day or two. The fish and frogs that were spared go on to have different lives because you decided to feed the ducks.

"Maybe one of the ducks is eaten by a crocodile or shot the next day by a hunter. Whichever time line it lives through, the end is predictable. The duck dies and decomposes into its constituent parts: into amino acids, fats, carbohydrates and water. One way or another the constituent parts end up all over the planet. The water recycles itself: it evaporates into the atmosphere then falls as snow or rain; it fills streams and flows into lakes and oceans. Plants absorb the water. Animals, including humans, drink the water.

"The water cycle repeats and repeats. Over half of our bodies is made up of water. That's a hell of a lot of water molecules. Have you ever wondered how many of your water molecules have been part of another human being? How many of our water molecules were part of Cleopatra's urine?"

"Gross." Dolly screwed up her face.

"Yeah, it sounds gross. Somebody calculated the number of molecules that were once in Napoleon's urine and are now in each person living today. That includes you, Dolly."

Dolly's face scrunched up again.

"Here's another one," Charlie said to Dolly. "Envision a large sandy beach on the ocean. While the tide is out, a child is playing on the beach and makes a line in the sand with his finger. The thin shallow groove remains in the sand for hours until the tide starts to come in. As the first small ripple passes over the groove, grains of sand slide into the tiny finger-width furrow. Another ripple comes in. Then two wavelets come in, and the groove disappears forever. So at the beginning of this short period of time, a time line, there is no groove but just a smooth layer of sand, and at the end of this time line, there is no groove but just a smooth layer of sand again.

"If a child uses his whole hand, he can dig a deeper and wider groove than with one finger. It doesn't take much longer for waves to obliterate the deeper groove and smooth the sand out again. If someone uses a shovel and spends more time, he can make an even broader and deeper furrow. It would take longer, but the repetitive action of the waves rolling over it would soon level that furrow too.

"Now what if a heavy-duty excavating machine is used to dig an even larger channel? It would take days or weeks of tides to smooth out the channel in the beach, but it would fill in. So that's like how time lines can diverge then merge back: quickly or slowly, very quickly or very slowly."

Charlie went on. "Just like with the beach, if the beginning of a time line is fixed and the end is also fixed, then what happens in between does not, cannot, determine the beginning or the end."

"I like that," said Dolly. "It's simple and gets your point across. In the beginning there's smooth sand. In the end there's smooth sand. In between doesn't matter to the beach or anything else in the grand scheme of things." Dolly continued. "Out, out, brief candle. Life's but a walking shadow, a poor player, that struts and frets his hour upon the stage and then is heard no more. It is a tale told by an idiot, full of sound and fury, signifying nothing."

"That's my favorite play. Macbeth's soliloquy describes my time lines well. The time line is self-healing. Is fate itself fluid? In the long term the fickle finger of fate may not be so fickle as events eventually lead to a preordained point."

"So what about time travellers that change events?"

"Distortions and changes in history that might occur because of the actions of time travellers can only affect events for a limited time. They can only stay in effect for a few years, 500 years, eons or just minutes, but the time line must eventually go back to where it was destined to be."

Charlie awoke the next morning. His brain had been processing time lines and existence. Will Our Universe keep expanding forever or will it end with a big implosion? Is there another possibility that man has not even imagined yet? Our Universe is over a billion years old. There has been plenty of time for galaxies to coalesce, planets like Earth to form and then lots of time for the evolution of life forms to take place.

Almost by definition, it's impossible for mankind to view Our Universe from the outside. Viewing Our Universe from the outside. What a thought! Only God could do that. But is there a God? He wondered why Whoever or Whatever had created humanity had also made us suffer continually with physical and psychic pain. Why would an all-merciful God create pain at all? To warn us that we are injuring ourselves? Could He not have rung a bell or made a quacking sound instead?

Did the Universe have a beginning? Will it have an end? Did Our Universe start with a big explosion? What was there before the Big Bang? Had there been a big implosion of another universe before our Big Bang? Will there be a big implosion at the end of

Saving Buddy Holly Blue Days Black Nights

Our Universe? Will it be the end of Our Universe and also the beginning of another universe? Is there a cycle of implosions and explosions as universes end and new ones begin? Implosion then explosion, implosion then explosion.

Maybe our definition of universe needs to change to include the possibility that there are multiple universes: universes in series and universes in parallel.

CHAPTER 23

Art was sleeping in on Sunday morning when the phone rang.
"Hello."
"Art?"
"Charlie?"
"Art, I'm going to kill myself."
"What! Charlie!" Art sat up and shook himself awake. "You are going to kill yourself? What happened?"
"The same old thing. I give up. I'm in pain all the time."
"What do you mean?"
"You know I feel so down and miserable so much of the time. It just hurts too much. I don't want to try anymore. I just give up."
"Where are you, Charlie? I can come over right now and we can talk. Did you fall asleep at the office again? You're at the office, aren't you?"
Charlie murmured in a whisper, "I am."
"Charlie, wait there for me. Please. The bad feeling will go away. It will go away. Please, Charlie. Don't do it. I'll come right over and we can go to Dolly's together. Okay?"
"Thanks for everything, good friend. Don't bother yourself. I'm doing what I've wanted to do for a long time. Bye, Art."
"No, Charlie! I'm on my way."
Art heard a dial tone.

Joan had heard Art talking and walked into the room. "What's going on Art?"

"Charlie called to tell me he was going to commit suicide. I'm really worried." Art was getting out of bed. "I have to go help him out."

"Tell Charlie I love him," Joan said.

After dressing hurriedly, Art ran out to his car and sped over to the office. He ran through the front lobby, past the security guard, who recognized him, and pressed the elevator button. He anxiously watched the numbers light up one at a time as the elevator took its painstakingly unconcerned time to descend to the lobby. The door lazily slid open. Art squeezed his way into the elevator as the door was opening. He jabbed the eighth-floor button. He jabbed it again and again. He pressed and held the button down in a vain effort to urge the elevator door to close faster. The elevator then crept upward to Charlie's floor where Art leaned against the open button until he was able to slither past the opening door.

He raced down the hall and into Charlie's office. No one was there. Art gasped for breath as he looked around the office trying to find a clue as to where Charlie had gone. Art strode over to the phone. He lifted the receiver. He pressed the redial button to see if the last number Charlie dialed was Art's house. Joan always answered within three rings. The phone rang four times.

"Union Station. Bookings."

Charlie had called the railroad station to check the train schedule.

Art called Dolly and quickly explained the situation.

"Dolly, can you get to Union Station on your own or should I pick you up?" Art asked breathlessly.

"Please come get me." Dolly felt too panicked to drive.

The traffic was light and Union Station was not far away. Art and Dolly feared the worst as they dashed into the train station. Was Charlie going out of town or was he going to jump?

They found him sitting on a green wooden bench looking down at the floor. He heard the clatter of their running feet.

Charlie looked up and saw his dearest friends slowing down as they approached him. He did not have the strength, mental or physical, to put up any kind of struggle. He stood up meekly and walked slowly as his closest friends, one on each arm, quietly reassured him like adoring parents comforting a child who had awakened screaming from a nightmare.

When they got to Dolly's place, Art and Dolly gently laid Charlie onto the couch.

"What happened, sweetheart?" Dolly worried quietly.

Charlie mumbled.

Dolly asked, "What did you say?"

Charlie looked down and mumbled again.

"Think about the waste of your knowledge and experience."

He shrugged. "I'll die eventually anyway. It hurts so much."

"What hurts?" asked Dolly.

"Everything."

"Everything?"

"Everything."

CHAPTER 24

Dolly and Art tried to convince Charlie to take a few days off but he was back at work the next day. He was afraid that if he skipped work because of his depression or anxiety, he might never go back to work again. Many times Charlie had begged his wife Sue to let him lie in bed under the covers. It was Sue's "Get up. Get to work. Just do it," that had forced him to persist another day. Dolly was more tolerant than Sue, but she nevertheless encouraged him. There was a tiny spark in Charlie that would not give up on life. The will to live was still there even when his craving to give up on life and die was at its fullest. Was it inherent in all human beings or something that had been ingrained in some? Even an insect tries to save itself from its own demise. For life to continue there must be that spark in our DNA.

His body and mind were fragile. He needed to heal from his recent crisis. It would have been easier to just lie in bed and keep his eyes closed. Tons of coffee and antacids were required to get through the next few days. He made a determined effort to avoid people and work carefully. He stayed in his office most of the day. If forced out of the sanctuary of his private office, Charlie would retreat back to its safety as soon as possible. From past experience he knew he would get stronger and improve if he could hang on.

The railroad station episode had been the low point of this depressive cycle and the lowest point of his life. Charlie had given up on life but when Dolly and Art put their arms around him at the railroad platform, Charlie started inching up slowly from his hellish pit of despair.

Charlie could not believe that he had gone down so far. This had been the most defeated and dejected point in his whole life. Lying down with his eyes closed at work allowed him to gather some strength. He took more than the usual number of naps. He was never sure if the heaviness of his eyelids was from physical fatigue or just his hiding from the sensations of the world. Probably both. He worked vigilantly with extra attention to detail and repeatedly checked his work. The day passed slowly, but nevertheless it passed. He remained physically and mentally frail, but as the days progressed his frailness went away.

For the last few years, the highs were not as high and the lows were getting lower. In the pit of his stomach, he was sure that there would be worse tomorrows. He had hit bottom at the train station and was now crawling out of his worst down cycle. As he slowly improved, he realized that he had been able to crawl his way through it and tried to convince himself that he would get through those tomorrows too.

Most people think of depression as a psychological problem that the sufferer can control by force of will. It is commonly thought of as a weakness of discipline and self-determination. People look down on depression as a personality flaw and not as the painful debilitating disease it really is. The signs and symptoms of depression have a biochemical basis that causes dysfunction of the whole body and not only the brain. Although it has a physical basis, people nevertheless disdain depression as a mind over matter issue. Often, they even shame those with the condition for not willing themselves out of the depression. In their frustration some people do not believe that one cannot just "snap out of it". Blaming the victim of depression is comparable to blaming someone for having a disease like rheumatoid arthritis or diabetes.

Saving Buddy Holly Blue Days Black Nights

There is a stigma associated with mental disease. Charlie's doctors warned him that he had to accept his depression for what it was but not to let anyone except his most trusted friends know about his illness.

Charlie's helplessness was frightening. When deeply depressed he even endured pain while he was sleeping. He dreamt of drowning. He was beneath an endless sea. There were miles of ocean below him. Just above him were the waves. The cold water penetrated his body, but this torment was not as bad as the heaviness in his chest from holding his breath. The panic and fear of the situation was agonizing. Just as he was about to breathe in water and die, an invisible hand would brutally thrust him to the surface. He took a gasp of air. It was an unsatisfactory breath that gave him just enough air to stay alive but not enough to relieve the heaviness in his chest. It was the discomfort that those with emphysema felt when they tried to take a deep breath but couldn't. The unseen hand would sadistically force him down under the water again. It held him there until he felt the tortured heaviness in his chest return. The unseen hand might even hold him down just long enough so that he would aspirate water and feel the burning pain of water in his larynx, bronchi and lungs. But this was not the end. The unseen hand would again lift him to the surface so that he could splutter and cough another breath. The cycle of torture continued as the sadistic invisible hand pushed him upward and downward in this nightmare of drowning agony.

CHAPTER 25

Charlie and Frank looked at Daphne as she walked toward them in the corridor. "What happened to you, Daphne?"

"I was a few minutes early so I took the long way past the garden near the parking lot. This bee started buzzing at me. He followed me all the way to the front door. Why would he do that?"

Charlie corrected her. "Most bees are female. The worker bees we see all the time are all females."

"Okay, why did she chase me?"

"Maybe it's your perfume."

Frank teased her. "Did you throw a stone at a squirrel or raccoon in the last few days?"

Daphne looked surprised. "No. Why would you ask me that?"

"Maybe a squirrel hired the bee as a hitman."

"You mean hitwoman," Charlie corrected again.

"Whatever." Daphne shrugged and marched off to her office still discombobulated by her experience with the bee.

Fred walked over looking troubled. "What do you guys think? Gertie's uncle has been visiting from out of town and he's staying at our house. He's been inviting old friends and war buddies over. He did ask our permission and we said 'yes', but after four days of his friends' coming over and staying all day, I find it's getting more intrusive. I've lost too much of my privacy. I didn't say anything before and I thought I hadn't let my frustration show, but yesterday Gertie asked me if I minded that her uncle had been inviting so many friends over? When I told her the truth, she got mad at me. She said that I wasn't a nice person. Do you guys think she's right?"

Charlie spoke first. "You didn't say anything and let on that you didn't like it?"

"I really don't think I did, but I was spending time inside watching TV in the evening when they were sitting in the backyard. I usually sit outside in the back after work."

Marcia said, "I think you're being nice. Doing something that you like to do is easy. Doing something you don't like to do is more generous."

"Maybe a white lie would've been a better answer, Fred. She shouldn't have asked a question like that if she wasn't prepared to handle the wrong answer."

"That's what they say about lawyers in court too."

"Our choices in all aspects of our lives are determined by everything that's happened to us before. And everything that's happened to each of us is predetermined by events that happened before we even existed," said Charlie.

"How can you reconcile free will with predetermined and inevitable?" Art asked.

"Even though it's predetermined by everything we've been exposed to and internalized, when it's time to choose, we must choose. Most of the time there are no perfect options and many times there are only bad options, so we have to choose the least bad. What we choose in the end is determined by what's happened to us before; nevertheless, when the time comes to choose, we have to choose."

"What about physical reactions and not just our personal choices?" asked Art.

"They also depend on what happened before and then affect what will happen next."

Fred jumped in. "So then everything has been determined by everything that has happened before, going all the way back to the Big Bang. What about the Heisenberg uncertainty principle?"

"I don't think Heisenberg's uncertainty principle even applies here. We must know when to think of things on a macro level or a micro level. It's not always straightforward, but we have to learn when to apply the right scientific principles to each particular situation. That's why we must make hypotheses and test them with experiments. There is lots of space within atoms, but you still can't walk through a wall."

"Here comes Mr. Rude. Sit down, Frank. Honor us."

Art asked Frank, "Did you ever go to your kids' talent shows when they were young?"

"Rarely."

"Would you go today? Would you go to your grandkids' school talent shows?"

"A kids talent show is an oxymoron. So, no. I would try not to go."

"Do you play with your grandkids?"

"I love them. I teach them stuff. Grandkids are easier to take care of than kids. You get to play with them, but their parents do the really hard stuff and make the hardest choices."

Art snickered. "Dogs are better than little kids. They both crawl on the floor, but when dogs are ready to go to university, they're dead."

Fred hustled in. "Sorry I was late, Charlie."

"What's up?"

"My father-in-law had a heart attack yesterday night. Gertie is freaked out. I had to bring some stuff to him at the hospital and spend time with him and Gertie."

"How's he doing?"

"He's feeling okay right now, but he needs bypass surgery. They're trying to arrange for a heart surgeon to do the surgery as soon as possible."

"Has he been feeling tired lately?"

"As a matter of fact, he has been complaining of fatigue for months now. Maybe even longer. Why?"

"I read that after bypass surgery, people feel a lot more energetic because more blood can flow to the heart muscles."

After Fred left, Charlie sat quietly thinking that if he needed life-saving surgery, he might refuse the surgery and get his life over with.

"Have you got fifty dollars to lend me until tomorrow?"

"It's Veterans Day today. The banks are closed."

"Do you know why Veterans Day is on November 11?"

"Other countries call it Armistice Day. November 11, 1918 was the day that the armistice to end World War I was signed. In Canada they call it Remembrance Day."

"I saw an anti-war demonstration on TV. The demonstration itself didn't bother me except when some of the demonstrators were booing."

"Demonstrators say that memorial ceremonies glorify war."

"You can be against war and against the decisions of politicians to send kids to war without denigrating the soldiers themselves."

"Remembrance Day and Memorial Day don't glorify war, just as a funeral doesn't glorify death."

"You look tired this morning, Charlie. It looks like your get up and go, got up and went," commented Fred.

"My middle name is tired. You know how tired I was this morning? I brushed my teeth and then took a nap before I flossed."

"What happened?"

"I didn't sleep well."

"Is something bothering you?"

"Nothing specific. My mind was just racing."

"Let's get you talking about Buddy Holly. That'll perk you up."

"What's the story about Buddy's in-your-face glasses?

"He used to wear plain glasses. Then he tried contact lenses, but they were really uncomfortable, and Buddy could only wear them for an hour before they fogged up. After that Dr. Armistead, Buddy's optometrist, suggested that he stick with glasses until something better was invented. Dr. Armistead brought back some sensational, really big glasses that he found in Mexico. He suggested that Buddy make them part of his image and that's what he stuck with."

Charlie perked up and continued. "After Buddy started wearing those legendary glasses, other musicians, mostly Brits, imitated him and started wearing similar glasses too. If you ever look at pictures of old British rock 'n' roll bands, you'll see lots of bands with one of the members wearing Buddy Holly thick black glasses: Peter of Peter and Gordon, Freddie of Freddie and the Dreamers, Chad of Chad and Jeremy and Elvis Costello. Manfred Mann's group sang "Do Wah Diddy"; his bass player and keyboard player both wore Buddy Holly-like glasses.

"Most of Buddy's hits were recorded in Clovis, New Mexico at Norman Petty's studios. Buddy and Roy Orbison met there. Soon after Buddy started wearing his glasses on stage, Orbison began to as well."

"Okay, Charlie. What was the first song that Buddy Holly released?"

Charlie perked up even more. "Buddy's first release in 1956 was 'Blue Days, Black Nights'. It was recorded in Nashville. 'That'll Be the Day' was recorded there too but the Nashville version never worked out. The version that Norman Petty recorded and promoted is the one that you hear. It was the one that got them on the charts and pushed Buddy and the Crickets to become big recording stars."

Frank grinned mischievously. "I was thinking that maybe if he were alive today, Buddy Holly would be dead by now."

Saving Buddy Holly Blue Days Black Nights

"Buddy's fans don't joke about him like that. We say that Buddy's music lives on through his songs and those who were influenced by him. That would include his fans and many singers that came after him."

Art finally cut Charlie off and changed topics. "Frank, do you ever bring Vicky flowers?"

"Vicky would always complain that I never brought her flowers. I don't like buying things that aren't practical. Once I walked by a flower shop and saw roses in the window, so I bought her a bouquet as a surprise. When I walked in with them she said, 'What did you do, Frank?'"

Fred walked over to the table looking haggard. "Guys, I'm upset. I have to get an urgent presentation done and after I was working on it all week, they changed it and now I'm going to have to work all weekend."

Frank said, "I told you they might do that. I hate to say I told you so. Actually, I am delighted to say I told you so."

Charlie spoke up. "Come on, Frank. Try being a life jacket not an anchor for a change."

Fred continued to complain. "After the hectic pace we've had here for the last few weeks, I feel like Boxer in 'Animal Farm' when he says that he will just work harder. That's me. I'll get it done. I will just have to work harder."

Charlie said, "I understand. Life is so hectic. We try to do our work, pay the bills, rush to relax, rush to eat and then get some sleep. We're in a rat race running one hundred percent flat out. We're doing more than we ever thought we could. Then something goes wrong: the car has a flat tire, the dog gets sick, or you have to help out a friend who has an operation."

"It's not fair."

"Fairness is defined in the eye of the beholder."

CHAPTER 26

Charlie's old friend Jim lived in England. Jim Rich, Art Simmons and Charlie Harding had been friends in university when they had all been studying engineering. Art and Charlie had taken mechanical engineering and then specialized in aeronautical engineering. The two of them had become sub-specialized in rocketry and space exploration. Jim became a civil engineer, working in construction. Jim would tease Art and Charlie with the old joke: civil engineers build things and mechanical engineers try to blow them up. While Charlie and Art remained very close friends and they both worked at SNI, Jim had moved to England; nevertheless, Charlie and Jim kept in touch.

Charlie phoned England. "Hi, Jim. It's Charlie."

"I know your voice."

"It's just before dinner time there, right? I'm always careful not to call you too late."

"Not like you did when I first moved to England."

Charlie told Jim about his brush with death on the way to work yesterday. He had been approaching an intersection when a car drove through a stop sign and almost hit him. Had he arrived at the intersection a second earlier the other car would have struck him on the driver's side. It could have killed him or maybe worse: he might have become quadriplegic or unable to communicate while still remaining conscious for the rest of his life.

"Your close call makes me think of Stan Smith. You remember Stan. He was in our first-year engineering class. He was killed in a car accident and his death really shook us. We were young and that was the first time many of us had encountered the death of someone we knew. It was especially upsetting as he was our age."

"It was staggering. We all had similar hopes and dreams for the future and then one of us was gone. We were shocked and scared. As we get older, we experience tragedies and come to be more familiar with losses to death."

"When my mom was in the hospital dying, she said to me, 'With God's blessing I will improve.' She was very sick, and I upset her when I said that I was mad at God because He was the one that allowed her to get sick. I can't understand how a loving God can make people suffer so much."

Even though he was on the phone Charlie nodded. "What's the point of life? You live your whole life to propagate your DNA and for someone to say a nice eulogy over you. Are you afraid of dying?"

"If you can reconcile with your physical body's fate, winding up as a skeleton after being left to rot in the sun or to decay under the earth as bacteria and molds use our bodies for nourishment, then it comes down to fear of the unknown."

A curious thought flashed through Charlie's head: do paleontologists dream about becoming fossils of the future?

Then he said, "The world is a giant compost heap."

"Giant compost heap. That's a good way to put it. So what do you want it to say on your tombstone?"

Charlie answered, "Nothing complicated, I guess. How about 'He was a nice guy'?"

"If I ever have a kid, I want him to say in my eulogy that my dad taught me math."

"So that will be one way that you live on after you die. Your son will then pass some of his math knowledge on to others."

"I remember Miss Jenkins in grade 2. She played baseball arithmetic with us. I still think fondly about her. So she will live on in my son too."

"I think people should put more emphasis on the positive experiences and memories of people who've died and not so much on how their lives ended."

"That's easier to say than do. So, what have you been up to, Jim?"

"Life has been too hectic."

"I know what you mean. These days, between work and our personal lives we are always going flat out, full speed, and then something unexpected happens."

Jim laughed. "I was taking classes to learn breathing and relaxation techniques. They did help. Unfortunately, at times I'd get so busy and find myself rushing to get to the relaxation classes. It was making me anxious just thinking about getting to them. I find my life less stressful since I gave up the relaxation classes."

"You quit relaxation classes so that you could relax."

"I still use the techniques of deep breathing and other calming stuff that I learned."

"So what's Lily been up to? She was working on her master's thesis."

"She got her master's degree and now she's working on finishing up a PhD."

"What's she going to do when she gets her PhD?"

"Her PhD's in history. If she doesn't get a teaching job, then she's considering a research job in politics or writing for a newspaper or magazine. We were talking about having kids and we decided that Lily should get her career started before we have kids."

Charlie was on the phone with Jim in England again.

Jim said, "What do you think of this? Time is like a stream going down a mountain: you can dam it up or divert it but the overall direction is determined by gravity. The water is headed for the ocean."

"Nice."

Jim continued. "I got your letter with the time line drawings. They make it even clearer to picture. I'm glad you sent them. I thought of another time line metaphor for you, Charlie."

"Go ahead. Shoot."

"A truck is being driven across the country at night. It hits lots of mosquitoes and moths drawn to its headlights. To the truck they are insignificant events. To the driver they are unimportant and trivial. But to the insects they are life shattering. The truck is going cross-country with different roads to choose from, and so which mosquitoes die is decided by which road the truck driver chooses."

Jim continued. "What if Buddy Holly had not chosen to get on that airplane? Maybe you could go back in time and try to warn Buddy about getting on the plane he died in."

"You're not the first one who's suggested that to me. I've thought about it. My work on time travel strongly suggests that as we rematerialize in the past or future, the information in our minds can be passed to those nearby."

"Rematerialize like in Star Trek when Scotty beams somebody up to the Enterprise?"

"Something like that. I think that even if I don't speak to Buddy, my knowledge about him could transfer from my mind to his."

"Tell me, Charlie, what was really so great about Buddy Holly?"

"He wasn't the greatest singer and not the best guitar player either, but he was also a songwriter. So if you put them all together, he was pretty darn good. Especially back then. There weren't many singers who played an instrument and wrote their own songs. He was a strong influence on early rock 'n' roll and then rock 'n' roll forever. Many of the British Invasion groups like the Beatles and Rolling Stones were inspired by him. The Beatles' name originated from the bug beetles and Buddy's group the Crickets. Paul McCartney is still a huge Buddy Holly fan. The Rolling Stones' first big hit in North America was 'Not Fade Away'. It was written by Buddy Holly under a pseudonym, Charles Hardin. Hardin was his mom's maiden name."

"Charles Harding and Charles Hardin Holly."

CHAPTER 27

Art walked into Charlie's office. "My cousin Graham is in the Orlando area for a convention. He's a doctor but he's a really nice guy. I don't know why I said 'but'. Graham is a really nice guy. Period. He lives up north in Albany. I'd like to take you along for dinner with us tonight, just the three of us. I'm sure you'll like him."

When they got to the restaurant, Art introduced Charlie to Graham. "Charlie, this is Graham Simmons and Graham this is Charlie Harding. I've known Charlie since early university. Graham's a distant cousin and we're good friends now too. When we first met, we hit it off immediately and since then we've connected many times. You're both great friends."

"It's a pleasure to meet you, Dr. Graham," said Charlie putting out his hand.

Graham reciprocated.

"I like being called 'Dr. Graham' by longtime patients. For you I'm Graham."

Art looked toward Graham, "I'm wondering. How do you stay so young looking?"

"I have a portrait in the attic that ages for me."

"Well, Graham, even when you take a trip you're here at a convention. Do you try to take other holidays?"

"I only go to conventions to learn about topics that I'm really interested in but I do try to tack holidays onto the end of the conventions. I bring my wife Patty and the kids along to some of the interesting places too. After I had kids, I've tried to slow down. It's been hard for me to control my workload and turn away people who want to become my patients. I hate the idea of not looking after everyone that calls to see me but I know that I should make an effort to balance my life. My father told me a long time ago that you can't buy time. I'm always torn between patients, my family and my own health. Can you imagine that a patient once said to me, 'What's more important, me or your son?'"

"Wow! Someone really said that?" said Art.

"I kid you not."

Charlie said, "I feel that I am buying time when I use faster toll roads."

"Charlie, tell Graham about time travel."

"Again, Art? Whenever you introduce me to someone new, you ask me to talk about time travel or Buddy Holly."

"I like to hear the different ways you explain your time lines. Just do it."

"I know that I get carried away when I talk about time travel. I don't want to go crazy and bore people. Art, don't you think I talk too much?"

"Sometimes you do get carried away about things but so what? You're a good friend and you're worth it." Art urged Charlie on. "He won't be bored. I know Graham. He likes learning about anything. Just like you. I'm sure he'll find your time travel ideas very interesting."

"Please do tell me about it," said Graham.

"Graham, I truly hate annoying people, but I do enjoy talking about this stuff so once I get going I can keep going on and on. I get so wrapped up that I forget not everyone is interested in all the details. What I lack in brevity, I make up in verbosity. Please stop me when you've had enough. I mean that."

Art jumped in. "Charlie does mean it, Graham. If you've had enough and want to change topics, don't be shy. Charlie, if I think that Graham's getting bored, I promise to stop you too."

Charlie began. "I have a theory that I've been working on for years. I got interested in it during university. To make it simpler for you, my concept of time travel is similar to what you see in movies and books."

Graham asked, "What happens if you go back in time and change something? What happens to today?"

"Like killing your grandfather and you were never born stuff? I believe that even if something's changed, it will resolve itself at some point as time moves on."

"Art mentioned something called time lines. What are time lines?"

"Time lines are parallel event possibilities, like parallel universes. All my life I tried to get my head around the concept of infinity within one universe. Now I have to envision multiple universes and parallel universes. It gives me the same headache that I get when I try to envision more than three dimensions."

Art asked, "We sense time as a direction but not really a fourth dimension. So above three dimensions what things do we see?"

"Maybe just the effects of what is in the higher dimensions. But I don't know. We are three-dimensional beings. So above three dimensions, we perceive nada."

"You speak Russian too?"

"It's just a nice word. Back to time lines, Graham. Let me give an example of what I call parallel time lines. There are multiple bus tours going from New York to LA. You can make stops in Boston, the Grand Canyon and Vegas, or you can stop in Detroit, Salt Lake City and Yellowstone National Park. You can go to Washington and visit all the museums there. There are multiple routes but the beginning and ending of the bus trips are the same. You still start in New York and wind up in LA."

Graham and Art listened to Charlie then Graham spoke. "Not like parallel in geometry but you have lots of choices of routes. Like the path a red blood cell can take through the body after leaving the heart into the aorta, then going through smaller and smaller arteries and arterioles and then back through larger and larger veins.

The blood cell eventually winds up back at the heart. There are a zillion paths for that blood cell to go through the body, but they still go from the heart and then back to the heart."

"That's a very good analogy. What's the big vein that goes right into the heart?"

There are two of them: one that comes from above and one that comes from below, the superior vena cava and the inferior vena cava."

Charlie asked, "Where are you from, Graham?"

"I live in Albany, New York."

"Oh yes. Art told me. It gets really cold up there in the winters."

"The cold doesn't bother me. The only thing I don't like about winter is driving in the snow. Now that it's spring and the snow is all gone, I've already started to worry about driving in snow next winter."

Art smiled devilishly. "Think positive, Graham. You might be dead by then."

Both Graham and Charlie guffawed.

Charlie said, "Pessimists are so much more realistic than optimists."

Graham said, "You're an engineer, Charlie. Maybe you can explain this to me. Sometimes I relax by staring at fires in the fireplace at my country cabin. I find it fascinating to see the flames rush upward. I've been trying to figure it out for years. I know that heat rises. But why?"

"Hot air rises because it's less dense than cold air."

"That's it? Of course! Density. Hot air is less dense than cold air because the molecules are further apart. It's so basic. Engineers know everything. I'm going to have to think of more stuff to ask you."

Art said, "Hey Graham, I'm an engineer as well. Why don't you ask me questions too?"

Graham replied. "I've just never thought of you that way."

"Good grief. Do you think of me in the biblical sense?"

Saving Buddy Holly Blue Days Black Nights

♪🎵♪🎵

Two years later, Charlie and Dolly, Art and Joannie would spend five wintry days with Graham and Patty at their cabin up north. The cabin was a short walk from a frozen lake. Charlie imagined that the lake looked similar to Clear Lake, Iowa on February 3, 1959.

Graham set the ground rules when they arrived. "So that's pretty much it. It's safe around here but don't stray so far that you lose track of the cabin. We don't want anyone getting lost, but we have good neighbours anyway."

Charlie and Dolly were out watching the ice fishermen with their huts out on the frozen lake. "I wonder why the ice looks blue way over there?" asked Charlie.

"I think that's open water. We shouldn't go anywhere near there."

"Okay, Dolly. I'm just gonna walk out a tiny bit right here to see if I can look around the bend over there."

Charlie pointed and then walked onto the ice. He had only gone about 15 yards when he heard the sound of cracking ice. His foot slipped and he felt himself falling. He lurched forward. His torso hung in the air for a second. Then he tumbled through the ice and into the frigid water. Dolly screamed for help. Charlie managed to scramble back onto shore. Graham and Patty ran over. Along with Dolly, the three of them dragged Charlie back and into the cottage.

Charlie began to shiver. Patty frantically pulled his soaked coat off and hustled him into a hot shower with his clothes still dripping icy water. Once his shivering stopped, Dolly and Patty took his drenched clothes off and wrapped him in big fluffy towels.

"Don't be shy," said Patty.

They threw a blanket over him and pushed Charlie close to the wood stove that heated the room. Charlie sat there with Dolly hugging him. He stared numbly through the glass of the wood stove. Wisps of ash bounced around inside the airtight fireplace. Gray-black ashes bounced over and against the glass. Charlie imagined the ashes as trapped souls trying to get away from the fire.

There was a lot less excitement the next day. The guys were vegging out by the fire.

Art said, "I think well of the teachers I've had throughout my life. When I hear that one of my teachers has died, I think of something they taught me or something really nice that they did for me. Teachers that were mean and thoughtless were rare."

"A toast to all our teachers, who live within us and within those that we pass our knowledge on to," said Charlie.

The three of them raised their glasses and had a drink. Then Graham said, "There was only one surgeon that I have a really nasty memory of. I was doing my final year of medical school. We were in the operating room, and he asked me to recite a patient's history in front of everyone in the room, the nurses and the anesthetist. As I started to speak, the old bastard continued operating and started talking to the nurses. I politely stopped talking and he told me to keep going. Once I'd restarted, he started talking to the nurses again. He may have thought it was funny that he could lord his power over me. He was being extremely rude and trying to embarrass me. I remember thinking to myself that he was the one being a jerk and that everyone in the room knew it, so I carried on reciting the patient history as he continued to operate and talk over me."

"Is he still alive?"

"No. He died a long time ago."

"When he passed away, you should just have said to yourself, 'Satan took his spawn,'" said Art.

"I tried to let my mind go blank, but I couldn't. He was an ass."

"That's a polite way to put it."

"Fucking asshole?"

"That's better."

"I thought of another story you guys might like. When I was an intern there were IV nurses in the hospital whose only job was to take blood and set up intravenous lines. When they had a difficult case, like in a patient whose body was swollen with fluid or those with fragile veins, they would call me. Ironically, I had much less experience than they had, but they'd call me for help anyway."

"What did you do?" asked Charlie.

"I tried my best. Maybe it was luck or skill, but I succeeded. Only once did I have to call the senior surgical resident, who actually had to make a skin incision to get at a vein."

"Keep going with other stories."

"I used to have a patient who was a very demanding lady. I was young and new to working in my own practice, so I felt intimidated by her as she was pushing me around like I was a kid. If I knew that she had an appointment the next day, I would be nervous the night before and even have trouble sleeping. On the day of her visit, I felt as if I were having a panic attack until she was gone. Because of her I totally stopped looking at the appointment book to see how busy I was or who was coming in. That's called anticipatory anxiety.

"Another thing that I've realized is that human beings are just human beings. I've seen politicians, policemen, judges and famous actors. At first it shocked me that when they came to the doctor, they were just human beings that were just as nervous and scared as any other patient. Unless you're a fireman, we all put our pants on one leg at a time."

"Sometimes at the end of visits, patients, especially new patients, say to me, 'You're such a good doctor.' So I say, 'You don't know that I'm a good doctor.' Then they say, 'But you're so nice.'" Graham smiled. My answer is 'I know I'm nice but that doesn't mean that I'm any good.'"

Charlie said, "So then what happens?"

"They laugh. Oh. You guys will like this one too. Sometimes a nervous patient asks me what I would tell them to do if they were my mother. I always say, 'I don't like my mother.'

Art said, "You really say that?"

"My mom always cracks up whenever I tell her that."

"When the news starts to overwhelm me, I take a break from it for a couple of months. I don't watch the news. I don't listen to the news. I don't read the news. I don't discuss the news. The news is like a soap opera. If you don't watch for a month, you find out that you hardly missed anything important. There are politicians carping at each other and there are different murderers and victims. I never worry that I'm missing something important. If World War III breaks out, I'm sure that somebody will tell me."

"Why do doctors give tranquillizers to relatives of a patient who just died? It's normal to feel very upset, isn't it?" asked Charlie.

"One of the maxims I learned in medical school was that even if you can't cure a patient, you can still relieve pain. When someone breaks their leg it's normal for them to feel pain and of course I treat their pain. Anxiety is also a painful sensation and even if I can't bring the relative back, at least I can decrease the amount of discomfort that's being suffered.

"Happiness can just be the absence of pain. I learned that once when I was on call as an intern and got a kidney stone attack. Kidney stone pain is considered to be one of the worst types of pain. Patty brought a large bottle of apple juice to the hospital. After I drank it and started to feel the pain going away, I felt so relieved and happy."

♪♫♪♫

"It must've been really upsetting to take anatomy and dissect dead bodies. What was it like to do that?"

"In studying and practising medicine, you have to get used to doing gross stuff. You do what you have to do. I'm not a hero but soldiers become heroes by doing what they have to do under dangerous conditions.

"I stopped eating chicken, and especially drumsticks, for a long time after studying anatomy. Eventually I was able to eat chicken again, but I never ate another drumstick again. It looks too much like the human shoulder joint."

CHAPTER 28

Charlie wanted an end to his life. He wanted to be dead and feel nothing. Absolutely nothing: no pain, no good feelings, and no bad feelings. He did not exist before he was born. He did not want to exist now, and he did not want to exist after he died.

Charlie wanted people to have fond memories of him. He hoped there would be lots of people at his funeral to mourn and say fine things about him. He felt it would be appropriate if he were buried on a chilly rainy day. But then many people would not come and those who did would be cold and wet. The fact that he had ever existed would be marked only by the things that he had written or created. He hoped that memories of Charlie would remain in the minds of those who had known him. It would not be long before the people who had known him would disappear, and those memories of Charles Harding would disappear forever.

One day in the distant future, in billions of years, the Sun would begin to burn out and die too. As the forces that held it together weakened, the Sun would expand. As it became larger and larger the Sun would engulf all of its planets and all that would remain of the Earth would be a mass of atoms and subatomic particles. One day even the Universe would implode upon itself. The thought that there would be an implosion of the Universe and his ultimate fate would be atoms and subatomic particles was comforting.

♪♫♪♫

Saving Buddy Holly Blue Days Black Nights

When you have surgery under general anesthetic the anesthetist says, "Go to sleep" and the next thing you remember is waking up. There is no sensation of anything in between. There is not even a feeling of emptiness. Charlie hoped that death was just an absence, a void. Dying during sleep was what most people wanted as their final exit.

For years Charlie had been thinking of and analyzing ways to commit suicide. There were lots of them. Charlie feared the act of becoming dead. How long did it take for Joan of Arc to pass out? It distressed him to watch movies with stabbings. The thought of grizzly wars fought with spears, swords and bayonets appalled him. Just as he could never imagine stabbing himself, Charlie would never slash his wrists. In ancient times falling on one's sword was an honorable method of suicide. Hari-kari was an honorable way for a Japanese samurai to die. But honorable was not necessarily quick and painless; in fact, a failed attempt to die by falling on a sword could cause an agonizing and prolonged death. Agony and a prolonged death were things that Charlie dreaded. Quick and painless were important.

Charlie was afraid of heights. It would be ironic if Charlie committed suicide by jumping from a building. He imagined how it would feel to leap to his death from an airplane or bridge. Would his life flash before his eyes? What was a shot bird thinking as it vainly flapped its wings while it was falling? The splat at the end with bones crunching and flesh tearing would be abrupt, but the dread of the descent haunted him.

His parents had sent Charlie to camp when he was 10 years old. Fourteen of the campers had gone on an excursion to a ranger tower. They had climbed up a flimsy ladder and then through an opening in the floor of the tower to get to the platform. They surveyed the forest as the ranger taught them about conservation and wildlife. When it was time to leave, young Charlie slipped away from the group. He pressed his back up against a wall. He watched the other kids lay down and extend their legs through the hole in the floor. He watched with panic and dread as the other campers dangled their feet searching for the steps of the ladder. His terror increased as one by one the other 13 disappeared downward. Try as he might he could never remember exiting the ranger tower.

Charlie studied methods of execution. There were countries where executions still occurred; nevertheless, painful executions were generally avoided. Guillotines and beheadings were quick and presumably caused instant death. But what if inside the severed head the mind was still conscious? A chicken with its head cut off could run around. Was it still feeling pain? Did it know what was happening?

Even electric chairs malfunctioned. Charlie had read accounts of failed suicides by electrocution in which someone didn't die but lost both arms. What if the electricity grounded improperly and his privates fried off? Charlie found this last image more amusing than scary. Charlie laughed at the bizarreness of some of his suicide ideas like jumping into the molten lava of an active volcano.

When people were burned at the stake, they died of suffocation not from the fire, but they could feel the agony of the flames searing their bodies. Again, how long did it take Joan of Arc to pass out? He had heard that suffocating himself with a bag over his head, especially with the proper gas inside, would not be painful. He doubted that and brushed the idea off.

Suicide by drowning? No way. Charlie had a recurring dream about drowning and had gone through that nightmare already.

He couldn't believe that people would actually hang themselves. In the old days execution by hanging involved strangulation and suffocation. Hanging had been meant to cause suffering as a deterrence and for revenge. In modern executions it was different. Today's scaffolds caused the condemned to fall so that the second vertebra smashed into the lowest part of the brain and brought about instant death. Nothing was perfect but even if they always worked properly, most people did not have access to a good quality scaffold.

Firing squads sounded reliable. He envisioned bullets ripping through his skull and chest and killing him instantly. Self-inflicted gunshots on the other hand were not as foolproof as people thought. A bullet through the head might not be fatal and leave the person with paralysis of his limbs and severe vision loss.

A variation of the gunshot scenario was suicide by police. Charlie could fake a bank hold up and hostage-taking while brandishing a toy gun, thus forcing the police to shoot him. What if he got shot in the guts and had a long agonizing death like those he had seen in western movies? It might be as devastatingly painful as ripping out the bowels of a traitor during medieval executions. Charlie's conscience did not like the idea of suicide by police anyway, as he had read how distressing it was for police to kill someone, especially since most police never fired their guns on duty during their whole careers.

A car accident: not really an accident. What would it feel like at the instant his body impacted the inside of the car after driving into a wall? He would have to remember to take off his seat belt and deactivate the air bags.

Having never lived through war, Charlie had lived a physically comfortable life and did not want to live through the harsh realities of a conflict with lack of water, food, modern medical care, indoor plumbing and the other amenities that he took for granted. If World War III ever occurred, he wanted the first bomb to drop right on his head.

With his knowledge of rocket fuels Charlie could make a bomb. He liked the idea of being blown to bits instantaneously. No autopsy. No decomposition in a coffin.

He absolutely did not want to survive a suicide attempt with physically painful injuries to supplement his painful depression.

CHAPTER 29

We read about actors taking time out for emotional exhaustion. Emotional exhaustion is a euphemism. It seems that a disproportionate number of artists, movie stars and TV celebrities are depressives or manic depressives. Comedy writers are adept at seeing different sides of situations as if their minds were stepping around an object like someone walking around a statue and getting a different viewpoint than when looking straight on. You either can do comedy, or you can't.

Charlie saw Frank walking over towards the table. "By the pricking of my thumbs something wicked this way comes."

"Fuck off," Frank retorted.

"Where did you learn to swear so much?" asked Art.

"I didn't have to go to school to learn how to put someone down. I met a guy who had a diploma in putdowns. After years of studying, he said that he had discovered the ultimate putdown. Do you want to know what he said was the supreme putdown?"

"I'd like to know very much."

"Fuck off. So, fuck off, Art. Fuck off Charlie."

Frank announced that he had won a few hundred dollars with his lottery ticket.

"If there was a god, then a bastard like you would never win anything."

"Go fuck yourself."

"Frank, you are so rude, crude and lewd. I sometimes wonder if you have Tourette's."

"Fuck you."

"You do swear a lot, Frank," said Daphne.

"Don't you worry about that at all, Frank?" said Marcia.

"No. Not at all."

"Maybe you should. You blaspheme a lot."

Frank said, "To a devout atheist, blasphemy is a victimless crime. For a while, I was doubting my atheism but now I'm a born-again atheist."

"Have you ever heard of Foulmouthed Frank?"

"No. Who's that?"

"Joan of Arc warned Foulmouthed Frank to stop swearing. He didn't and soon after he fell into a well and drowned."

"Foulmouthed Frank. That's a perfect name for you. Most of the time you act like an offensive obnoxious horn dog," said Charlie.

"I didn't come to work to be nagged. If I wanted to be nagged, I could've stayed home."

"You can be very obnoxious, Frank. If there were truly justice, you would fall into a well."

"So why do put up with me?" asked Frank.

"Because you're worth it, Frank."

The others agreed. "Yes you are, Frank."

"That's really nice of you guys to say. I appreciate it, but don't ever say anything nice about me again."

"We promise."

Charlie said, "I don't remember his name, but do you see that guy over there? He used to have a problem in his nose. When he picked his nose, he would stick his fingers so deep up his nose that I thought he was going to pull out his pituitary gland."

Frank looked over. "Now that his nostrils have been stretched so wide, I'm worried that when he breathes, he'll suck all the oxygen out of the room and someone will suffocate and die. Speaking of dead, so many people I know have been dying lately that I should get seasons tickets at the funeral home."

"It must be tough to lose friends and family."

"If you don't laugh at tragedy once in a while, you'd be crying most of the time. When you have a couple of close friends die it makes you wonder if maybe it's time to cut down on saving and start spending more. I wonder when the average age of my friends is going to be deceased. As I'm getting older, I'm starting to measure my past life in decades and my future in months."

"Frank, you're not really that old."

"Yeah, Frank. You don't look a day over 80."

"After you retire, a big problem could be if you lived too long and ran out of your retirement savings."

"Is there anything good about getting older?"

"Your doctor visits get more interesting."

Daphne said, "I saw this old guy, he looked about 50, with a red sports car."

"50 isn't old," said Charlie.

"Let me finish. I saw this old balding guy driving a sports car. What a waste of a car. He was driving a red convertible sports car with the top down. He had a big smile on his face. The guy thought he looked so cool."

"The 50-year-old worked for his sports car. A 19-year-old got the sports car from his father or grandfather. Who deserves it more? The older guy who worked for it and earned it. Let him enjoy it."

♪♫♪♫

Charlie and Frank nodded as they passed in the hallway. Charlie stopped and turned back. "Are you mad at me, Frank?"

"No. I'm just in a bad mood today."

"How am I supposed to know the difference?"

"I'm not mad at you. Why do you ask?"

"You haven't made fun of me for a couple of weeks. I assumed that you were mad at me."

"I haven't had anything to make fun of you about. I guess I've had more important things to fuck around with."

Frank had always made jokes about his wife Vicky, but his friends knew that he was fooling around.

Someone had asked Vicky how she put up with him. "I love him and the longer we are married the more I love him."

"What do you see in him?"

"He makes me laugh."

"That's what Jessica Rabbit said about why she loves Roger," said Charlie.

Frank said seriously, "My favorite sound is Vicky laughing. It's nice to be married. Find a good woman and hope she sticks with you." Then Frank grinned. "Sometimes Vicky even says that I look sexy. She married me for mind but she stays with me for my body."

They laughed and Charlie said, "She has to stay for something because you've certainly lost your mind."

"Did you tell her not to get her cataracts fixed?" Art teased.

"Fuck off!" Frank's standard retort when he had been outmaneuvered.

Art said, "My cousin Graham told me about a lady who sued her eye surgeon and the hospital because she got wrinkles after her cataract surgery."

"Come on."

"The lady said she didn't have wrinkles before her cataract surgery. Graham swore that it's a true story."

"So how did you meet Vicky?"

Frank said, "They say that all's fair in love and war. But not with me. A long time ago a friend of mine told me that he was breaking up with his girlfriend. They had dated for six months and they had even set me up for double dates. When he told me that he was breaking up with her I told him he was making a mistake and that he would never find anyone better. That was Vicky."

Daphne had been listening carefully. "When I get married, I want to have a big wedding. I want to have all the pigs and whistles."

Everyone except Daphne howled with laughter.

"What did I say?"

CHAPTER 30

Charlie's depression was compounded by anxiety. He had free-floating anxiety: fear without reason. The anxiety was even worse when he was depressed. He had a recurring dread of things going wrong, even when there was nothing going on to worry about. Before he was put on tranquilizers the anxiety was much more excruciating than his depression. Even on tranquilizers he still had an inner turmoil, anxiety and queasiness. Ripples of dread would flow through his body for no reason at all. Ripples of apprehension fluttered in the pit of his stomach. The fluttering became nausea and sometimes retching. In order to control his urge to vomit, he used some of the breathing tricks that he had learned during Sue's prenatal classes. He would breathe deeply just as Sue had been taught to control her labor pains. If things got extreme, he would pant. Breathe. Breathe. Pant, pant. Breathe. Breathe. Pant, pant.

Before he had been put on tranquilizers for his anxiety, when Charlie had a terror attack, he felt like a bug-eyed victim in a horror movie. Although Charlie didn't believe in the God who had given him his poorly controlled depression, he nevertheless thanked God for the tranquilizers he was taking. With the tranquilizers his full-blown anxiety attacks went from a stark feeling of terror to a milder but relentless inner fear.

Anxiety caused him to wrap his arms around his shoulders and embrace himself tightly. He found scabs on his shoulders and upper arms where he had torn at the skin in an effort to distract himself from the psychic discomfort.

At work Charlie was in control and outwardly calm. Outside of his work life, stresses could overwhelm him. When the TV didn't work, he panicked. What if he couldn't figure it out? Would it ever be fixed? Sue took control. After she checked out the connections, she called a repairman. Before the repairman arrived, she promised Charlie that if the television could not be fixed, she would go shopping for a new TV with him. Sue was able to calm Charlie's panic attack by telling him the obvious.

Charlie had read about a professional hockey player with anticipatory anxiety. He had won the Vezina trophy for best goalie more than once. He would throw up in the dressing room before games; he would drink a glass of orange juice and then he would get out on the ice. The butterflies in his stomach dissipated after his first save. This great goalie said that the best thing that could happen was for the first shot to hit him in the facemask.

Because of the anxiety associated with the fear of what a new day might bring, mornings were the worst part of the day for Charlie. Even though he had dealt with and survived every crisis in his school, social and work life, he was scared. Some evenings the thought of going to sleep knowing that he would have to deal with anxiety in the morning really frightened him. So his choices appeared to be to go to sleep and face the anxiety of the next morning or stay up and be more exhausted than usual. He had two bad choices to pick from: sleep or stay up. In the end, of course, sleep won out.

Charlie had episodes of sleep paralysis. He was nodding off and became caught between wakefulness and sleep. His mind was still awake, but his body could not move. He was paralyzed. He desperately tried to move a leg, a hand, a toe, to break out of this terrifying state. His mind raced with harrowing scenarios. What could he do if an intruder barged in with a knife or an ax? What if a fire started? What if he stopped breathing? What if a vulture saw him and thought he was dead?

Lying in bed one Saturday morning, Charlie was sleeping fitfully as life's worries were going through his head. His desperate and hopeless thoughts were being magnified by his anxiety. As he was lying there, he sensed the presence of something nearby. He thought someone was coming toward him with a knife held in their hand. Charlie could not move. He was frozen and paralyzed. His brain's motor control seemed separated from his conscious will. He was partly awake but unable to move. Someone was in the room. Would he ever be able to get up? Was he in the presence of something evil? He concentrated on his left hand. He willed his left arm to touch his thigh. He awakened. Charlie rolled over and saw Sue quietly slipping out of the bedroom.

With his chronic anxiety and depression Charlie's teeth clenched. In early university he had done lab experiments on rats. He remembered that the rats' teeth always appeared to be clenched. As part of the experiment the rats were "sacrificed". To "sacrifice" them was such a gentle euphemism for killing the animals in the name of science. Their organs were harvested. "Harvested" was another delightful euphemism. Just before it died, the rat's mouth would be ajar with its clenched teeth ghoulishly visible. When Charlie was struggling with the pain of his depression or anxiety, he could feel the tightness of his jaw muscles and grinding of his teeth. He thought of the rats. Would God sacrifice or harvest him? Would it hurt?

CHAPTER 31

As a teenager Charlie had been a fan of horror stories. Sometimes when he was contemplating his own death his mind would flash back to a story that he had read. After years together, a husband and wife had become so enmeshed that they could feel each other's thoughts and even their pain. When his wife died, the husband not only felt her last breath but after she had been buried, he was tortured by his perceiving the sensations of his wife's body decomposing in her coffin.

Charlie had convinced himself that there was nothing after death and that by committing suicide he would sink into an oblivion in which there would be no thought of past or future torment. Yet he still had a niggling fear that if he committed suicide, he would suffer eternal punishment. He knew that in most religions those who committed suicide were damned. What if he committed suicide and had to endure eternal pain? Maybe he would be punished like Prometheus, by having his liver eaten by an eagle every day only to have it regrow overnight to be eaten again and again for eternity? What if he found eternal torment instead of eternal rest? Charlie worried about going to Hell. He had learned religion in Sunday school, and he had gone to church with his parents on holidays. Sometimes they said grace before meals. He was caught in a Catch-22 of suffering agony in life or agony after death: the eternal torment of Hell versus the torment of his life.

Saving Buddy Holly Blue Days Black Nights

He liked the idea of dying by accident. Maybe by an air conditioner falling out of a window and landing on his head. If it were unexpected, there would be no anticipation and fear. Also, if there was an afterlife, it might get him off on a technicality. It was like a Jew, a Hindu or even an atheist's being baptized by the Mormons after death: it was an insurance policy.

Ironically all religions consider those of other religions to be pagans and infidels. Religions have had different attitudes about suicide: some find it honorable, and some find it profane, immoral and blasphemous. Orthodox Jewish cemeteries do not allow those who have committed suicide to be buried there. Less Orthodox Jewish cemeteries allow those who have committed suicide to be buried in a corner of the cemetery. Where he would be buried was not of much concern to Charlie, but Dante had put those who had committed suicide in the seventh circle of Hell. They were encased in a tree, unable to speak, with harpies breaking off their limbs. Their limbs would regrow to be repeatedly and agonizingly broken again and again, forever.

Sisyphus was consigned to an eternity of pushing a giant boulder up a hill only to have it roll back down after he reached the top. Tantalus was forced to suffer an eternity of hunger and thirst with water and food just out of reach. Ixion was bound to a wheel on fire and cursed to spin across the sky forever.

Some Muslim scholars have said that even suicide attacks are forbidden. Those that have killed themselves must keep killing and torturing themselves in hellfire by repeatedly suffering their own suicide methodologies.

Buddhism prohibits suicide and assistance with suicide. By the principle of karma, the same conditions that led to suicide in one life recur in following lives, so there is no escape.

In Charlie's worst case, as well as physical pain there would be eternal psychological pain like that of a neuronic whip.

CHAPTER 32

Charlie was at a wedding. Depression was bogging him down. It happened at birthday parties too. He felt aloof from the celebrating and happiness going on around him. He felt like an outsider in a sad little universe of his own, observing people acting like they were having fun. Were they faking mirth and merriment? He longed to be someone who could just be part a world that was happy when there was something to be happy about and only sad when there was something to be sad about.

Fred asked Charlie, "Are you still jogging to that tape of Buddy Holly songs that I gave you?"

"Definitely. Sometimes at the end of a run I get pushed to go longer if one of my really uplifting songs is still on: like 'Tell Me How' or 'Rave on'."

"What about 'Peggy Sue' and 'Oh Boy'?"

"Of course."

"Did Buddy write all of those?"

"'Oh Boy' and 'Rave On' were written by two other Texans, Sonny West and Bill Tilghman."

"Is there anything else they wrote that I'd know?"

"Not really."

It was just Charlie and Fred together. "It's not any of my business," said Fred, "but just for the sake of conversation, are you religious?"

"Not really but I used to be, and I remember a lot of what I learned. I still think about it and read about it. Whether you believe or not, religion is a large part of our culture."

"Some of the greatest movies ever made were about biblical themes."

"The religions of the world no longer satisfy me with their explanations of reality. There's so much we don't understand about the Universe that has nothing to do with spirituality."

Art overheard them as he sat down next to Fred and Charlie. "'There are more things in heaven and earth, Horatio, than are dreamt of in your philosophy.'"

"Hi," said Fred.

Art continued. "Sometimes I think of God as the master plan for the Universe."

"Hi, Art," said Charlie. "That's not the dictionary meaning of God. You are using the word God as something else than what God has been thought of for thousands of years. I don't believe that the main religions of the world and most people who refer to God mean that God is a master plan. The definition that most people are talking about when they say 'God' is an omnipotent and omniscient being who created the Universe. You can't possibly believe that people are worshiping a master plan or that this plan gave the Ten Commandments to Moses."

Fred said, "If there's a master plan then everything in physics could be quite simple, mathematically I mean. We may be looking at things the wrong way. You know, like numbers written with different bases. Look at pi. Pi appears to be an infinite string of digits, but what if the base of the number system itself was pi itself. Then it would be written as just the number 1. The infiniteness of pi would disappear. All the laws of physics and chemistry might be simplified if we understood the mathematics that was used to create the master plan of Our Universe."

Art laughed playfully. "But we don't know the base for the Universe's numbering system. We use base 10 because we have ten fingers. If we knew what numbering system God was using when he created the Universe, we would know how many fingers God has."

"There is lots more we will learn about the Universe as technologies advance but there must be limits to what we can know that are determined by the properties of the Universe itself. I look forward to seeing the amazing things that will be invented."

"It's impossible, but depositing checks without having to go to the bank would be so convenient."

When I'm older I expect to be saddened that I won't live to see even more of what man discovers about physics and the Universe."

Charlie enjoyed the laughter in the cafeteria with the lunch gang. Even when he was down, the laughter could lift his spirits temporarily.

Frank Funk was hilarious. His self-deprecation and sarcasm were like that of Rodney Dangerfield. Frank was in his late 50s and like everyone else at SNI was very skilled and dedicated to his job. If laughter was the best medicine, then Frank was the best medicine for Charlie. Charlie had almost fallen off his chair laughing more than once. Everyone had to be careful not to choke on their food when Frank was in top form. He kept everyone in stitches with his lewd and sardonic stories. His complaints about his sex life were legendary. "Prostitutes are supposed to be more reliable than wives but with my luck if I hired a hooker, she'd have a headache."

Frank had a litany of excuses that he said his wife used to fend him off when Frank wanted to have sex. "She complained that she was having a heart attack or that her headache could be a stroke."

"You should have said, 'Let's hurry. This may be our last chance.'"

"Her last resort, her nuclear option is explosive diarrhea." Many of those at the table spit out their food as they howled with laughter. Charlie fell on the floor.

"Frank, have you ever called one of those sex chat lines?"

"Just once," said Frank. "She said, 'Not tonight, honey. I've got an earache.'"

Frank tried to stifle a sneeze, but he couldn't.

"Bless you."

"I get blessed all the time. But what's the use? If I'm so blessed, why can't I get laid?"

"Hey Frank. You used to have a dog. Did you feel uncomfortable having sex when your dog was in the room?"

"Come on, Art. Dogs have been watching humans fuck since the beginning of time."

"Hi, Frank."

"Frank does not look happy."

"He never looks happy."

"The only good thing about getting old is that you have an anecdote for everything, but getting old sucks. Vicky's hormones are going crazy. Now she gets fucking hot flashes. She calls them hot attacks. "If another asteroid hits and our species has to depend on women like Vicky to repopulate the earth, Homo sapiens would become extinct."

"Shit, Frank. Your wife must have a harder life than Job did."

"Speaking of shit," said Frank, "Vicky is whining again about constipation. When I wake up in the morning and my wife is singing, I know that she had a good dump. One day she's going to have to take a dump by Caesarean section. You guys and girls are laughing now but your time will come one day too. The worst way to die is death by constipation."

Eyes rolled up.

"And just wait for it guys. In a couple of years, you'll have prostate troubles as well. Prostate and constipation: double, double toilet trouble."

"Now he's quoting Macbeth too."

CHAPTER 33

Every stone in a cemetery has a story buried beneath it. Whether the person interred under the headstone was famous or infamous, educated or not, rich or poor, baron or peasant, each person under that stone had a unique life. Each life had its own trials and tribulations, human interactions, relationships to animals and nature, good and bad luck. Numerous biographies and autobiographies have been written, but just because one person's life is written in a book does not make that individual's life, its countless details, its molecules and atoms, more important to the Universe than the countless details of any other human's life; in fact, not even more important to the Universe than the life of an insect or the existence of a rock. Nevertheless, that particular individual had lived every detail of it, and it was the only life he had.

Human life is precious but how much is a human life actually worth? It depends on whose life and to whom. How many lives of others have kings expended to keep their kingdoms? How much would those who died for those kings have given to save themselves?

When an eraser wipes the chalk off a blackboard what happens to the information that was on the blackboard? When a person's physical body dies everything that person had ever thought disappears with it: all the knowledge accumulated over a lifetime, stories that had been heard, a favorite color, even their sense of fair play and justice.

Luck influences how history will judge a commander in a war. Generals can invoke similar strategies in similar circumstances and get different outcomes. There are many events on the battlefield that a general does not control: decisions of other officers, individual decisions made by his own men under battle conditions, as well as the resolution and perseverance of the soldiers fighting against him. Whether a general is considered great is determined in retrospect by the result of his strategy. General Lee was advised by General Longstreet to bypass the Union army near Gettysburg and go on to Washington. Lee chose to attack at Gettysburg and his loss there has been considered a tactical error that was the turning point in the American Civil War. Lawrence of Arabia was told to bypass Turkish troops and go directly to Damascus. He attacked instead and was judged a hero as he defeated the Turks and then went on to Damascus. So, it is the result of the battle and not just the strategy that determines history's representation of a leader's greatness.

Genetic information is copied and passed down from generation to future generations. In every surviving strand of DNA and in every person's ancestry there have been close calls with death that would have caused the extinction of that ancestral line. With evolution, survival is a combination of being fit and being lucky. Since the dawn of civilization, two mothers have given birth to a male child. They loved, fed and nurtured them. Both boys had mothers and fathers who cared for and adored them. After they grew up, the two boys left their parents to join different armies. As borders moved back and forth throughout history, the army that each of them joined was determined by which side of a river they had been born on, at what time in history they had lived or which religion their parents had taught them to believe. At two different locations on Earth, they both spent hours and hours, days and days, weeks and weeks, months and months learning the skills of warfare. They learned about weaponry: how to use it and how to defend against it. They were trained in the skills of fighting, killing and surviving.

They built up physical strength in their arms and legs. They built up their hearts and stamina. One day the boys met as soldiers opposing each other on a battlefield. They fought until one of them was about to deliver a death thrust. But his foot slipped on a loose stone and he was the one who died instead. He was the one who had all of the love that had been lavished upon him by his mother and father and all the knowledge and skills he had mastered over his lifetime snuffed out forever. And so one of the boys came home on his shield and the other carrying it. One soldier lived to have children. The other's DNA disappeared forever.

CHAPTER 34

Frank walked over to their usual table and sat down with Charlie, Art and Fred. "Vicky and I saw the Buddy Holly movie on the weekend. Can you tell me why he went on the plane that crashed? I know that he was on a bus tour but I don't get why he was on an airplane."

"You're right, Frank. Buddy was on a tour with a lot of rock 'n' roll stars. You've heard of The Big Bopper and Ritchie Valens. Dion and The Belmonts were on that tour as well. The Big Bopper and Ritchie Valens were on the plane that crashed and died along with Buddy Holly."

"What was it that Ritchie Valens sang?" asked Frank.

"You mean 'La Bamba'. Or maybe it was 'Donna'. Those are his biggest hits. You know the song 'Chantilly Lace'? It was a Big Bopper hit." Charlie went on to explain that it sometimes got confusing when reading about him because the Big Bopper's real name was J.P. Richardson and a lot of his friends called him 'Jape'.

"I remember those Big Bopper songs and I still hear them on the radio. So, what were they doing on the plane? Why weren't they still on a bus?"

"The simple answer is that they were afraid of the cold. It was extremely cold and they were almost freezing on the buses. Even worse, their buses were breaking down. Carl Bunch the drummer got frostbite and wound up in hospital. It was going to be an eight-hour bus ride to their next gig. There were some other issues about Buddy's wanting to do laundry, but I think it's pretty obvious that it was another frigid bus ride that got them to go on that fateful plane ride."

"Good grief. You know an awful lot of details," said Fred.

"Here's a trivia question," said Charlie. "Who knows where Roger Maris lived?" There was no answer. "He was brought up in Fargo, North Dakota. Maris was living in Fargo in 1961 when he hit 61 home runs for the Yankees. It's the twin city of Moorhead, Minnesota where Buddy was going to play the next day. He would have landed at Fargo Airport if his plane hadn't crashed.

"There were only three spots for passengers on the plane. Buddy had recently broken up with the Crickets and for this tour he got two other musicians to be billed as 'The Crickets'." Charlie went on. "One was Waylon Jennings. You've probably heard of him. He ultimately became a huge country star. Waylon was supposed to be on the plane but gave his seat to Big Bopper because Bopper had a cold or the flu. Waylon's kindness saved his life."

"I like these words from one of his songs," said Fred. "'I've always been crazy but it's kept me from going insane'."

"I guess that's Frank's theme song."

Frank gave Fred an exaggerated angry look.

Charlie continued. "You saw in the movie that Tommy Allsup, Buddy's lead guitar player, gave up his seat to Ritchie Valens. You remember the coin toss in the movie. Years later Tommy opened a restaurant called the 'Heads Up Saloon'."

Frank asked, "What about the song 'American Pie'? I heard somewhere that the song was about Buddy Holly and the others who died in the plane crash."

"That's right. Some people mistakenly say the plane was called 'American Pie'. But that's not true. The plane did not have a name. It just had a number."

"Do you know the number?"

Charlie smiled. "Does a bear shit in the woods? N3794N."

Saving Buddy Holly Blue Days Black Nights

"What color was the plane?"

"In the Ritchie Valens movie 'La Bamba', the plane is blue and white. That's wrong. It was a red and white V-tailed Beechcraft Bonanza."

Charlie speech tempo was speeding up. "What else do you want to know about Buddy Holly? There is tons more that I can tell you."

"Was the movie pretty accurate?"

"The two Crickets in the movie had the wrong names."

"Why would they do that?"

"There were two versions of the movie being filmed at the same time and copyright issues screwed things up before the movie was finally released.

"Buddy's drummer, Jerry Allison, was married to Peggy Sue. Sometimes Buddy called her 'Song'. I bet you didn't know that Buddy Holly and his wife Maria Elena honeymooned in Acapulco with Jerry Allison and Peggy Sue. Peggy Sue and Jerry were married about a month before Buddy and Maria.

"The original name of the song was supposed to be 'Cindy Lou'. Lou was Buddy's sister Patricia's middle name and Cindy was Patricia's daughter."

Frank controlled his urge to say something sarcastic. "Buddy must've played with some other famous rock stars."

Charlie was talking even more quickly now. "Buddy toured with a lot of well-known rock 'n' rollers. Chuck Berry, Little Richard and Jerry Lee Lewis. Umm. The Everly Brothers and lots of others. There is the Canadian singer and songwriter Paul Anka."

"So, what happened to the Crickets after Buddy died?"

"Jerry Allison and Joe B. Mauldin, Buddy Holly's long-time bandmates stayed together with the name the Crickets. They were the drummer and bass player. The two of them played together for decades, with different lead singers, as the Crickets. One of those that played with them is Sonny Curtis. He was an old pal of theirs from way back. Sonny Curtis was a prolific songwriter. His biggest claim to fame was probably writing the Mary Tyler Moore Show's theme song. Also, have you heard the song 'I Fought the Law'?"

"Of course, I've heard of it. It's one of my favorites. It's sung by the Bobby Fuller Four and was a hit in the early 60s."

"Sonny Curtis wrote it. Do you know which group recorded it first?"

"Since you're asking, it must be the Crickets."

"You got it. It was written by Sonny Curtis and recorded by the Crickets after Buddy Holly died. The singer on it is a fellow named Earl Sinks. I've heard the record and he sounds a lot like Buddy. I like the Bobby Fuller version better than the Crickets' version that I heard. It's one of my favorite dancing songs. The Crickets even backed the Everly Brothers on some of their tours and records; in fact, Jerry Allison played the drums on another one of my favorites, 'Til I Kissed You'."

"So cool. I love the drumming on that song."

"The Everly Brothers were friends of Buddy. Phil Everly was one of the pallbearers at Buddy's funeral. There's a barely known story about a song that Phil Everly wrote. They got a fellow named Lou Giordano to record it. It didn't do well but when it came out Billboard Magazine wrote that the 'gals behind him lend a wild sound.' The two gals singing the background vocals behind Giordano are actually Phil Everly and Buddy Holly singing in falsetto. It's really funny to listen to it knowing who the gals singing in the background really are."

I've always liked the Everlys. I'd like to hear that song with them singing falsetto."

Charlie said, "For sure. I have it and can bring it to work next week. It's called 'Don't Cha Know'."

CHAPTER 35

Charlie was on the mailing lists of Buddy Holly fan clubs and through these he learned of Paul McCartney's annual Buddy Holly Week in England. Former Beatle, Paul McCartney, was a big fan of Buddy Holly, and the Beatles were named after Buddy's band the Crickets.

One night Charlie dreamt that he was at McCartney's Buddy Holly Week. In his dream he had been depressed prior to the trip to England. Early in the week he heard a band playing Buddy Holly songs like "Peggy Sue" and "That'll Be the Day". He was so moved emotionally by the experience that he began crying quietly. As he whimpered softly with his face in his hands, someone with a Liverpool accent came by, tapped him on the shoulder and asked, "Are you alright?"

Charlie looked up in the dream and saw Paul McCartney himself. Charlie murmured softly, "You are so nice. My wife would kill to see you."

Paul smiled, "You're alright then I see. I hope you enjoy the rest of the shows. Be well."

"Thanks. Thank you very much for your kind thoughts and this great week."

As the dream continued, Charlie saw Maria Elena and Peggy Sue. He was dying to go over and speak to Buddy's wife and the girl in every song. This was the chance of a lifetime, but Charlie was self-conscious going over to them. It became obvious to the two women that he was cautiously eyeing them but was too bashful to approach. The ladies whispered to each other and laughed.

"Don't be shy. We came a long way to be here, and we suspect you did too."

"Come on. We won't bite."

In the dream, Charlie's heart raced. He went over to them sheepishly. They playfully smiled and teased him as they tried to put him more at ease.

"I see you have a camera. You do want your picture taken with us don't you? Maybe this gentleman will do the honors for us."

"It would be a great pleasure to take a photograph of you with these famous and lovely ladies," said the Englishman.

Charlie was becoming more excited and less self-conscious. He put out his right hand. "My name's Charlie."

The Englishman took Charlie's hand and said, "Charles too, ironically."

Charlie went over and stood between Mary Elena Holly and Peggy Sue Gerron. His arms were close to his sides.

Peggy Sue smiled and the room lit up. "Come on folks. Do you want the picture to show us with our arms at our sides and looking like a picket fence?"

The ladies each put one arm around Charlie's shoulders, drew close to him and then smiled for the camera. Charlie whispered in disbelief, "I don't believe this is really happening. Someone please pinch me." And one of the ladies did, on his butt.

Charlie cried out, "Who did that? I'm never going to wash again."

They all laughed just in time for the camera.

"Thank you. Your turn, Charles," said Charlie.

"Unfortunately, I don't have my camera with me."

"Don't worry. I'll take your picture and send it to you."

After Charles got his picture taken too, sans pinch, Charlie got his address and again promised to send him the photos. "Don't worry, Charles. I keep my promises."

Saving Buddy Holly Blue Days Black Nights

Charlie shook hands with Charles, Maria Elena and Peggy Sue. He thought about not washing his hands for a few days but soon remembered that shaking hands was the most common way to catch colds. He let the ladies' handshakes linger on his hand and fingers, but he did wash them before dinner. His butt could wait until later that evening. When he woke up Charlie tried to remember which one of the ladies in the dream had pinched him.

CHAPTER 36

Marcia and Daphne walked over to the group's lunchroom table. "What did we miss, folks? What are you guys laughing about?"

"Frank was telling us that his biggest fear was having a stroke and not being able to talk," Fred answered.

"He doesn't have to worry about that," said Marcia.

"Frank will still be talking when they put him in his grave."

"And after I'll come back and haunt all you guys."

"We put up with you, Frank, but you know that you're weird."

"No I'm not."

"Guys, Frank said he's not weird."

"Come on, Frank."

"I'm not weird. I'm eccentric."

"What's the difference between eccentric and weird?"

"Money. If I didn't have a good job, I'd be weird."

Marcia looked across the cafeteria. She said, "Hey who's the new guy in the corner over there. He's cute."

Charlie pounced, "You female chauvinist pig. You girls all think like that. You treat men like sex objects."

"Yeah. We have minds too," Fred asserted with mock disdain.

"Get outta here, you guys. Can't a girl just look?"

"Slut!" teased Frank.

"How can you talk to us like that?"

"Don't be silly. I think of you girls as nieces with big boobs."

Marcia rolled her eyes and turned to Charlie. "Charlie, I've got work for you to check. Do you have time to look at it today?"

"Let's see that." She passed a folder of papers over to him. Charlie glanced at them. "That looks okay. I can whip that into perfect shape this afternoon." When Charlie was up, everything was easy. "Okay, Art. We better get back to work. I want to get Marcia's stuff proofread before I go home today."

Art drank the last of his coffee. "We're outta here."

On the way out, Charlie whispered to Art, "Marcia's really on the ball but her grammar and spelling aren't very good. Other than that, whatever she does is excellent."

"Have you got any ideas about what conventions we can go to next year?"

"I'll check it out. Most of the conventions we go to are pretty good."

"When I go out of town for conventions, with the neighborhood all lit up outside the hotel window, I have trouble sleeping," said Frank.

"Why don't you wear a sleep mask?"

"I'm afraid that when I wake up I'll freak out and think that I'm blind."

Marcia walked over to the table and said, "Hi, Frank. I was thinking about you."

Frank flashed a devilish smile. "Oh really?"

She laughed and said, "Not in the biblical sense."

Frank made an exaggerated disappointed frown.

She walked behind Frank's chair. "Oh, Frank," she cooed. "Let me massage your shoulder."

Daphne got up and put her hands on Frank's other shoulder.

Art noticed what was going on and said, "Leave him alone, girls. He can't even handle one woman, let alone two."

Frank said, "Hey be quiet. Leave the girls alone. A little more to the left please, Daphne." Then he said to Marcia, "Hey Marcia, how's your boyfriend doing? Maybe you need an Adonis like me on the side."

"Come on, Frank, you're almost 60 and she can't be more than 30."

"That's okay. He's just my type: a pathetic lecherous grandfather figure."

The cafeteria loudspeaker called out. "Frank Funk, phone call. Please take line three. Frank Funk, phone call on line three."

Frank tried to look miserable as the ladies' hands slipped off his shoulders. He ambled over to a phone mounted on the wall and picked it up. "Hello."

It was Vicky. "You have to help me." She sounded frazzled. "I'm in the car and I don't know which way to turn."

"Where are you?" asked Frank calmly.

"I'm at the corner of 10th Street and 15th Avenue. Which way do I turn, left or right?"

"Vicky, are you going north or south?"

"I don't know, Frank. Quick. Just tell me if I turn left or right."

This had happened before. Frank started to become exasperated.

"Help me, Frank," pleaded Vicky. "Just tell me. Do I turn left or right?"

"How can I help you if you don't know which direction you're going?"

"Just tell me. Do I turn left or right? Quick."

"Oh, just go right."

Frank gave Vicky a kiss through the phone and walked back to the table shaking his head. "It was Vicky asking me to be her navigator again."

"Were you able to help her?" someone asked.

Frank shrugged. "I don't know."

"What do you mean?"

"There's a 50-50 chance I was right."

Frank looked frustrated.

"Come on, Frank. It's so obvious. We know that after all these years you and Vicky are madly in love and crazy about each other.'

"You seem a little dazed today, Daphne," Frank said. "Did you get your brains fucked out last night?"

Daphne looked at Frank with a sly grin. "You're always talking about sex. You know what they say: 'Those who can do, while those who can't, talk."

"She's right, Frank." Charlie chimed in.

"Don't be such a big talker, young asshole. I was upset when Vicky became a born-again virgin. Vicky has done a complete 180 about sex recently. I think her hormones have gone nuts again. Suddenly she's horny all the time. She keeps telling me that with monogamy, comes responsibility. She's killing me. My pecker has been flying little white flags and writing suicide notes."

"What a martyr. Someone should invent a pill to stiffen your dick."

"If they invented a pill like that, I'm sure it would cause blindness."

Charlie was giving a pep talk. "They just dumped an important project on us. Our budget has been getting tight lately and there's a lot of money at stake here, so this is major stuff. We need to have it done quickly. I've already divided it into smaller chunks so we can all work on it simultaneously. I brought copies for everyone so we can see what the others are working on too. We'll meet in two days to collaborate. We all have to work our butts off so we can get it all done within a week."

"We've got this, gang," said Daphne enthusiastically. "Remember, if you're not part of the solution, you're part of the problem."

Gerald I. Goldlist

"Who said that?"
Daphne answered quickly. "It was Hitler."
"That was the Final Solution, you idiot."

CHAPTER 37

You cannot have a perspective of the ageless or the eternal if you are constantly using the perspective of a mortal

–K.G. Mills

♪♫♪♫

Graham, Art and Charlie got together whenever Graham came to Florida.

Graham said, "Life isn't fair. A person's life can be ruined by being in the wrong place at the wrong time. Someone slips getting off the bus and accidentally bumps into the person ahead of him. The person hit takes offense, turns around and punches the person who slipped. The fist hits his temple, cracks through his skull causing a stroke and immediate death. A moment of weakness or just one mistake can ruin a career."

"Do doctors get in trouble if the patient dies?"

Graham replied, "If it was even close to reasonable treatment then a reprimand, a fine or a short suspension might be the punishment. But if you really want to lose your license, you screw a patient, even with consent, and you're gone. It's about asymmetrical power dynamics, where the perpetrator occupies a more powerful or dominant position in relation to the victim. It's like Bill Clinton and Monica Lewinsky.

"In some small towns a long time ago," Graham went on, "it was considered acceptable to ask a patient you saw just once, out on a date. Now it's considered professional misconduct. You kill a patient, you get a reprimand; you screw a patient, and you lose your license."

"To be successful in life you have to work hard and be lucky. Even though you worked hard, if a meteor lands on your head you don't succeed. A fly pays with its life for being an irritant."

"I heard about a young fellow who went to my med school. He was celebrating a long weekend with his friends at a pool party. He dove into the shallow end of the swimming pool, hit his head and broke his neck. He was a brilliant kid with a super career ahead of him. He has to live the rest of his life as a paraplegic in a wheelchair."

Graham, Art and Charlie continued to talk.

I never try to console a patient by saying that things could be worse and that others are worse off. The fact that someone else has a medical problem that's even worse, does not make a patient's problem less bothersome to them. I could tell anyone who complains about their lives about Usher's syndrome."

"What's that?"

"It's a syndrome in which people are deaf as kids and become blind in adulthood. I have a patient with it. He became totally deaf as a child. A lovely man. He's brilliant. He has worked around his deafness and he has a great job. He was just at the ophthalmologist, who told him that he has started to lose his vision and ultimately will go blind. Now that disease makes me wonder about the existence of God."

"Our friend Jim lives in England," said Charlie. "When Jim's mother died, he was angry that her God had allowed his mother to get so sick."

"Do you believe in God?"

"It depends on what you mean by God. Definitions are very important in any discussions. If we aren't using the same definition, then we are talking past each other and so the conversation becomes pointless. The word 'God' has different meanings to different people. This can cause confusion and heated debates. 'God' can be defined as a personal god that created everything and also cares about each of us as individuals. Others define God as the creator of the universe but other than that, stays out of our individual lives. Various religions and people use 'God' to mean different things. There's a considerable difference between being in awe of His power to create the Universe, and being in awe and praying to Him for His help."

"Did our Universe come from nothing or was there a Creator of the Universe? Atheists say that even if there were a Creator, what existed before the Creator or how was the Creator created? In our minds we conceive of everything having a beginning and an end. It's something we probably can't fathom but maybe Our Universe was not created but has always existed. We can talk about infinity and forever, but we really can't envision them in our three-dimensional view of the Universe. Maybe we are part of an Always instead of a universe that began and might end."

"Headache time."

"What are the odds that we came to exist? They are very low. That is one of the key arguments for Intelligent Design. A Creator must have made things happen as they did to put us here at this point in time or existence. The Earth's orbit is so precise that if it changed ever so slightly, it would be the end of life on our planet."

Art said, "I took a comparative religion course in college. Some of my so-called tolerant classmates got pretty upset when the teacher asked us to define a religion. A young lady — I remember her name — Susie answered that a religion is a cult that made it. That invoked a lot of hissing, booing and anger from some of our classmates."

Graham said, "Like with politics, it can be risky to discuss religion. You can get shunned and lose friends. I think a lot of folks might get mad about what that girl said but it was a comparative religion class, so I would've expected that even if they were challenged, they'd be more respectful."

"It's interesting how people come to a specific religion. Historically millions were forced to convert. A few convert to a religion by choice but in general they take the religion of their parents."

"In some form or another, the derogatory term 'infidel' seems to exist in all religions to describe those of a different religion. Freud said that religious intolerance is associated with the belief in one god."

"Do you pray?"

"I don't pray. I wish."

"Can you really reconcile science with religion?"

"Other scientists can, but I can't."

Graham said, "I talked to a pious Jewish classmate in medical school. He followed his religion diligently. He had his faith but when asked if he believed in God he said, 'I am part of a people, some of us call it The Tribe, that has a history that goes back thousands of years. But I am still a man of science.'"

"Did you ask him what he meant?"

"No. I didn't push it."

"The fact that humans know that we will die is a big burden for us to carry around. Man has always invented religion. It gives a purpose for the endless struggle of life to exist and then to die."

Art said, "The Fountain of Youth and immortality is a theme in almost all human cultures. There is always that tiny hope that we will not die, ever. So as far as I know the only person to get to heaven without dying was Elijah. Even atheists must still have a tiny grain of hope that death isn't the end. Animals have fears but I doubt that they think about dying like we do. They are afraid of getting hurt and have the instinct to avoid pain and danger. Animals don't worry about dying and their mortality, so they don't even need the concept of heaven."

"How do you know that?"

Art said, "I discussed it with my dog."

"When we learned about man's mortality, mankind became afraid of death. We had to find ways to cope with this fear. One of the ways is belief in an after-life and a soul that does not die."

Graham said, "I learned that most of my patients come to terms with death as they get older. For some, the upset is less about their own deaths but what family events they will miss. Others say that they will miss living through exciting future events and discoveries."

"I respect the rights of others to worship or believe as they choose. You can believe whatever you want as long as you don't impose your beliefs on me."

Charlie said, "Some people can be obnoxious about pushing their religion or even their atheism on someone else. I am not talking about saying 'Merry Christmas'. I am thankful for and accept all good wishes from people. And I'm not a fundamentalist atheist. It isn't that I'm against God: I just don't believe He exists. If God's existence can be proven to me, then I would believe in Him. Should I be saying 'Him' or 'Her'?"

"Wouldn't it be amazing if one day we proved that God exists?"

"Or prove that He doesn't exist. That would be awesome too."

"Charlie, when you say 'God', do you capitalize it in your mind?"

"Usually."

"Our Universe is believed to be at least 10 billion light years in diameter and contain a vast number of galaxies. It has been expanding since its beginning in the Big Bang about 13 billion years ago. It's been speculated that Our Universe will ultimately spring back and implode into a tiny ball, and then explode outward with another Big Bang, to form another universe. How many times has this already happened? Or, if it doesn't implode, will Our Universe keep expanding forever?

"Now that we know that our own Universe seems to have had a beginning like the Big Bang maybe we should be considering the existence of other universes besides ours. The Totality of Existence could include multiple universes including ours."

"Tell us another doctor pet peeve of yours."

Graham said, "This bugs all doctors. We've just finished the patient's visit. We've dealt with the issues that they came in complaining about. The doctor gets up to leave the room and move on to the next patient. Only then does the patient say, 'By the way, is this important? Occasionally the vision in one eye blacks out for about a minute.' Then we have to sit down and look into this potentially serious and maybe urgent problem. It's frustrating but it's not the patient's fault. They don't know what could be potentially serious or whether their question will take a long time to tackle. They had expected the doctor to say, 'Don't worry about it.'"

"No wonder people complain that doctors are always behind."

"I was walking by the room of one of my patients in palliative care with terminal liver cancer. That's the end. Game over. I overheard my patient ask her daughter to get her a piece of cake, but the daughter said that cake wasn't good for her. I called the daughter outside and reminded her what palliative care meant. Then she understood. I can't get mad at people as they just don't always see the big picture."

"People don't seem to have common sense these days."

"Common sense is only common after someone teaches you about it or you have experienced it yourself."

"Here's one for you, Graham. What does it say on the hypochondriac's grave?"

"I don't know. Go ahead and tell me."

"I told you I was sick."

"Good one. Now here's a medical tip for you guys. Contrary to what some people think, when a doctor says, 'I'm going to make a special project of your case,' you should go pick out your cemetery plot."

CHAPTER 38

Whenever Charlie heard the song "Time Warp" on the radio he would reminisce about the times he had heard it during those first honeymoon years of his marriage to Sue. He was intrigued after seeing people doing choreographed dancing to "The Time Warp". He knew the song was from a movie but because of the long lineups of midnight cultists Charlie was thwarted from seeing "The Rocky Horror Picture Show". Although it was with Sue that he had first heard the song "Time Warp", he never did get to see the movie with her.

One evening Dolly called. "Hey Charlie, are you interested in doing something different later this week?"

"You mean you want me to get dressed up like a girl before I come over to your place?"

"You're on the right track, Charlie."

"Excuse me? What do you mean 'on the right track'?"

"You've always asked why I can wear your clothes but you can't wear mine."

"Dolly, you sound so serious that you must be kidding. What do you have in mind?"

"How about taking me to that weird movie that we've heard about. The one you've wanted to see for years. Pamela at work, you don't know her, told me that since we both love rock 'n' roll music, we should go see 'The Rocky Horror Picture Show'. It's been playing for a long time now and she tells me that it's not sold out in the middle of the week anymore. Come on, Charlie, let's go Thursday night. What do you say?"

"I'm thinking about it."

"Pamela's daughter convinced her to go. She said we would love it. The music is wonderful. You know that you like at least one of the songs and you will finally get to see how they dance to it in the movie itself. She said the story is weird but really lots of fun. From what she said I'm sure we'd like it. Come on, let's do something silly."

"Okay, let's go!"

"It's a cult musical. The young folks see it over and over. Pamela told me a lot of the kids in the audience dress like the movie characters and throw stuff like rice and confetti. The movie starts at midnight."

"I'll stay extra late on Wednesday and then I can leave work early on Thursday and grab a nap. Then we can have a late dinner before the show. I'll call you just before lunch Thursday."

"It's a date, Charlie. So what are you watching on television?"

"I'm just flipping channels. There's nothing that I'm finding interesting. How was your day? Anything exciting?"

"Nothing special. I'll clean up here a little bit more and then get to sleep soon. I want to get my beauty rest so I can look ravaging for you. I'm glad you're finally going to get to see 'Rocky Horror' tomorrow. It should be interesting and a lot of fun. Maybe you should get to bed early too. Why don't you lie down and listen to quiet music?"

"I don't like listening to quiet music. You know I basically only like rock 'n' roll. Quiet music just puts me to sleep."

"Bingo!"

"You make a good point. I need some extra rest after the last week. Quiet music on the radio? Maybe I will."

♪ ♫ ♪ ♫

Saving Buddy Holly Blue Days Black Nights

Charlie and Dolly were at the "Rocky Horror" movie. They smiled and chuckled at the antics of the audience. Some had flashlights and others, candles. The audience was throwing confetti and playing cards, queens and jokers. The kids knew all the words. They were singing and chanting at the screen in unison. Many were dressed in costumes that mimicked those of the characters in the show. The songs included driving rock 'n' roll tunes that dripped with satire.

Charlie elbowed Dolly in the ribs during one of the songs.

"Did you catch that?" he whispered excitedly.

"What?"

"That neat line in the song. You missed it. I'll tell you later."

On the way home they discussed the movie itself and the "Rocky" enthusiasts. They had laughed at the audience, more correctly, with the audience. The audience had added so much to the evening.

Dolly remembered. "You elbowed me during the show. Why? You said you'd tell me later."

"When? Oh yes! Yes! Yes! "Do you remember the rock 'n' roll song that Eddie sang halfway through the show?"

"It was a great song. I liked most of the music but found the songs in the first half to have a stronger rock beat. Actually the whole show was great. I bet you liked those better too."

"You're right. Me too. I liked the first half better."

"You know, all in all the show was a wonderful wild farcical fantasy."

Wow. I like that alliteration. 'Wonderful wild'. 'Farcical fantasy.' Oh, you obviously didn't catch the cool line that I really liked."

"So, are you going to tell me?"

"Of course, but I've decided to buy the tape of the show's music and you can hear it yourself. For your listening pleasure we can buy it right now and listen to it in the car."

"Nothing's open now."

"You're right. We'll find it on the weekend and then we can play it over and over until you guess the line I'm talking about."

"You love to play guessing games. Okay, I'll wait and play along."

They found the tape on the weekend and listened to all of it. When they came to Eddie singing "Hot Patootie Bless My Soul" Charlie had to play the relevant part several times before Dolly smiled knowingly. There it was: "Buddy Holly was singing his very last song."

"Buddy Holly! Of course," said Dolly. "I should have known, Charlie. You cute, dumb, stupid jerk. I love you."

"Your love will not save you from hearing me sing, Dolores. I'll play it again." He put his arms around Dolly and waited for the critical lines: "Buddy Holly was singing his very last song. With your arms around your girl you'd try to sing along."

Dolly hugged back and waited until the song was over. "Charlie, I looked it up. Do you know the name of the actor who plays Eddie in the movie?"

"No, I don't think so."

"He's a singer too. He sings 'Bat Out Of Hell' and 'Paradise by the Dashboard Light'."

"Oh, I know who you mean. What's his name? I know. Meat Ball. That's his name, Meat Ball."

Dolly laughed. "You jerk, Charlie! His name isn't Meat Ball. It's Meat Loaf."

"You called me a jerk again." Charlie pouted.

"But you're my jerk."

"Okay, okay, okay. You're right. Meat Loaf, not Meat Ball. Well they're both food."

"Right. They're both food. And he does get eaten in the movie."

"Yeah. He does get eaten in the movie. Cute."

"Do you think he was chosen to play the part as a play on his name?"

"Who knows?"

CHAPTER 39

His first psychiatrist had tried to treat Charlie's depression and anxiety without drugs. The talking and thinking strategies helped Charlie deal with his depression and anxiety when the symptoms were mild, but they were inadequate most of the time. While using these cognitive therapies Charlie acquired insight into his depression and knowledge about depression in general. Unfortunately, cognitive therapies did not adequately control Charlie's symptoms. Charlie's doctors soon realized that Charlie needed anti-depressants and anxiolytics and so they tried many medications to manage his psychiatric issues.

Psychiatric drugs work on neurotransmitters in the brain. These same neurotransmitters are not only in the brain, but they are present all over the body in nerves and organs and thus they unfortunately can cause scores of unwanted effects. Charlie's doctors chose the medications, but Charlie had to live with the side effects. And the drugs certainly had side effects. He worked with his doctors to find doses that balanced their efficacy against the severity of their side effects. After years of experimenting, Charlie wound up on a cocktail of drugs.

It disturbed Charlie to look at the bottles of pills that he was taking. He brooded over what would happen as he got older and needed medications for other medical problems. He felt that he was cheating at life by taking pills and altering his mental functioning.

He came to terms with this by accepting that he was taking drugs to function within society and not to run away from society.

Charlie was extremely wary of illicit drugs. When he took a decongestant to control cold symptoms, its stimulating effect decreased his need for the energizing effect of caffeine. Cocaine is an even stronger stimulant than what is in cold medicines. When Charlie found out that cocaine caused a feeling of energy as well as a sense of happiness, self-confidence and well-being, he realized that these were the opposite of depressive feelings. Charlie was certain that if he tried cocaine even once, he would become addicted instantly.

Depression is associated with early morning waking. Anxiety is associated with fitful restless sleep. The psychiatric drugs that Charlie took interfered with getting good quality sleep. So it was impossible to know how much his medications contributed to his poor quality sleep.

There was an antidepressant that could trigger dangerous side effects or even death when taken with certain foods. His doctors never put him on that. He was put on another medication that made him extremely hungry and he started to gain weight. The doctor got him off that drug very quickly as he had seen other patients gain massive amounts of weight, balloon in size and become grossly obese while on it. Fortunately for Charlie, exercise, willpower and the fact that his anxiety caused recurring anorexia, enabled him to lose the unwanted weight. Except when he was on one medication, his weight was not a problem for him. Some people gain weight, and some people lose weight when they are depressed. Some become anorexic and some crave solace from eating. These two groups cannot understand each other.

Charlie was aware that he would probably encounter side effects when he started any new medication. He also got withdrawal symptoms as he was tapered off one drug and started on a new one. He tried to begin new medications just before a holiday or a long weekend, hoping that he would be adapting to the new drug and its side effects before he went back to work. He figured out that he would be more likely to notice side effects if he knew in advance what to look for, so he tried to avoid reading about its side effects when he started on a new medication. Dealing with side effects was a constant issue for Charlie. Milder ones were only annoying. They were distractible: distractible by speaking, jogging or dancing. Light-headedness was a side effect that caused him to sit or lie down. Lowering the dose of these drugs or waiting for his body to adapt to the new drug decreased the light-headedness.

He had mild involuntary movements like tapping his feet or drumming his fingers. Charlie was too young for age-related tremors or movements so Charlie thought some of them might be nervous habits but some of them were also a side effect of medication. When he was among people, they thought this was just a way that Charlie concentrated and thought deeply. He felt as if he were slurring his speech. He did not feel like it was drunken slurring; in fact, it was more an internal impression of slurring rather than something other people could notice.

He would unexpectedly hyperventilate while feeling lethargic and hot. It was different than a calming cognitive relaxation technique or the shortness of breath from a good physical work out. He wondered if he was hyperventilating to take in more oxygen or to exhale more carbon dioxide. Maybe his body was trying to get rid of drug breakdown products and toxins.

Many modern antidepressants increase serotonin in the brain. Serotonin is a neurotransmitter that affects mood, appetite and anger. Unfortunately, it also has effects on body functions like sleep cycles, body temperature and blood pressure. There is much more serotonin in the gastrointestinal tract than in the brain and ironically it can cause both diarrhea and constipation. Nevertheless, the side effects of the drugs that were finally settled on caused less agony than his depression.

Charlie had an unusual but horrific reaction from one of the serotonin drugs. It caused a constant burning, zapping and itching sensation under his skin. It intensified after a few days and he had to stop going to work because of it. When he complained to his doctor about this symptom, his doctor told him that the burning and tingling were almost certainly from the extra serotonin in his skin. He reassured him that it would gradually disappear over less than a month.

A few weeks later, Charlie was lamenting that the burning and buzzing in his skin would never go away. He was tortured by the searing pain in his hands and feet. The scorching sensation would reverberate through his being. Charlie had started this harrowing medication weeks before Easter. One day he fell asleep on the couch and dreamt. He dreamt about a crucifixion. He saw nails going through flesh and through bones, causing excruciating agony. He dreamt of bystanders watching a wretched man screaming and shrieking with pain and waiting to die. In his dream, Charlie was one of the bystanders at the crucifixion but when he looked up at the victim he saw his own face. Charlie awoke screaming. He was alone in bed and drenched with sweat. He could bear it no longer. Charlie called his doctor and told him that he had thrown away the pills.

On one particularly tough day Charlie had to drink even more than his usual large amount of coffee to keep going with his work. He had a different nightmare that night. In this nightmare, he was tied up spread-eagled being tortured at the hands of the Inquisition. He saw his own abdomen being cut open. Then he saw his bowels being pulled and squeezed. He could feel a literally gut-wrenching brutal pain. As he felt this intense torment with each pull on his bowels, he watched in horror as his entrails were dragged out of his body and draped over his chest. Charlie woke up and realized that the cramps were real. He got out of bed and rushed to the bathroom, barely making it in time.

Thus Charlie had suffered and continued to suffer from the side effects of medications. He had been on a whole arsenal of drugs. There were pills to control his anxiety and pills to control his depression. And there were pills to control his coffee-induced diarrhea as well as pills to control the other side effects of his medications. With all the mental torment of his depression and anxiety as well as torture of pharmaceutical poisons, Charlie wondered why he could not just do away with his gruesome life.

CHAPTER 40

We are all ignorant; just about different things

–Mark Twain

♪♫♪♫

Art wasn't with them this time.

Charlie said to Graham, "I was thinking about our conversations and it amazes me how people can be brought up in two different parts of the world, live different lives, have never met and wind up having so many similar values and ideas."

"When I got into university, one of the toughest things I had to deal with was the realization that I would never be able to learn everything. In high school it seemed as if what was in our textbook was all that there was to know about a subject. It took me a long time to accept the fact that I couldn't learn everything, even about one subject, and that I would have to compromise about how much time and effort I could put into any given subject."

"Yes. We have to choose to try to know a little about lots of things or try to know a lot about a few things."

"I think many doctors specialize in order to cope with the explosion in knowledge that has been going on. I've had specialists say to me that they are in awe of family physicians, who have to keep up with so many different facets of medicine."

"Have you heard of the Dunning-Kruger effect? The less we know about a subject, the more we think we know."

"I've never heard that it really has a name, but it explains why people with a limited knowledge of something are so sure that they are right."

"These days almost every field requires some degree of specialization. Art and I are engineers and look how specialized we became in our work. Do you remember when people started to joke that doctors were becoming so specialized that there would be surgeons for the right hand and other surgeons who only operated on the left hand?"

"I remember when doctors started subspecializing. An ophthalmologist told me that there are more than five subspecialties within ophthalmology itself."

"Five subspecialties about eyes. Unbelievable."

"When I was an intern, one of my teachers admitted to me in a moment of candor that he sometimes felt scared to come back to work after a holiday. He was afraid that he had forgotten everything and that he wouldn't be able to practice."

"Wow."

"Yes. Imagine that. He was one of the top specialists in the hospital, in fact, in the state. In my early years of practicing on my own I would sometimes feel anxious about my work and knowledge. I would think back to what he had told me and it helped me cope with my anxiety."

"Were you competent?"

"Definitely. Very importantly, I also know when I can't give proper care to a patient and need to refer to a specialist. It's great for me and the patients."

"So you don't feel that you have to deal with all the problems that come to you?"

"No. But what problems you have to deal with without help can be determined by where you practice, for example, whether you practice in a big city or an isolated town. One of my classmates terrified me when he told me that he removed an appendix with a textbook open in the operating room. He explained that he had been visiting a village in the Brazilian jungle and the closest surgeon was days away. It was a matter of his operating with his limited skills or letting the patient die. Knowing when to refer is part of knowing how to deal with the patient's problem. Even specialists refer some problems to other specialists for another opinion or for surgery that they don't do."

"Like lawyers work in specific areas of law: real estate, divorces, commercial law or medical malpractice."

"Malpractice. That's a scary word for us doctors. It's not just being exposed for something going wrong in care. A bad result isn't always, or even usually, the doctor's fault. An example would be getting sued for a penicillin-induced allergic reaction in a person with no history of exposure to penicillin."

"That makes sense. That's not what I think of when I think of malpractice. I think of something like doing surgery on the wrong part of the body or making a huge error in diagnosis."

"Lawyers sue what they call deep pockets, deep pockets that have a lot of money. Although in the end insurance companies may pay the dollars, the doctor suffers the loss of self-esteem, embarrassment and stress that can lead to divorce, alcoholism and even suicide. I know that in Canada the standard for malpractice is what a reasonable doctor would do under similar circumstances. But that doesn't mean that the innocent but unfortunate patients don't suffer huge health consequences."

"Do you have any ideas of how we should deal with an injured patient and an innocent doctor?"

"For those circumstances I like the term 'medical misadventure'. I think it would be better to have a fund to compensate patients for medical misadventure. This would help the unfortunate patients and decrease litigation costs for everybody."

"That sounds like a reasonable idea," said Charlie.

"The devil will be in the details. But I want to get back to your time lines. I was imagining what happens after you throw a stone into a lake. How long does it take for its effect to disappear? Ripples travel for a distance but they ultimately disappear as they become mixed in with the regular motion of the lake. It may affect a few minnows but ultimately they make basically no difference. Whatever was going to happen on the other side of the lake happens regardless of the stone's ripples at this end."

"That's a good example of a fixed beginning and end. The stone hits the water on one side and on the other side things go on as they would have anyway," Charlie said. "Here's a question. Why is the weather not what was predicted two days ago? Why does it seem that there is a limit to how far ahead we can predict the weather?"

Graham said sarcastically, "Could it be that the gods on Olympus sneeze and cause a typhoon or disastrous windstorm in Athens? Their sneezes would be a lot more powerful than the flapping of the wings of a butterfly."

"The Norsemen believed that when the god Thor got angry he threw thunderbolts. Thunderbolts are in mythologies all over the world, even in Native American mythology."

"Do the sneezes of the gods on Olympus affect weather in the long term time line? Does the hurricane caused by Aphrodite's sneeze affect what will ultimately happen to the Earth, the Solar System, the Galaxy, Our Universe?"

"You're kidding, right Graham?"

"Yes, I am. So, are you pretty sure that time travel will work?"

"No scientific theory is proven until repeatedly tested and reproduced. Even then the theory can be disproven and superseded as new knowledge is discovered."

"Obviously, Jonas Salk and his family took a huge risk when they volunteered to take the first polio vaccine."

"Inductive reasoning can never prove something 100%. The likelihood of something being true increases with more confirmation but you can't be absolutely sure. The theory of evolution has been proven repeatedly because fossils of predicted intermediates have been found: but still not 100%."

"If you're going to warn Buddy Holly, your knowledge of the crash must remain intact. With time travel what do you think happens to thoughts?"

"I think thoughts can follow the body. I know it sounds crazy, but I think that memories could transfer to a nearby person when you materialize after travelling through time."

"That could result in strange effects, especially if a person travels from the future with knowledge of future events and passes them on to someone."

"They could know the results of sporting events and place bets that would create new time lines for them."

"When you travel back in time, maybe you should bring a biography of Buddy Holly with you. Or a copy of the newspaper headlines about the crash."

Art was with them this time.

"If a tree falls in the forest and no one is there to hear it, did it make a sound? What about when ice splashes into the sea in Antarctica with no penguins around?"

"It depends how you define sound. Remember that in all discussions using the same definitions of what we are talking about is essential to understand each other. Are you talking about the sound waves created or the perception of the sound waves by a person? If sound waves, then yes, they make a sound. If hearing, then no."

Charlie said, "Before 1969 people used the expression 'That will happen when there's a man on the Moon,' to mean that something was impossible. After the Moon landing, that expression just faded away. Can you imagine what we will be able to do if computers can be made that are faster and smaller than what we have now?"

"I know we put a man on the Moon, but will we ever be able to put a man on Mars?"

"Mars seems a hell of a long way to go."

"There are things that I can imagine and wish for. It would be great if we could deposit money, even checks, without having to go to the bank but I really can't see how that could happen."

"That'll be the day."

"Very clever, Graham." Charlie smiled.

Graham went on. "There have been tremendous medical advances since the nineteenth century. Advances in the twentieth century have accelerated. Before antibiotics people used to die from severe ear infections that spread into the brain. What new medical advances will there be? Will man discover how to regenerate arms and legs like salamanders do? Will brain and spine injuries be repairable? Will all our body parts become replaceable?"

"Will we find out if anything can go faster than light? Will fusion energy be harnessed as safe and economical? Will new energy sources become available? Maybe one day there will even be driverless cars. Maybe we will find new sources of food. I know it's ridiculous but maybe we could create meat without killing animals."

"I like that idea."

"And if we find out that it's possible, would medical science one day allow us to live forever?"

"If people could live forever, would some commit suicide?"

Charlie considered whether with his recurrent mental anguish he would want to live forever. Definitely not. But what if his depression became curable? That would change things.

CHAPTER 41

Through the British Buddy Holly Society Charlie had found out about the three-day Buddy Holly Tribute Party that took place every year at the Surf Ballroom in Clear Lake, Iowa. Charlie decided to go. This was the last venue that Buddy Holly, Ritchie Valens and The Big Bopper had played as part of the Winter Dance Party tour before their ill-fated plane ride.

On the last leg of their flight to Mason City Airport, only minutes away from the Surf, Charlie and Dolly were on a 19-seater Beechcraft airplane. The cockpit curtain was open to the passengers, so Charlie peered in and saw that the plane was a Beechcraft. Charlie said to the pilot that Buddy Holly had crashed in a Beechcraft Bonanza. The pilot reassured Charlie with a smile and said, "Don't worry. This is a really good plane."

They rented a car at the airport and drove to the motel. Charlie had never driven this model car and so the next morning he got flustered when the car engine wouldn't start. The engine wouldn't even turn over, so he thought that the battery had died in the extreme cold weather. He ran back to the motel lobby and asked the owner of the motel for help.

John, the owner, said, "I have some booster cables but let me have a look first."

John got into the car. When he turned the key, the car started. Charlie was pleasantly surprised. "I wonder what I did wrong?"

"Some of these newer cars need you to have your foot on the brake pedal when you turn the key."

"That's probably it."

There were afternoon exhibits for the fans plus dances in the evening. Dolly and Charlie had thought that Charlie was one of the biggest Buddy Holly fans in the world, but at the Surf Ballroom exhibits they quickly realized that it was not the case. They met people who had been at the original Winter Dance Party show in 1959. They had literally been in Clear Lake and seen Buddy play for the last time. Others had seen Buddy and the other musicians a few days earlier at concerts in Davenport, Iowa and Duluth, Minnesota. Bob Dylan was not at the reunion dance party but he had been at the concert in Duluth. Bob Dylan had once dated a girl named Echo. Buddy's first girlfriend was Echo McGuire. She was very religious and wouldn't dance so sometimes when Echo and Buddy went to a high school dance she would allow Buddy to dance with another girl.

That afternoon Charlie shared his car incident with new friends that he had made at the Surf. He made fun of his own mistake and they all laughed with him.

Charlie was excited. He met others who were just as excited as he was. Many had been coming to the Surf Tribute for years. Charlie was in the autograph line standing in front of Sonny Curtis, who was a current member of the Crickets. He was one of Buddy's old friends and a well-known songwriter himself. Charlie stood there like a star struck teenager when Sonny said, "Y'all want me to sign that?"

That year Iowa was one of the ice boxes of America. It must have been like this in 1959 when Buddy, Ritchie Valens and the Big Bopper wanted so badly to get off the poorly-heated bus that would be travelling from Clear Lake to Moorhead, Minnesota. Charlie left a can of Coke in the motel room next to the window to keep it cold. When Charlie picked up the Coke can the next morning, he felt ice floating in it. He ran out in his pajamas and started the car to warm it up. After dashing back to the motel, he realized that he had another car fiasco. In his haste he had locked the keys in the running car. This time John couldn't help so he called Dolly and Charlie a cab and said he would have to get a locksmith to open the car door.

As the cab pulled up John told Charlie not to worry. "Just have a good time and I'll take care of the car. Don't stress. You can pay me back later."

They arrived on the second day of the Ballroom festivities just as they were beginning again. When the manager of the ballroom heard about Charlie's second car plight and that his car was back at his motel, he told Charlie that they had a limousine available for the festival and that he would arrange for the limousine driver to take Dolly and Charlie back to the motel later. Charlie's second car story made him the butt of even more jokes that day. On the way back to the motel they got a limousine to take them to the post office so they could get cardboard tubes to protect the posters they had bought.

When they visited the crash site, it was minus 40°. This is the temperature where Fahrenheit and Centigrade are irrelevant: minus 40° is the same in Fahrenheit and Centigrade. With the wind chill factor it was minus 60°F. Dolly wisely stayed in the running car while Charlie foolishly tripped through the snowy field to the monument that marked the spot where the music had died. When he finally got back to his car Charlie had no feeling in his baby finger. Charlie was afraid that he had gotten frostbite until he got the feeling back in his finger a half hour later.

♪♫♪♫

Saving Buddy Holly Blue Days Black Nights

Over the three days there were many entertainers including Elvis impersonators. But there were no Buddy Holly impersonators. It was as though Buddy impersonators would be sacrilegious. The bands and singers like Bobby Vee and the Crickets seemed genuinely appreciative of the fans reveling as they watched them perform. There was delight on Tommy Roe's face as the crowd gleefully danced to their teen idol singing "Sheila" and "Sweet Pea".

Over the years the Surf Ballroom had showcased many musical stars and there was memorabilia all over the building. The Surf Ballroom was owned by the Dean Snyder family that also owned a construction company in Iowa. Members of the Snyder family were at the three-day Buddy Holly Tribute too. They mingled eagerly with the visitors. Everyone there was a rock 'n' roll fan as well as a Buddy Hollic.

On the final day of the Winter Dance Party, as Charlie was leaving, Kathy Snyder waved goodbye to Charlie and called out, "Bye, Charlie! If you ever write a book, don't forget to put the car and limo story in it."

CHAPTER 42

As he lay in bed at night, anxious thoughts and images raced through his mind: his health, his job, friends, Dolly, Art, Joan, Sue, Davy, to warn Buddy about getting on that fateful plane. Charlie would lie in bed with his eyes closed but still awake and exhausted, trying to sleep. Wherever the wakefulness center was in his brain, it wouldn't flip its switch to off. It was like trying to turn a light's dimmer switch to off but not being able to get past the final click to shut it. He was in a vicious cycle: anxiety interfered with Charlie's sleep; his anticipation of being tired at work the next day made his anxiety even worse and this in turn made it more difficult for him to relax and sleep.

During their marriage when Charlie had moaned in his sleep, Sue had desperately tried to console him by squeezing his hands and kissing his face. Little did she know that her caressing and kissing were being integrated into his nightmares. Charlie felt his hands being crushed by a vice and his face being attacked by demons.

Dolly awoke with a start.

Charlie was awake and said, "What's wrong?"

"I had a horrible dream. I went out of town with Joanie and she screwed up our reservations. We couldn't find a motel and so had to sleep in a barn. We were dressed in our nightgowns but were sleeping on piles of hay. I woke up in the dream with a little dinosaur coming out of my pussy."

"What!"

"I woke up in the dream with a little dinosaur coming out of my pussy. I was pulling the dinosaur out of my pussy and the dinosaur had an evil smirk on its face and was shrieking. I was screaming for help but Joanie wouldn't help. She even left me there. She came back later, and I was still fighting to get the dinosaur out.

"Joanie had gone shopping and said, 'You owe me five dollars.' I said, 'Can't you see I'm busy?' I kept trying to pull the dinosaur out of my pussy. Joanie opened my purse and took five dollars out of it and walked away. I was yelling at Joanie. 'You fucking bitch! Help me!' Then I woke up."

"That's a pretty wild dream."

The next day they were talking about Dolly's dream. "Maybe I should get it analyzed?" said Dolly. "Could you ask your doctor about it?"

"I'm not sure I can tell him that with a straight face."

"Okay, Charlie. Then promise not to tell anyone at all about my nightmare."

CHAPTER 43

Dreams are a composite of life events, hopes and fears.

♪♫♪♫

In a colorless but vivid dream Charlie met Buddy. He told him about cover versions of Buddy's songs. He told him about the cadences that he liked and that his favorite version of "Not Fade Away" was by the Rolling Stones. He told him who the Rolling Stones were. Charlie advised Buddy to stay off small planes and instead opt for buses. Was it possible to transfer information to the past?

They discussed his vision. Buddy said that he had 'stigmatism. Charlie said, "I think it's called astigmatism not 'stigmatism."

"Well, that's what we called it," Buddy said.

"Why didn't you try contact lenses?"

"I did. Dr. Armistead got me contact lenses."

"How did that work out?"

"It didn't work out. They were really uncomfortable, and I could only wear them for an hour before they fogged up. After that, Dr. Armistead said that I should stick with glasses until they invented something better."

Charlie knew that one day they would invent contact lenses that were easier to wear than those that Buddy had tried.

Buddy continued. "Dr. Armistead went down to Mexico and brought me back some cool glasses and that's what I stuck with."

Charlie told Buddy that after he had begun wearing his really big in-your-face glasses, other musicians followed his lead and became less inhibited about appearing with glasses.

Buddy had died at the age of 22. He lamented to Charlie that he was sorry about the things that he had missed in his life: having children, relatives growing up, his brothers, his sister and his wife Maria Elena.

Charlie also dreamt about what he would miss if he died soon: getting depressed again, growing old, watching relatives and friends getting sick and dying, maybe losing a child, a broken bone, vomiting with the flu. He hated the helpless feeling of vomiting.

Charlie awoke thinking over the possibilities of travelling back in time and convincing Buddy not to fly on February 3, 1959. If he could warn Buddy and keep him off the plane that crashed, he could prevent Buddy's premature death along with those of the Big Bopper, Richie Valens and pilot Roger Peterson. If anyone could do it, Charlie had the scientific background to figure it out.

CHAPTER 44

Charlie visited Buddy Holly's grave in Lubbock, Texas. He saw the guitar picks pushed into the earth in front of Buddy's headstone. They were put there by Buddy fans who had come from all over the world. It reminded him of the small stones left on headstones he had seen at Jewish cemeteries.

He had once dreamt about a future in which the cemeteries were filling up as more and more people were born and died. In that dream, the future cemeteries were so packed that people were buried vertically and later one on top of the other. Bodies were exhumed and moved. The first burial sites of corpses were not their final resting places. When he awoke, he had thought about the remains of soldiers buried in other countries having been returned to their home countries and re-interred. He wondered if more war dead would ever return from Europe or Korea to be buried in their final resting places, again.

While in Lubbock Charlie was introduced to Peggy Sue. He asked her if he could sing to her. She good-heartedly agreed. Charlie sang "Peggy Sue" to Peggy Sue. Buddy's nickname for her was "Song". So he sang Song's song to Song. He had seen pictures of Peggy Sue but none of them did her justice. Peggy Sue's smile lit up the room.

Saving Buddy Holly Blue Days Black Nights

He visited disk jockey Bill Griggs, the Buddy Holly biographer and expert, who knew more about Buddy than Buddy had. Bill had moved from Connecticut to Lubbock and even named his daughter Holly.

He went for hamburgers with Buddy's niece Sherry at the Hi-D-Ho drive-in restaurant where Buddy played well before he got famous.

He sang in a Texas bar. They didn't throw bottles at him. He sang in a Lubbock diner. They didn't throw food at him.

Dr. J. Davis Armistead, the optometrist who had found and prescribed Buddy's world-famous glasses, showed him around Lubbock. Charlie had read about General Lewis Armistead, who had bravely fought and died at Gettysburg."

He shook hands with Buddy's older brother Travis, who had fought at Iwo Jima. Travis made guitars as a hobby, and he made one for Charlie.

He heard from Larry Holley, who was Buddy's oldest brother and had also fought in the Pacific during World War II. Larry had been among the assault troops waiting to invade Japan just south of Nagasaki a couple of days before the two atomic bombs that ended World War II were dropped. Had the planned landing occurred, Larry later found out, 95% casualties had been expected. Larry would not have lent Buddy the money to buy his Fender Stratocaster. President Truman would have had to answer to Ella Holley along with countless other American mothers and wives for not deploying the atomic bombs that would have saved the life of Buddy's eldest brother and Lord knows how many other American boys.

CHAPTER 45

Art said to Frank, "Charlie and I are going out for dinner with the girls Thursday. You and Vicky can come along too. The reservations are at eight so you can stay in your coffin until after sundown."

"Thanks for asking but Vicky and I are busy on Thursday. But please invite us another time."

"Frank said 'please'. Have you turned over a new leaf?"

"Don't push your luck, smart ass. So, Charlie, what new Buddy Holly stuff have you learned? What was his favorite food?"

"Buddy's favorite food was okra."

"What's okra?"

"It's a vegetable. He liked it fried."

Anything else to report today about Buddy Holly?"

Charlie explained the various spellings of Holley and Holly again. "People know that Buddy's last name was misspelled on his first Decca contract. His parents' name was Holley with an 'e' but on the contract it was spelled the way we know it now. I saw a picture of Buddy's high school yearbook and they spelled Holly without an "e" there too. That could be confusing to someone who doesn't know the true story."

♪♫♪♫

Saving Buddy Holly Blue Days Black Nights

Art and Charlie were at the restaurant. While they waited for their girls Joan and Dolly to arrive, Art ordered the wine.

"Art, so now that you have this so-called wine hobby, teach me something."

"Well, it's more complicated than red with beef and white with fish and chicken. You have to match the wine properly to how the food is prepared: like the sauces and stuff. In magazines and on some wine bottle labels, they suggest what they call pairings. This is a fancy way of saying that this wine goes well with certain dishes. I suppose they use their experience and then try them out."

"Or maybe they just make it up," Charlie suggested. He then asked, "Well, what happens if the, uh, if the pairings are wrong?"

"Some people don't care, as long as they get to drink it. Remember in college that mail order wine course I took?"

"Oh yeah. You even got a diploma for that. You were so, so proud."

"Recently I decided to make wine a bit of a hobby again."

"Being a Buddy Holly fan, I've always wondered about Texas zinfandels," said Charlie.

"Well, you know Texas is not known for zinfandel. California is."

Charlie smiled. "I knew that. That's why I asked you."

"Texas may be big in many ways, pardner, but it fails big time with wine grapes. If you could even find a Texas zinfandel, I have a perfect match for it. It would make the wine seem to taste great."

"You're kidding?"

"I have a perfect match for a Texas zinfandel."

"Okay, so what is it?"

"Well to make a Texas zinfandel taste good you would have to pair it with cow patties."

"Is that a beef dish?"

"Cow patties or cow pies. You know, cow dung."

"Hey Art, I like Texas."

The wine arrived. The waiter poured and Charlie breathed it in. "It has a nice smell."

Art corrected, "Bouquet, not smell."

"Well its bouquet smells nice. I think it smells like chicken," Charlie clowned.

"We should wait for the food but let's take a sip to see what it tastes like. Oh. The girls are here. Let's wait for them. Do you think they did a lot of shopping? What am I saying?"

"Hey, Dolly. Hi, Joan," Art waved Dolly and Joan over to their table.

"What were you girls up to?" asked Art.

Dolly and Joan sat down, and Dolly said, "We were window shopping."

"Well not just window shopping," said Joan. "Eyes are for looking and credit cards are for buying."

Art put his head down on the table and whispered, "I love you, Joannie."

Joan went on. "I bought a blouse. That's all."

Art lifted his head off the table. "So, what did you buy me?"

"Nothing," said Joan with not a hint of facial expression.

"Nothing?" said Art. "I see that you are high maintenance and I am zero maintenance."

Charlie noticed the awkward pause and said, "Art, you have an uncanny knack for being able to act stupid even when you're not drunk."

"I know."

Charlie continued. "I'm glad that we are here today. I had a root canal not that long ago. It hurt like hell. It's great now but the dentist's assistant told me that if I had been born hundred years ago, I'd have no teeth. Advances in modern dentistry allow me to continue eating steak."

Dolly said, "Steak once in a while is okay but to be healthy, we all need to eat a balanced diet."

Art said, "Charlie and I always eat a balanced diet when we go out together. We put olives and sliced tomatoes on our pizzas. And when we go to a football game we eat our favorite vegetables, potato chips and popcorn."

"You guys should be eating more organic fruits and vegetables."

"But just like MSG on Chinese food, pesticides enhance flavor."

Both women laughed.

"I've never worried about becoming a vegetarian. I think that cows and sheep wouldn't hesitate to eat us if they were hungry enough."

"I wasn't keen on the idea of shark fin soup but after I saw the movie "Jaws", I began eating it as revenge.

Art said, "My idea of living dangerously is having spaghetti while wearing a white shirt."

"I try to buy him disposable shirts, the cheapest I can find," said Joan.

"What would vegetarians do if they discovered that vegetables feel pain?"

"Lord knows."

The waiter brought the menu. Art ordered much less than the others. He knew that Joan had big eyes. When it came to menus, she was a good orderer but she only ate 2/3 of what she ordered and so Art would eat the rest.

After they'd ordered and the waiter had gone, Charlie said, "I was reading the newspaper and I think this recycling thing may be going too far. I like the idea of recycling newspaper and glass. It sounds simple enough but what's next? Recycling lightly used toilet paper?"

CHAPTER 46

Art and Charlie were with Graham again.

Graham said, "I've given even more thought to your time lines. How about a football shaped time line analogy? It has more possible paths because it's three-dimensional."

Charlie said, "I like that three-dimensional football idea. It would be like many strands of spaghetti going from one tip to the other."

Graham gagged.

"Are you okay, Graham?"

"I'm okay. Go on," said Graham.

Charlie went on. "So multiple time lines are like a mass of intertwined spaghetti strands running through a football, with some going along the outer edge and some going straight through the football and some twisting and turning their way through the football."

"A mass of intertwined spaghetti. I can envision that," said Art. "Did Buddy like football?"

"There was a football team at his high school in Lubbock, but I've never read anything about Buddy's having been particularly interested in team sports. I know that he liked to fish and hunt. He also liked swimming and water skiing."

♪♫♪♫

"Have you ever pronounced anyone dead?"

Graham nodded thoughtfully. "Oh yes. Then I have to talk to the family. That's very difficult," Graham said slowly.

"Medically, how do you determine if somebody is really dead?"

"We look at physical signs like pulse and breathing and brain waves. My favorite definition is how my second-year pathology professor phrased it: 'Death is when the soul leaves the body.'"

Charlie said, "When you're dead, you're dead. Except for passing on your genes to future generations and your lasting impact on people that you've interacted with throughout your life."

Graham said, "I had a patient with severe sweating who developed a chronic rash in his groin. We sometimes call it crotch rot."

Art opened his eyes widely. "Crotch rot? Is that the medical term?"

Graham smiled. "We call it that sometimes but no. The medical term is tinea cruris, but I thought you'd like crotch rot better."

"Oh, okay," said Art with a half-hearted smile.

Graham continued, "It's caused by a fungus. It's a constant battle as the fungus keeps coming back and we treat it again. I know that one day the fungus will win the war when the patient dies."

Charlie had watched battles in war movies. Afterward, dead bodies were tossed into heaps. He imagined himself as a body in the middle of a heap. Charlie had mused about his own body's decomposing. Which parts of his body would decompose first? Hair and nails? Probably later. Bowels with all their bacteria? Probably quickly. Bones? Maybe never. Eyes? Gross. Skin? Muscles? Spleen? What did the spleen do anyway? His body would be broken down by insects and bacteria into the basic building blocks of life. Thus, from the top of the food chain to the bottom of the food chain. And then back up the food chain in a cycle that had been going on since the formation of life on Earth. Dust to dust and back.

Charlie said, "I sometimes think of the world as a giant compost heap."

"That sounds appetizing. On that note let's go have lunch and talk about creationism versus evolution."

Charlie continued the conversation. "When we think about the existence of evolution we wonder about the odds. There were incredibly low odds of things happening exactly as they did, but even with the very low odds when you multiply them by infinite time, the result is more than zero. We are each lucky to have had a life. The odds of the universe, galaxy, planet, evolution and all the wars since the beginning of history aligning just right for each of us to exist are incredibly low."

Lucky? mused Charlie.

"So you are saying that no matter how low the odds were, the necessary events that brought us here together to have this discussion, must have happened or someone else might be having this same conversation. The odds of another chain of events happening may have been just as low as that of us all being here talking."

"Yes."

"Evolution is related to fate, whether it's guided by an invisible hand or whether it's just like playing craps. Some win and some lose. Some walk away from the table with money and others walk away having lost everything. If the odds are one in one million to win the lottery, then it's extremely unlikely that any specific person will win. But in the end, someone does."

Art spoke. "After the fact, once something has already happened the odds of its happening are no longer relevant. No matter how unlikely it was before, the odds of its having happened are now 100%. Let's imagine that a battle is about to occur. Before a brigade of soldiers charges up a hill, the odds of any particular brigade soldier's surviving that charge are only 1 in a 100. Then the brigade of 3,000 soldiers attacks and they charge up the hill. After the bloody battle, they have taken the hill and as predicted there are only 30 survivors. Even though they were 1% before the charge, the odds of the survivors being alive after the charge is 100%. After the charge each soldier who survived can say, 'I don't know how I made it but I did and I'm here.'"

Charlie told the others, "When I visited Lubbock I met Buddy's brothers, Larry and Travis. They both fought in the Pacific during World War II. Travis fought at Iwo Jima. Larry was with the assault group that was just about to invade Japan. They were expected to lose 95% of their men in the invasion. Then the Hiroshima and Nagasaki atomic bombs were dropped and the War was over.

"I also met Buddy's eye doctor, Dr. Armistead, when I was in Lubbock. What a nice man. He told me that he also was in the Pacific during the War and he didn't understand why he made it back while others didn't. It was interesting that one of Dr. Armistead's relatives was a general who had died at the Battle of Gettysburg. There's a memorial for him on the battlefield. Dr. Armistead told me that another relative of his, Colonel George Armistead, had commanded Fort McHenry during the War of 1812 and became known as the 'Guardian of the Star-Spangled Banner'. You must know that's where Francis Scott Key wrote 'The Star-Spangled Banner'."

Art said, "Of course. But did you know that ironically the tune of 'The Star-Spangled Banner' was taken from an old British drinking song?"

"Really?" said Charlie. "I didn't know that."

"I can never get a straight answer. In the end, who won the War of 1812?"

"It depends on who you ask. Americans say that we won, and the British say that they did."

"Does that mean that 'history is written by the winners' doesn't apply here?"

"Well if both sides think they won, then it does apply."

Art said, "If we keep meeting, we are going to solve every difficult issue on the planet."

"There are an infinite number of possibilities in the universe. Not all things are predestined except for the beginning and the end. There are just multiple pathways from the beginning to the end."

"Yes. Time lines."

"Graham, why don't you come over to SNI sometime and we can show you around. I'd like to introduce you to some of our coworkers."

"The last day of the convention is pretty quiet. I'll be leaving for home on Tuesday morning. Can I come over tomorrow?"

So on Monday, Art introduced Graham to Frank Funk. "Here's my friend Frank."

Frank shook Graham's hand. "Pleased to meet you. Any friend of Art's is a friend of mine." Frank could control his mouth around new people and when he had to.

"Nice to meet you too."

Art continued. "This is my cousin Graham from up north. Graham's been spending time with Charlie and me while he's been in town. Today we brought him over to show him around SNI."

Frank asked Graham. "Has Charlie discussed time lines with you?"

"Does a bear shit in the woods?" said Art.

"What about Buddy Holly? Did Charlie mention anything about Buddy Holly to you?"

Graham smirked. "Does a bear shit in the woods?"

Charlie suggested that the three of them go to the cafeteria for coffee.

After they picked up their coffees and sat down together Graham asked Frank what he did at SNI.

"I work as a statistician. I do stuff for a lot of departments. So, what do you do?"

"I'm a doctor. I practice family medicine."

"Maybe you can tell me why hospital food tastes so bad?"

"I've wondered that too. When I was a medical student, I had spaghetti and meat balls in the hospital cafeteria one time. Only one time. The meatballs tasted like sawdust. Now when I see spaghetti and meatballs on a menu, I gag." Charlie and Art looked at each other. "I think hospitals even age the salads to give them a brown tinge before they set them out in the cafeterias. We've considered having the salads carbon dated."

"Graham, what changes do you see in the future of medical care?"

"I've looked at older medical texts and I'm only talking about the 50s and 60s. We've had so many improvements in medical care in the last few decades. Patients don't realize how lucky we are to live in the twentieth century. And the advances are continuing all the time. One day medical science might stop mankind's continued evolution. As negative genes become treatable, genetic fitness could become irrelevant. There will be no more survival of the fittest."

"The end of evolution. How will we pay for the stuff?"

"Good question. Maybe the price of gene therapy will decrease as it becomes more common. Some of the antibiotics we prescribe have dropped so much in price since they came out years ago, that the pharmacist's dispensing fee is higher than the drug itself today."

CHAPTER 47

Dolly and Charlie were watching one of Charlie's time travel movies. "Back to the Future" was about a mad scientist and his young friend who travel back and forth in time.

"Now I have it!" Charlie burst out.

"What?" asked Dolly.

"Doc's voice is the same as Judge Doom's."

"Judge Doom?"

"Judge Doom is the villain in 'Roger Rabbit'."

"'Roger Rabbit' the movie?"

"Yup."

"It's a kids' movie, right? A cartoon."

"The hero Roger Rabbit is a cartoon character but no I wouldn't call it just a kid's movie," said Charlie. "I just realized that Christopher Lloyd, who plays Doc in 'Back to the Future' also does the voice of Judge Doom in 'Who Framed Roger Rabbit'.

"I've never seen the Roger Rabbit movie."

"Let's watch it together, Dolly. It's one of my all-time favorites. I've watched it about twenty-five times."

"Twenty-five times?"

"Hyperbole. Would you believe five?"

♪♫♪♫

After they had watched the movie, Charlie said, "Dolly, isn't it amazing how the movie has dialogue and interaction between cartoon characters and human actors? Can you imagine how much work there was integrating real people with the cartoon characters? They somehow spliced the cartoon characters and people together. The actors must have done their scenes and interacted with thin air. They must have imagined the characters they were talking to and interacting with. Every time I watch it I'm amazed."

"It must've taken tons of time and money to make the movie."

"I read that it was very expensive."

"It even has cartoon characters in it that you don't see very often anymore, like Pluto and Goofy and Tweety Bird and Sylvester the Cat."

"'I tawt I taw a puddy tat.' And Porky Pig. 'That's all folks!' And Roadrunner too. And Wile E. Coyote." Charlie smirked. "I always root for the poor coyote, but he always gets clobbered. I wish there was an episode where Wile E. actually catches Roadrunner. I wonder what Wile E. would do. I heard once that some do-gooder group tried to ban the Roadrunner show because it was too violent and it could be a bad influence on kids."

"What! You're not kidding, are you?"

"I'm not kidding. I sure turned out really violent, didn't I? I won't even step on an ant." Charlie continued, "So did you notice why Jessica said she loved Roger?"

"Because he makes her laugh. I think that's one of the things that makes us so good together too. We make each other laugh."

"For sure. That's because there is so much about you to make fun of."

"Watch it, Charlie. You're my sweetie, but God'll get you."

"It's not my fault," Charlie smiled evilly. "The Devil made me do it."

In the movie, Jessica Rabbit was a cartoon character drawn as an idealized human vamp. She oozed sexuality. Her eye makeup appeared to have been painted on by an artist. She was a cartoon character and of course it had been literally painted on by an artist. As a humanoid temptress she was very striking. She had lavender eye shadow generously and widely applied. Her eyes were accentuated by thick black eyelashes and a generous track of eyeliner. Her long auburn hair came down well over her shoulders and reached down her back. Her hair was thick, flawless, surreal.

Dolly said, "I love her hair. I wish I had hair like that."

"Screw the hair. Hubba, hubba, hubba. I think her best feature is her rack."

"Charlie, don't be disgusting. She's only a cartoon character, but her knockers are more than ample and they do flow right out of her dress."

"But she wasn't bad, just drawn that way."

"Did you like her luscious red lips?" Dolly asked.

"I'll go with the bazooms. Nice booby trap."

"You pig." Dolly exhaled seductively, "Oh Charlie, I love you because you make me laugh."

"She walks like she has two dislocated hips. Why do girls wiggle when they walk?"

"I think it's anatomy but I know that high heels make girls wiggle even more," explained Dolly.

"I like girls in high heels, but I still think you girls are nuts to abuse your feet with those things."

A few days later the phone woke Charlie up from a nap. He had been dreaming about Jessica Rabbit. It was Dolly on the phone.

"Guess who I was dreaming about?" said Charlie trying to mask his guilt about his dreamy unfaithfulness.

"Me?" flirted Dolly.

"Not exactly. I was daydreaming about Jessica Rabbit."

"You are so bad," Dolly scolded playfully.

"I suppose," Charlie conceded.

"At least you're only an adulterer in your dreams."

"That's true, but not very often." Charlie went on. "You know they could have made the movie into a raunchy adult cartoon flick. They should have gone crazy and made it restricted to adults. Although there is a lot between the lines, it would have been a lot of fun to make it a totally X-rated movie raunch."

"Are you crazy?"

"Is that a rhetorical question? Hurry home and let me take your clothes off slowly. Really slowly. Maybe you should wear a low-cut top that accentuates your boobs, sort of like Jessica Rabbit wears."

"Are you crazy?" squealed Dolly.

"Another rhetorical question?"

Later after she returned home, Dolly went to look at the movie box's cover. She studied Jessica's picture. Jessica had an hourglass figure with large hips, a wasp waist and a voluptuous in-your-face bosom.

"Very interesting how Jessica is drawn," said Dolly to Charlie. "She has long dark butterfly eyelashes and peekaboo hair that always covers her eye. She has purple lavender eye shadow and sensuous rosy red lips."

"Good grief. Girls have the most phenomenal ways to describe colors and makeup. Can you wear makeup like Jessica's?" asked Charlie.

"I can't do the arched eyebrows. I don't have green eyes and my hair doesn't sit that way. But I can use lots of mascara to get those long dark butterfly eyelashes, I can get lavender eye shadow and I can wear scarlet red lipstick"

"Sounds good to me."

CHAPTER 48

Why do people cry at funerals? They are crying for themselves: because they have lost someone and because they are frightened about their own mortality. Most people do not understand that the sadness of mourning a loss is normal and lifts sooner than depression. Comparing sadness and depression is like saying that getting wet and drowning are the same thing.

When Charlie was working while depressed, his physical and mental sides could be out of sync. Even if the mental aspect of his depression was not as bad, he could still feel physically exhausted. The physical side of depression was like walking in water up to his chest. When necessary, he could press on with work and interacting with people. Maybe it was adrenaline. Once he was alone his physical depression would take over and his body collapsed. He would put his feet up on his desk, lean back and hope to sleep. As he did not want to be embarrassed by a coworker finding him napping, he tried to remain alert for the sound of approaching footsteps. He imagined that this was the way an exhausted alley cat slept after barely getting away from a pack of dogs.

♪♫♪♫

Saving Buddy Holly Blue Days Black Nights

Guilt lived in his brain. He experienced guilt because he was better off than so many other living things on the planet. He felt guilty that there were those that had never even been born to have a life. But his life was so full of anguish. How could anyone have been worse off?

They say that the good die young. Buddy died young. Why hadn't Charlie? He had tried to be good but maybe Charlie wasn't as good as he thought. Charlie knew he was depressed when he felt that those who did not live into adulthood were the lucky ones. They would no longer have to struggle to eat, learn, work, suffer through illnesses and injuries, and then go on to die anyway.

Sometimes when Charlie woke up sweating just before sunrise, he went to a window that faced east and saw the morning star Venus. It was a glorious thing to behold. But on bad days, no scene looked beautiful. When he walked around trying to absorb beautiful sights, sounds and smells that he had sensed in the past, he perceived no beautiful sights, sounds or smells. He found that the word 'anhedonia', the inability to feel happiness, described him perfectly.

Buddy Holly's song "Not Fade Away" was the Rolling Stones' first North American hit song. Charlie had lots of Stones' songs on his exercise tapes too. They included "Get Off My Cloud", "I Can't Get No Satisfaction" and "Jumpin' Jack Flash". Their song "Paint It Black" spoke to Charlie on a personal level. "I have to turn my head until my darkness goes." "I look inside myself and see my heart is black." "It's not easy facing up when your whole world is black."

♪♫♪♫

People say that they don't want to spend the rest of their lives dying or waiting to die. They mean to enjoy your life as best you can while you have it. To Charlie it meant get your miserable existence over with by committing suicide.

Charlie took the long route home. He drove by the cemetery, stopped and looked longingly at the headstones. Then he felt a shiver on the back of his neck.

CHAPTER 49

Charlie and some of SNI's other staff were at a conference in Atlanta.

"It's a nice city. Did you notice how all the streets in Atlanta are named after peaches and peach trees?"

Art complained about some of the lectures. "There were a lot of problems with the slides for a while," complained Art. "Thankfully they got that cleared up."

"I thought the projectionist was focusing in Braille," deadpanned Frank.

"Hey, Mike, come over and sit with us," said Frank. I introduced you to the other guys earlier at the coffee break but you haven't met Charlie Harding. Charlie, this is Mike Fry. Mike, Charlie."

"Hi. Nice to meet you, Mike," said Charlie.

"Likewise, Charlie."

The socializing often was what made a conference memorable and interesting. There were some heavy-duty discussions about professional and college football.

"When did you move down to the Orlando area?" Charlie asked Mike.

"More than ten years ago. I work more directly with the actual rocket launchings than you guys do. It's interesting that you work down there for a related company in the same field but we've never met each other before."

Charlie said, "I'll bet we've crossed paths or been in the same room in the past somewhere but just never met each other before."

"Come on guys, let's get some dessert," said Art.

After dessert, it turned out that not only had Charlie and Mike been living in the same city for the last few years, but they also had been born and raised in the same city as well.

"Mike, tell me then, which high school did you go to?"

"I went to Eastern Tech."

"I went to Northern Collegiate, not far from there," said Charlie.

"It's interesting for us to finally meet and have lunch together in another city altogether after having worked and gone to school so close to each other." Mike continued, "I even had a few friends at Northern Collegiate; in fact, one of them broke my leg," he chuckled.

Charlie replied with feigned incredulity. "Come on. You must be kidding. I would have thought it was the other way around. You Tech boys were the tough guys, not us nerdy Northern boys. How could one of us Northern kids have broken your leg?"

Mike answered, "Oh, no! It was an accident. I said he was a friend of mine back then. It was in a football game."

Something clicked in Charlie's brain. He visualized something he had not thought of or even dreamed about for twenty-five years. Charlie was seeing a profoundly detailed vision of long-ago events.

"Junior football," Charlie said. "You were a running back and wore number 22. You were pulling out to your left and then our middle linebacker, number 36, tackled you and broke your leg."

Charlie was stunned by what he had just witnessed in his mind and the scene he had described to the group. The table was eerily quiet.

Mike was staring at Charlie in disbelief. "How did you know that?"

Charlie shuddered. "I was there. I was one of the fans at the game. It really bothered me back then, but I haven't thought of it for twenty-five years. I remember that one of the Eastern players had been injured near the end of the game. It was a meaningless play near the end of the game. The outcome was settled. I remember that our player had tackled this poor fellow viciously and I was upset as I watched him being carried off the field on a stretcher."

Mike interrupted, "No, no, no. The two of us went out for supper the night before the game and he teased me that he was going to break my leg the next day. But he was just joking. It was a clean tackle and a fluky fall. I can't even remember his name anymore."

"I remember," said Charlie. "The linebacker had curly blond hair and his name was Ray."

"That's right! Ray," said Mike. "Ray and I had been good friends for a while. Because of my cast and crutches I spent more time studying and my marks went up. I can't get over how you could remember my injury in such detail."

The rest of the table was still quiet. They had just passed through the twilight zone. He was not afraid, but Charlie could feel that the hairs on the back of his neck were standing up.

Charlie tried to explain. "I think memories are ingrained in our brains forever. We just need something to trigger an association with it and then the memory can come back into our consciousness. I don't know what happened but when you said broken leg and football and game against Northern, I began to see the play in my mind just as it had looked when I was there as a teenager. It was like I was watching a movie. It was so vivid."

Charlie continued, "Listen, Mike. Give me your address. I'm going to find a picture of Ray for you in one of my old high school yearbooks. I'll see if it mentions the football game we're talking about. I don't know how much detail there would be but I think they wrote a little about each game. We didn't have very good football teams at Northern. Remember, we were supposed to have all the smart guys, not the tough guys. Anyway, I'll send you what I find for sure. Just give me your address and I promise to look for it."

"Thanks, Charlie. I'd appreciate that but don't waste too much time on it if you don't find it. I guess you just had an amazing déjà vu."

Charlie responded, "I believe that technically a déjà vu is a feeling of having experienced something before that you actually did not experience before. Today I re-saw something that I actually did experience a long time ago. What I just experienced was weird. Linguistically, however, 'déjà vu comes from the French words meaning 'already seen' and what I described was certainly 'already seen'. So, linguistically a déjà vu, but technically not a déjà vu."

Charlie always felt a compulsion to correct errors, but he tried not to give into his perfectionist urges. The problem was that when he heard something that was not exactly right, he felt an imbalance in the universe, an uncorrected free-floating error. And so, he felt driven to correct it and re-balance the universe.

Fred covered for Charlie. "Charlie is being pedantic again."

"Sorry, the Devil made me do it."

Everyone laughed.

Fred continued, "What Charlie just experienced is kind of creepy. It gets me thinking of one of Charlie's time travel ideas. You know, Charlie, the thoughts of someone traveling in time getting messed up with the thoughts of a nearby person as he materializes in the past."

Charlie said, "I have thought about that for a long time. If their memories get amalgamated, how would these memories of past events be integrated? Which would dominate? That would be really confusing to deal with."

Fred asked, "So what do you think would happen within the minds of two people that were literally at the same place at the same time? How would the brain handle the two memories? There would be two different views of the same event. You guys were at that same football game years ago and obviously you two have different perspectives of that long-ago game. Which would the person consider to be the real memory? If two sets of memories are intermingled, maybe they both would be true memories but from different points of view."

"Oh no. I think I'm starting to get a headache," interjected Mike.

Charlie said, "I still have to try to work that out. Let's forget it for now. Hey, I'm going to buy Mike a drink."

Mike replied, "Not now. I'll fall asleep during the afternoon talks but tonight we'll go out together. I'll buy you a couple of drinks and then you can buy me some. Okay?"

"You're on. Shall we let these guys come along?"

"Why not?"

CHAPTER 50

The report had to be ready. It was Charlie's responsibility to get it done and there could be no excuses. It was a presentation about what had been done so far on one of SNI's newest projects. Over the last few days, he had met with all the supervisors involved in the project and had read and reread the summaries. He had all the information he needed organized, but he still had to make it coherent for the investors. He had to show them that their funds were being used wisely and how their money would lead to a significant return on their investments.

He had been in a down cycle for weeks. Charlie was putting the finishing touches on his presentation but in his depressed state progress had been slow. Now it was getting late, and Charlie was getting more tired. The neurons in his head were bogging down. What he should have been able to do in a few minutes was taking much longer. He wrote and rewrote sentences. Then he rewrote them again.

Cups of coffee gave him bursts of energy. His stomach had already been churning when he came in to work. The coffee made the churning worse and induced some retching. He poured yet another cup. This time it came from the bottom of the pot and had significant dregs floating in it. He drank it anyway. Soon after he was rushing down the hall to the washroom and barely made it. He emptied his bowels into the toilet bowl. The painful contractions stopped then returned. After they eased off and he was only feeling a mild tension in his abdomen Charlie thought the cramps were over and went back to his desk. He was wrong. It took several more trips that evening before Charlie got final relief from the pain. This was not the first time that coffee had wreaked havoc on Charlie's intestines. Charlie had been forced to choose between fatigue and abdominal cramps many times.

Charlie returned to his office, sat down and slumped over his desk one more time. He tried to pull his knees to his chest into the fetal position and hugged himself. The caffeine was keeping his brain active even after it had let go of its grip on his guts. He finished his work. Then a hopelessness crept in. He knew that now that this report was done there would come another day when he would have to go through this hell again, making a deadline in the face of physical and mental anguish. Hopelessness weighed on his mind. Hopelessness weighed on his total being. Everything was for naught. The world would end. He would die. The solar system would only last another five billion years. All was hopelessness and pain, mental pain and utter hopelessness. He had to end his suffering. How could he get out of this? He had to get out of his predicament.

The report was done. There was no moon that night and it was very dark outside when the final draft was put on his secretary's desk. In the morning she would read through it and call him if she thought corrections were needed. There would be none.

It was finally the end of another hellish chapter in Charlie's existence. He was profoundly beaten down by the mental and physical efforts of a day that had been compounded by the bouts of retching and horrific cramps. Charlie dragged himself over to the coat hangers. He slipped on his jacket in slow motion as the fatigue and depression weighed oppressively on his brain and on his limbs. Every step was an effort as if he were going through quicksand. He walked down a few flights of stairs. Charlie never took an elevator if it was less than four flights: 2 calories per trip times 4 trips per day times 365 days per year equaled 3,000 calories per year. That was almost one pound. It was also good for his heart. It amused Charlie that he could worry about weight and health while only minutes earlier he had been contemplating suicide.

He made it to the street. He had finished work. Survived yet another day. He realized that when he got home, he would not have the wherewithal to go to the refrigerator and get leftovers for supper and so not long after he left the SNI parking lot he turned his car into a small strip plaza. He got out of the car and walked toward the restaurant. Nothing had made him feel good that day. Now sadness permeated his being and so eating was not something that he looked forward to that night. It was just another task to get done.

It was midweek late, and the other stores were closed. As he passed the darkened laneway, he heard the murmur of mumbled words and turned slowly, mechanically toward the dimly lit lane. In the gray darkness he discerned the presence of a man. The stranger was grubby and shabbily dressed. He was not tall.

"Gimme your wallet."

Was this what he had always wished for? Was this his way out? He had never had the guts to kill himself but had always wished that someone would do it for him. Would it hurt? Maybe. But then it would be over. Finally. Charlie did not move. He raised his eyes and looked toward the sinister lane. He could not discern the would-be mugger's eyes.

"No," said Charlie. Just a simple subdued "no" was all that Charlie uttered.

The dark figure moved closer.

Charlie repeated, "No."

He stood there waiting for his demise. Finally, his wretched existence would be over. He hoped that the end would be swift and painless. Maybe by bludgeoning, less likely by pummeling, hopefully by bullet. An accurate bullet would be the death of his dreams: swift and painless. The pain would be acceptable if this was really the end. Charlie steeled himself. His breathing increased. His pulse sped up. For years Charlie had longed for this moment. As the realization that the moment he had been hoping for was imminent, his mind and body became calm and relaxed.

Charlie was offering no resistance, nor had he complied with the request for money. He waited, somewhat hunched at his shoulders. Two worn-out creatures in darkness and gloom confronted each other near the entrance of the alleyway. Charlie felt that his life was utterly worthless and even worse, painful and tortured. But his tattered adversary thought more of life than Charlie did. Charlie waited, but alas the mugger ran away.

CHAPTER 51

Charlie said to Dolly, "There's no urgency, but what do you think about spending a few days together in a hotel sometime just for fun?"

"What do you have in mind? You know my work schedule is pretty flexible. Just give me a few weeks notice and I can arrange the days off."

"There's a new hotel in Biloxi called the Beau Rivage. I was thinking that we could fly there because the drive is about eight hours."

"Remember the time we drove across the state on Alligator Alley?"

"That's a great highway. Straight as an arrow across the Everglades. We drove at night and we made great time. Do you remember the sign that said, 'Panther Crossing'?"

Dolly smiled. "How could I forget? When we saw the sign, I told you to slow down and you said if you hit a panther, you wanted to kill it, not just make it mad."

Charlie smiled too.

"OK, Charlie. I'll leave the flight and hotel details to you."

"The Beau Rivage is right on the water and the view should be beautiful. Because it's right on the Gulf though, we shouldn't go during hurricane season."

"So when will you feel safe?"

"Let's go in the early spring. I think late March will work. It won't be too hot outside, which is even better."

"Okay. Go ahead and arrange it."

"I'll check the exact dates with you before I book the hotel and flights. The hotel has a casino and restaurants right inside the hotel. We should put a strict daily limit on how much money we gamble. We'll buy our limit of chips when we get to the casino each day. Then we can make small bets and quit for the day when we run out of chips. If we can go two hours before losing our day's limit, that would be about the cost of going to a show and dinner so it's just the cost of entertainment. And if we get carried away with the gambling and blow our budget, there's even a McDonald's nearby. The Mardi Gras Museum is not far from the Beau Rivage. I checked and we can easily walk there."

Dolly and Charlie checked into the Beau Rivage and were just about to leave the front desk and go upstairs.

"What room is it again?" Dolly asked the desk clerk.

The desk clerk repeated the room number for her.

Dolly said, "Could you repeat that please? I can't understand your accent."

The desk clerk looked Dolly straight in the eye and said, "Lady, here you are the one with the accent."

When they were upstairs in the room, they both took naps to recover from their flight. Dolly woke up first. Soon after, Charlie was lying in bed awake and watching Dolly through the bathroom door. She was getting ready to go out for dinner. Dolly had taken her shower, brushed her hair and was putting on makeup. She stared at her image in the mirror, puckered up her lips and kissed toward her own image in the mirror three times.

"You seem quite the narcissist. Do you love yourself that much?" asked Charlie.

"Charlie, you fool. I'm puckering my lips to smooth out my lipstick."

"Really? I've seen you do that so many times. I thought you were kissing yourself in the mirror."

"Girls do that to smooth out their lipstick."

"I'm glad to hear that. I really thought you were admiring yourself in the mirror."

Charlie looked at his watch. "Hey, Dolly, you better hurry up or we're going to be late for our dinner reservations."

"Don't worry," Dolly replied calmly.

"Don't worry?" Charlie cried out incredulously. "You're buck naked!"

"I'm ready! I'm ready! I just have to put my clothes on."

It was their second night at the hotel. They had dinner in one of the hotel restaurants and then after they had lost their quota of gambling money at the blackjack table, they went back to the hotel room.

"You like wearing my shirts, don't you?" Charlie asked.

"They're comfortable. I like wearing them."

"And my boxer shorts too?"

"Of course, they're very comfortable."

"Let me try on your panties," said Charlie.

"And how will you get them on without squashing your balls?"

"I could use duct tape to keep them safe. So how about I wear your panties? What about one of your pink bras too?"

"That's not alright. You may not wear my underwear," frowned Dolly dramatically.

"Why not? You wear my underwear."

"I can wear your clothes, but it doesn't work the other way around."

Charlie responded with an exaggerated pout. "Women get away with so much."

"Tough, Charlie," taunted Dolly, "but life's just not fair. Men let women get away with a lot because we look good and all you guys really want to do is get into our panties, not wear our panties."

Charlie grinned. "I do have a stash of your panties that I keep as trophies. And come to think of it, you do look good in my shirts and boxers."

"I know," said Dolly, with faked coyness.

"Well if you know, then I don't have to give you compliments anymore."

"No. That's not true." A look of feigned alarm came over Dolly's face.

"Oh don't worry, my sweet little goofette. I like to give you compliments."

"Then let me try on my new dress."

"Did you pay on my credit card or yours?" Charlie asked with mock trepidation.

"We're joint now, dummy."

"Oops."

"I bought the dress just for you. Let me show it off," cooed Dolly.

"Not now please. Can't we just stay in bed and you know?"

"Let me show you the dress. We can skip the sex today."

"Wait a second. With monogamy comes responsibility."

"Okay. We'll get to that later."

She hopped out of bed, walked quickly to the hotel room closet and came back strutting her new dress.

"Does this dress make me look fat?"

"Cat's got my tongue," evaded Charlie.

"Does this dress make me look fat?" repeated Dolly.

"I plead the fifth. I have the right to remain silent. Anything that I say can and will be used against me." Charlie answered impassively, trying to look serious.

"Come on Charlie, tell me the truth. Do I look fat in this?"

"You look fine. You always look great. Anyway, it's not the clothes that make you look fat: it's the fat that makes you look fat. Actually, I really like the dress. I'm not kidding but what would you say if I said that the dress did make you look fat?"

"I'd say, 'Couldn't you lie?'"

"You are so bad." Charlie grinned.

"I'm not bad. I'm just drawn that way," purred Dolly.

"Oh Jessica, does that mean that you're not a bitch but just drawn that way?"

"Do you want the last thing you see in your life to be the stars that Roger Rabbit sees when he gets hit with a frying pan?"

Dolly stuck her tongue out at Charlie and then grabbed the newspaper from the nearby table. She rolled it up and hit him on the top of his head. Charlie curled himself into a ball and covered his head with his hands for protection.

"Don't hit me on the head. You'll make me stupid."

"I think it's too late for that, Charlie. By the way, I am not a bitch. I've just been in a bad mood for a couple of years."

Charlie jumped at Dolly, pinned her arms to the bed and forced a kiss on her.

"I can't breathe." Charlie backed off and then Dolly demanded, "Kiss me again."

Charlie kissed her again.

"Wait a second," said Charlie. "Do you remember the movie 'Basic Instinct'?

"Yes."

"I'm just checking, but would you ever kill me after we have sex?"

"Do you think I'm a Praying Mantis?"

Charlie leaped at her again.

"Why don't you wear more eye shadow to give you that seductive Jessica Rabbit look when we go out?"

"I can't wear that much eye shadow outside. I'd look like that evangelist lady on TV. What's her name?"

"I know who you mean. Tammy Faye something."

Dolly jumped up off the bed, pulled her dress up over her head and then plopped down on the bed next to Charlie. She rolled over with her back toward Charlie and sheepishly said, "Please scratch my back."

"What's it worth to you?" asked Charlie.

"Anything you want."

"Anything?" Charlie raised his eyebrows.

"Okay. Anything."

Charlie was proud of the fact that he'd never broken a promise and so he teased, "Is that a Charlie promise or a Dolly promise?"

"Just scratch my back, please. I have this terrible itch. Please," begged Dolly.

"Okay."

Charlie's fingers ran down Dolly's back.

Dolly moaned contentedly. "Ah. That is so good. Now can you scratch under my bra too? A little to the right side please."

Charlie obliged.

"Yes, that's it. Do it again right there."

"Now to the left." Charlie obliged yet again.

"It feels so good. Oh yes. Yes! More! Don't stop! Don't stop! I'm begging you!"

Charlie smiled and continued to scratch, being careful not to break the skin of Dolly's alluring back.

"Thank you. Thank you. Do it again a little closer to the center." Charlie indulged her one more time.

"That was orgasmic," sighed Dolly.

Charlie smiled. "I thought that because Eve got Adam thrown out of Eden, women are condemned to suffer labor pains. But if women are supposed to suffer so much, then why do you girls get multiple orgasms?"

Charlie's grin got even bigger. "Women have a special bounce to their step and special smile after they get laid. I think it's called orgasm face."

They decided to go out shopping the next morning. Charlie was just about dressed and ready to go, so he called to Dolly in the bathroom, "Are you almost ready?"

"I'll be a couple of minutes. I just have to put my face on."

In the other room Charlie looked up at the ceiling, rolled his eyes and hit his forehead with the palm of his hand.

"Charlie, just let me put myself together."

"Wait until they invent replacement body parts for everything. It's going to take you a whole day to put yourself together."

Early that afternoon they were wandering around the toy store looking for gifts to bring back for Art and Joan's kids. They had found one gift and split up to hunt for one more. When Dolly located Charlie again, she gave him a quick peck on the lips and smiled.

"I found a gift for you too, Charlie. Have a very merry un-birthday." She held up a T-shirt with a sultry picture of Jessica Rabbit emblazoned on it.

CHAPTER 52

Charlie had been with his current psychiatrist for a long time. "I told you that I am moving to a new teaching position. I made a detailed summary for the doctor that I am transferring your care to. I think it's a good idea for me to leave you with a synopsis of what I told him. The summary I gave him was quite detailed so don't worry about that. You have long-standing chronic depression and anxiety. We've tried lots of medication and you're moderately controlled and for now this is about as good as it's going to get."

"I understand."

"There are always new drugs and treatments coming along but there is nothing else right now to try. I explained to you that the movie 'One Flew over the Cuckoo's Nest' grossly exaggerated and misrepresented electroconvulsive therapy. We tried ECT but it did not work for you."

"I know that it works for lots of people. It was not a big deal to go through but it just didn't work for me."

"You still have significant mood swings but your depression is reasonably stable. Although you have side effects from your medications, you put up with them."

The psychiatrist continued. "You have discussed with me many times that you are hoping to go back in time to save Buddy Holly by warning him off the plane that he crashed in. It does not seem realistic to me, but time travel is something that you've worked on for a long time and is something that you are an expert in. So it doesn't appear to be a delusion and you are not psychotic."

"I don't know if it will work until I try it."

CHAPTER 53

Life was relatively good. Charlie had not had a down cycle for months. He thought that with his experiences he might be able to help others cope with their severe depressive episodes, so he considered volunteering at a suicide help line. He discussed the idea with his new doctor and the two people he trusted most, Dolly and Art. In the end he decided to go ahead and help out.

Charlie was trained by experienced support workers. He had sat in and listened to his teachers' phone calls. Then he was supervised on his own phone calls. Charlie was on his first unsupervised call, his first solo flight. He was aware of how some words could make a depressed person feel worse while others were helpful and supportive. Charlie listened but spoke little. He knew that letting the caller talk frankly was important. He felt terrible for the caller. He could feel the caller's pain. He had lived it many times. The vast majority of callers did not commit suicide and they ultimately got help, their depression lifted and long-term supports were put in place. They never told Charlie how his first solo caller had ended his life that night.

At first the anxious fluttering in his gut was unsettling but it could have been just an isolated incident. When it started happening again and again Charlie knew that another down cycle had begun.

He had suffered through down cycles countless times and dreaded what was coming.

He tried to convince himself that he would get through this down cycle just as he had done before and that when this down cycle ended there would be some good times again. He considered whether, whatever pleasures might come his way in the future, it would be worth suffering the ghastly torments again. Charlie made the firm decision to never suffer the agony of another down cycle of depression again. Charlie would not wait until he was so depressed that he did not have the strength to carry out his plan. He was not going back to that bleak place of dark despair and desolation.

The time machine was ready.

He had told both Dolly and Art many times that if he died, they shouldn't feel sorry for him. Instead, they should think of his being at rest from a tortured existence and no longer feeling pain.

He had discarded all his proposed suicide methods except one. His decision had been made. It was firm. The recurrent miseries of his life would soon be over. He felt an inner calmness.

Two major goals of Charlie Harding's had been to end his own miserable existence and to save Buddy Holly. Charlie stared at the newspaper headlines of the February 3, 1959 plane crash: the Mason City Globe-Gazette front page dated Tuesday, February 3, 1959 and the Clear Lake Mirror-Reporter dated Thursday Feb 5, 1959. Having read these pages so many times, Charlie had memorized the details. He knew that the pilot of the Beechcraft Bonanza who had died in the plane crash with Buddy Holly, Ritchie Valens and The Big Bopper was a young man named Roger Peterson. Charlie even knew the names of Roger Peterson's immediate family.

Charlie had started his crusade to meet and try to save Buddy Holly a long time ago. Charlie knew that Buddy Holly would marry Maria Elena Santiago at Buddy's parents' home in Lubbock,

Saving Buddy Holly Blue Days Black Nights

Texas on Friday, August 15, 1958. Charlie set his time machine to Lubbock, August 14, 1958.

Charlie considered the fact that he himself would not likely find out how his quest would turn out. Theoretically everything was correct. But until it was actually tested, he could not be sure that his time machine would work. The time machine was ready. He rechecked the settings. He got into the time machine. He sat down. Then Charlie was gone.

Buddy was walking with his brother Larry when Buddy felt a cold shiver on the back of his neck.

"Buddy?" said Larry.

"I feel like someone just walked over my grave."

CHAPTER 54

In October, 1957, Buddy Holly and the Crickets did a live show in Vancouver, Canada. He was interviewed by the well-known west coast radio deejay Red Robinson.

"'That'll Be the Day' was your first big hit. How long have you and the Crickets been together?"

Buddy answered, "Jerry Allison, the drummer, and myself have been playing together for about four years. We went to grade school and high school together. Then Joe B. Mauldin and Niki Sullivan joined us."

Red continued. "Your song 'Peggy Sue', that you do as a solo is doing real well. "What do you and the Crickets have coming up for records?"

"We got one just released the other day by the Crickets called 'Oh Boy'"

"That's terrific!" Red said excitedly. "We'll be playing it just like the other ones. That'll mean that you've got three songs on our charts when that comes out: 'That'll Be The Day', 'Peggy Sue' and 'Oh Boy'. How do you think 'Oh Boy' compares with the others?"

"I like 'Oh Boy' better than 'That'll Be The Day', Buddy replied.

As you fellows are from Texas and visiting us up here in Canada, tell me what the weather is like in Lubbock these days?"

"It's not quite this cool."

"I bet. And it's only October."

A week later, the Crickets were interviewed by deejay Freeman Hover in Denver, Colorado.

Freeman asked, "Now the name Crickets. Where does this Crickets thing come in?"

Jerry Allison answered. "Well, we were trying to think of some name that hadn't been used before. So we came up with Crickets, and sure enough it had been used before."

"Buddy, I was looking to get a copy of your new record 'Oh Boy'. You got a copy in your room or any place we could have?" asked Freeman.

"No, sir, we don't. Norm can't even get one of those things."

"Norm's a fine lad," Freeman said. We had the privilege of meeting him about a year ago when we were down in Clovis, New Mexico, visiting a relative. We visited his studios there and had a wonderful time. He did some fine work for us too. How did you happen to tie in with my friend Norm Petty?"

"Well, we've known Norm for quite some time. As you probably know, Lubbock and Clovis are about a hundred miles apart and when we are at home, we spend most of our waking hours over in Clovis. We went over there and were making a dub to send in to various companies and see if we could possibly do anything in the line of the music business. Norm asked us if we'd like him to represent us to Brunswick Records in New York. And so we told him, 'Yeah, go ahead. We can't lose.' So he sent it in and Bob Theile, the A & R man for Brunswick okayed it and put it out, and the kids all over the United States did the rest."

It was a month later, on December 1, 1957, that the Crickets performed on the world-famous Sunday night variety show hosted by Ed Sullivan. Niki Sullivan was still with the Crickets as a guitar player at the time. He left the Crickets within weeks of the performance.

The Crickets had performed two songs, 'That'll Be The Day' and 'Peggy Sue'. Ed Sullivan called Buddy over.

"Buddy Holly! Buddy, I want to ask you a question. How old are all of you fellas?"

"Well, there's two eighteen, one twenty, and I'm twenty-one."

"Where do you come from? Lubbock, Texas?"

"Lubbock, Texas, yes, sir."

"You go to school down there?"

"Well, we did, until we got out of high school, finally."

"Have you been a big hit from the start?" asked Ed.

"Well, ah, we've had a few rough times, I guess you'd say," said Buddy," but we've been real lucky, getting it this quick."

"Tex, very nice to have you up here. Let's have a very nice hand for these Texas men."

CHAPTER 55

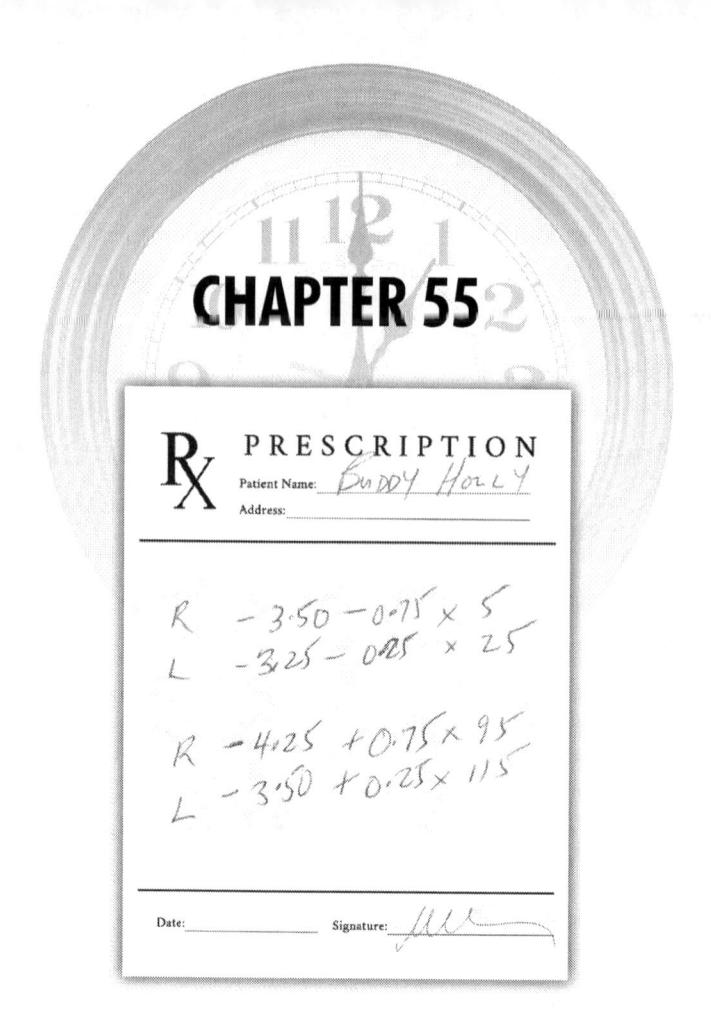

PRESCRIPTION
Patient Name: Buddy Holly
Address:

R −3.50 −0.75 × 5
L −3.25 −0.25 × 25

R −4.25 +0.75 × 95
L −3.50 +0.25 × 115

Date: _____ Signature: _____

While they were in New York in the fall of 1958, Jerry Allison, Buddy's drummer, had found out about an eye doctor who specialized in contact lenses and who looked after many New York celebrities, singers and movie stars. Buddy had his teeth capped just a couple of months before to hide teeth that had been discolored by Lubbock's water. He had been really pleased with the results, so when Jerry said that he had found an optometrist that might be able to fit him with better contact lenses, Buddy seriously considered it.

"Buddy, you are going to be thrilled that you won't have to wear glasses on stage anymore. You know the gals are gonna love you even more without glasses."

"Well, I'm still not sure about putting those things into my eyes again. You remember that when I tried contact lenses back in Texas, I could only wear them for a few minutes at a time before they fogged up and started feeling scratchy. Dr. Armistead finally said I should just stick with glasses."

"But I heard this here doctor is one of the best."

"And I assume one of the most expensive," said Buddy. "But if it works, I can afford it now. I'll give it one more try even though they were a real pain last time."

Buddy called and arranged for a late morning appointment so that he would have time to get to the show later in the day. The boys went along with Buddy.

The cab arrived in front of Dr. Highgild's office. Buddy paid the fare, left a tip and they all stepped out onto the street.

"I'm real nervous about this but here goes nothing," Buddy said as he walked through the opulent entrance. Expensive doctors have expensive doors.

They entered a waiting room with five large luxurious leather chairs. The receptionist sat behind a desk. Lisa was a buxom belle; in fact, buxom was an understatement. Her name tag teetered precariously above her cleavage. Her inter-mammary cleft was amply displayed as her white lab coat was unbuttoned from her midriff up. Her blouse left little to the imagination and she put on quite a show for any red-blooded American male in her vicinity.

"Hello, Mr. Holly. You are right on time," Lisa said formally but with a bright friendly smile. "I already have your information. Lisbeth, the doctor's assistant, will see you first. She will ask you some questions and do some preliminary tests before the doctor sees you. She should be ready for you in just a few minutes."

The boys sat down on the spacious leather chairs in the waiting room. A patient, a smiling young lady approached the receptionist from the back of the office. She was a pretty blonde girl with a ponytail.

"When did the doctor ask you to book your next visit?" asked Lisa.

"Six months," replied the smiling patient.

"You must be doing well."

"Oh yes. I just love my contacts. Is there a charge for today?"

"No," replied Lisa. "The first three months are included in the initial payment that you've already made. For the next visit in six months, you will be billed our regular rates again."

"Thank you. I prefer the afternoons. Wednesday or Thursday, please."

Lisa showed her the appointment card.

"Is this okay?"

"Perfect."

As the blonde young lady left the office Jerry smiled and said, "Cute girl. She reminds me of Peggy Sue."

Joe B. whispered, "Did you see the hardware on that chick Lisa?"

A Jerry whispered back, "She is well-endowed all right."

Lisa's desk had a modesty panel to hide her legs. "I wonder what her hips and legs look like?"

Joe B.'s eyes bugged out further, almost bulging out of their sockets like those of a cartoon character.

Joe B. was screaming in a whisper so that Lisa could not hear him.

"Did you see the broad in the back? She's more wow than this one!"

After a few more minutes of whispering, Jerry ventured boldly over to Lisa at the desk.

"Excuse me, Lisa, ma'am," said Jerry, exhibiting his Texas manners.

She looked up, smiled tantalizingly as she said, "What is it, honey?"

Jerry blushed but continued, hesitating at first and then becoming more bold. "I thought that most contact lens wearers were young women. How come Dr. Highgild has such gorgeous staff? Aren't his lady clients jealous?"

"Well, thank you. Aren't you a dear," she purred. "You're pretty cute yourself, young man." She was in her late 20s. "I don't assist the doctor but too bad you're not getting your eyes checked. Lisbeth could certainly take very good care of you."

Had Lisa really winked? Then almost on cue Lisbeth, the bombshell that Joe B. had noticed earlier, appeared in the corridor. Like Lisa's, her intermammary cleft was riveting with Lisbeth's name tag hanging on for dear life. Lisbeth was a stunning broad – broad was definitely the right word for Lisbeth. Lisbeth was a 36D-22-36. The girl had a wasp waist that made her look like a voluptuous cartoon beauty. Her auburn hair touched her shoulders and it was so flawlessly perfect that it seemed as if it had been drawn that way by a painstaking artist. Her eyes were green. She had eyelashes coated with thick black mascara that were accented with thick black eyeliner. Her eyelids had been painted with lavender blue eye shadow. Bright red lipstick completed the image of her alluring face.

"Follow me, Mr. Holly," Lisbeth purred. There was a lot of purring going on in this office.

"Follow her, Buddy," snickered Joe B.

"I will do some preliminary questioning and testing," Lisbeth continued. Then Dr. Highgild will check your prescription. When he has decided which contact lenses are best for you, Susan over there will show you how to put them in and take them out. Don't worry. Susan is the most patient of us all."

Buddy looked over at Susan and beheld another dazzling broad. He sheepishly followed Lisbeth to one of the examining rooms. The door to the doctor's private office was ajar and Buddy nervously tried to peek inside. After they both were seated, Lisbeth very professionally took Buddy's medical history. Thank goodness he didn't have to talk about VD. His eyes were continually being pulled away from Lisbeth's eyes toward her name tag. Buddy was sure that Lisbeth knew that he wasn't just checking her name over and over again. But he couldn't help it. It was a reflex encoded on the Y chromosome.

Lisbeth batted her long butterfly eyelashes as she asked Buddy, "Could I have your glasses for a moment so that I can measure their strength?"

Saving Buddy Holly Blue Days Black Nights

Buddy handed them over sheepishly. His eyes were naked. As Lisbeth turned to examine the glasses in the lensmeter, Buddy got another peek at the wasp-like contours revealed by her tight-fitting outfit. Even without his glasses the blurred image was making his pulse race. That darned Y chromosome.

Lisbeth used a plastic paddle to cover his left eye, turned on a projector and then asked Buddy, "Which line can you see well enough to read?"

"Without my glasses? The second line."

"What do the top two lines say?"

"The top letter is an 'E'. The first letter on the second line is an 'S' and the second letter looks like a curved stick. Is it an 'L'? Below that I can't make out anything."

After Lisbeth put his glasses back on him, Buddy was able to read to the third line from the bottom. She wrote the information down and then Lisbeth escorted Buddy to the examination room into which Buddy had earlier peeked to get a glimpse of Dr. Highgild. Dr. Highgild was in his 40s but seemed older to young Buddy. There was a picture of the doctor's wife and his two boys on the wall. They exchanged greetings and then Dr. Highgild had Buddy sit in the examining chair.

Buddy looked down at Dr. Highguild's notes. He wondered why the prescription was different than Dr. Armistead's.

"Sir, why are the numbers different on Dr. Armistead's prescription?" Buddy asked.

"It's just a different way of writing the same thing but they are exactly the same. I work in what is called plus cylinder form and Dr. Armistead works in minus cylinder form. That's how I learned at school. I have to convert to minus cylinder anyway because that's what we use to calculate the contact lens power. Don't worry. I know what I'm doing. If you told me something about music, I would trust you even if I didn't understand it."

Buddy nodded. "Yes sir. Thank you. I think I get the idea. It's like F sharp and G flat are the same sound just written a different way."

"That's right."

Dr. Highgild did some calculations on the paper chart. The doctor then examined Buddy's eyes. After a few passes of a small flashlight from one eye to the other, he had Buddy sit forward and put his head into a large microscope. Buddy's head rested on a chin rest covered with a flimsy piece of paper for cleanliness. After more bright lights, a blue light gizmo came very close to Buddy's eyes. He didn't feel anything at all.

After the doctor had scribbled some more notes Susan, the assistant that Lisa had mentioned earlier, entered the room. Dr. Highgild told Buddy that he would see him again soon. Susan took Buddy into another smaller room. Susan saw how nervous Buddy was and suggested that he take a few big breaths to relax himself. At first Buddy thought that she had said big breasts.

Buddy recalled his previous experience with contact lenses in Lubbock; nevertheless, he was stoically able to deal with the situation. Given his trepidation, he was still not at all like the patient Dr. Armistead had told him about, who had put his head down, cupped his hands over his eyes and then said, "Okay. Go ahead. Put them in."

As Susan was inserting the contact lenses, Buddy's eyes would drift down and glance over at her cleavage, thus proving again that even in front of a firing squad, the male libido would still notice the bust of a hot wench walking by. That darned Y chromosome again.

Jerry and Joe B. were waiting in the reception area and Lisa would periodically look over and give the young fellows the eye. Lisa was about ten years older than the guys but was enjoying flirting with them.

"Too bad you fellows don't have appointments. Lisbeth could check you guys out too," purred Lisa. Purring again.

Behind Lisa the boys noticed Lisbeth moving around at the back of the corridor. She was wearing red stilettos. Joe B. and Jerry leered at Lisbeth. As Lisbeth breathed, her chest heaved sensually.

Saving Buddy Holly Blue Days Black Nights

The vastness of her bust placed her center of gravity so far forward that it seemed next to impossible for her to remain upright on her spiked heels and not fall forward onto her face and breasts. The boys began to argue and giggle about physics and gravity. They invoked mass, density and levers. They laughed and debated whether her bosom would cushion her fall if she tipped over.

Eventually Buddy was back in Dr. Highgild's examining room. The contacts had been too uncomfortable for Buddy. Contacts were not going to work for him.

Buddy said, "I guess my eyes are real bad. I have too much stigmatism."

Dr. Highgild said, "The word is 'astigmatism' not 'stigmatism'. You have a little astigmatism but it's almost insignificant. Astigmatism is a little hard to explain. It sounds bad but it's just another type of glasses. Actually, you're moderately nearsighted. That means that without glasses you see things better up close than far away. Your eyes are completely healthy otherwise."

"But I'm almost blind, doc."

"People find it hard to understand but being blind means not being able to see even with glasses. That's blind. It's what we call best-corrected vision that's important. In other words, what we can correct your vision to with glasses determines whether you are defined as legally blind or not. Your glasses may well be a nuisance, especially in your business but, young man, your eyes are healthy."

The doctor gave Buddy a prescription.

"This is your glasses prescription. It's similar to what you are wearing now. Keep it in your wallet in case you break yours."

Buddy came back to the reception desk where Lisa presented Buddy with the bill. Buddy paid cash. As he stood over her desk, he took another sneaky glance at Lisa's Jane Russell figure. Then he went out the door with Joe B. and Jerry.

♪♫♪♫

Jerry hailed a cab and on the way back to their hotel, they discussed the events of the last hour.

"Those things felt just as bad as the ones that Dr. Armistead tried back in Lubbock," said Buddy.

Joe B. said, "Listen, Buddy, at least you could afford to try again and now you know that you have to accept that you'll always wear glasses."

"You're right. Sometimes you gotta try and fail just so you know that you did your all. After I tried contacts, Dr. Armistead back in Lubbock told me he would be on the lookout for some really fancy glasses for me. He said that the next time he was in Mexico he'd try to find something really cool. He told me that it might be a good idea to make glasses part of my image." Even if they come up with something newer and better than glasses or contact lenses, I don't know if I'd do it."

Jerry said, "No, Buddy. You want to be remembered as a musician and not for your glasses. Maybe one day they will invent a simple operation to get rid of glasses."

The cabbie looked in the mirror as the boys indulged themselves in playful horse play. Boyish good-natured fun permeated the air as good friends enjoyed the silliness and mirth.

The conversation turned to the girls in the doctor's office. They discussed the pros and cons of an inch here and there: 36-24-36 versus 37-25-36 versus 38-26-36. Joe B. Said that he thought adding an inch to the waist was well worth it to get an extra inch on top, but Jerry said that he preferred a 24-inch waist because 36 inches in the boobs was more than adequate. They argued about the age-old question of whether more than a handful was a waste.

Joe B. said, "Listen guys, let's face it. They all were very nicely proportioned."

Jerry was astonished and said, "Nicely proportioned! Give me a break, boy. Stacked is the word. Stacked, stacked, stacked! If one of them got too close to you, she could poke your eyes out."

Joe B. said, "And the necklines went down almost to never never land."

Jerry said, "Lisa reminds me of Jane Russell."

Buddy said, "I remember a few years ago when Elvis was in Lubbock, a few of us went out with Elvis and saw the movie 'Gentlemen Prefer Blondes'. Jack, Sonny and Don came along with me and Elvis. Jane Russell and Marilyn Monroe starred in that movie."

Joe B. said, "Susan makes me think of Rita Hayworth."

Jerry said, "Yeah, I agree that Susan looks a lot like Rita Hayworth. But Lisbeth, I don't know who she reminds me of, but she has one hell of a booby trap. Hey, Buddy, what do you think?"

Buddy looked dreamily out of the cab window and toward the horizon and said quietly, "You know, that Lisbeth chick reminds me of Jessica Rabbit."

"Who the heck is Jessica Rabbit?"

Buddy had a strange, confused look on his face as he answered quietly, "I don't know."

CHAPTER 56

Buddy and Maria Elena, his wife of only six months, were living on Fifth Avenue in New York City. The Crickets, Jerry Allison and Joe B. Mauldin, had split with Buddy in November, 1958. Buddy had been talking about going on a tour to make some money, but Maria did not like the idea of Buddy's going on the Winter Dance Party tour.

"You don't need to do this," she said. "It's not the right thing for someone like you to do. You're a big star and shouldn't be touring on buses."

"I'd take you along but you're still getting nauseous from the pregnancy," Buddy replied. "This will be like the Summer Dance Party that I did last summer."

"I want you here to give me support."

Buddy said, "I know. It's only a three-week tour and I need to do this. I want to bring some money in. It's time for me to go to work. I'm not going to keep asking your aunt to lend us money. I want to start paying her back. Aunt Provi has already lent us and given us plenty."

"Buddy, remember when you asked my Aunt Provi to let us go on our first date? Since my mom died over twenty years ago, she's been like a mother to me. Helping their kids and making their lives easier is what my people do. Aunt Provi always told me that what was mine was mine and what was hers was mine too. She was joking but she meant it. She tells me that it makes her feel good to help us. She just wants to make our lives easier. We should pay her back but there is no rush."

"My family is like that too," said Buddy. "Larry always helped me with money when I needed guitars and stuff, but I still think it's not right to keep taking from Aunt Provi when I could easily go out and make money. Norman owes us a lot of money, but I can't wait for that anymore. The idea that lawyers and accountants are holding things up drives me nuts. In Lubbock I was taught that a handshake was a deal," lamented Buddy. "I always trusted Norman. I just can't believe he's cheating me. Norman said he is being screwed around by the record companies and business folks in New York."

Maria had lived and worked in New York since she was a little girl. "New York is not Texas," she said.

"Vi treated me and the boys like family. Norman sometimes treated me like the son he never had. I know that Jerry said he thought we were being ripped off by Norman when he added his name as a writer to songs. Norman explained that it was only fair. He let us use his studio for a lot of time that he didn't charge us for. Getting writer royalties for songs was how he got paid back for that session time. He told us that if the records never sold, he would never get paid for a lot of his work. Maybe we made a mistake in trusting Norman, but it made sense back then. I always trusted Norman. I think I still do." Buddy went on. "Without Norman, who knows where I'd be in my career. When I went to Nashville, the session turned out real bad. They really screwed up 'That'll Be the Day'. The Crickets didn't really start making it until we went to Norman. I miss those guys."

Maria said, "You said that Jerry, Joe B. and you had misgivings about splitting up. I remember they said they didn't want to move to New York like we did."

"I'd love to get back together with them. We were so good together. Jerry and I have been friends since junior high school."

"I wouldn't be surprised if they called you to get back together again," said Maria.

"I sure would like that. What a silly way it happened. First one dumb word then another one and before we knew it, we had split up. Maybe I'll call them and we could work out something. It's only been a couple of months and I really miss those guys."

Maria was starting to accept that Buddy would not back down about going on the Winter Dance Party tour. "Who are you going to get to play with you if you go on this tour?"

"I know an awful lot of good musicians. I'll ask Waylon and Tommy."

Maria Elena dreamt about a ball of fire falling out of the sky. She awoke screaming.

CHAPTER 57

The bus rides on the Winter Dance Party Tour were far from glamorous. As the buses were poorly heated, the musicians would sleep in their clothes and coats for heat. For the most part, the tour was: get on the bus, do the show and get back on the bus.

Buddy was daydreaming. Would the heaters work well enough so that they didn't have to burn newspapers in the bus again to keep warm? Transportation between shows had been an immense problem as their buses broke down repeatedly. On their way to Green Bay for the February 1 show, their bus had broken down. A passing truck driver saw them and alerted the sheriff's office. Deputies had come out and saved them. The driver and his passengers had been fortunate that none of them had lost a limb or died of exposure. Carl Bunch, their drummer, got frostbite and had to be admitted to hospital. Wisconsin's winter was so bad in 1959 that people died.

There was little time between shows and travelling for them to get enough rest or get their clothes cleaned. Waylon Jennings would later say that they smelled like billy goats. Buddy had hoped to get to Moorhead, Minnesota early after the Clear Lake show so he would have time to do laundry and get some good quality sleep.

Buddy complained to Ritchie, "All this freezing cold weather is really starting to upset me."

Ritchie had a cold and sighed. "I'm sick of this cold too. I wish I was back home in California."

"We should have been on a southern tour at this time of year. Now I know what the expression bone-chilling means."

"Bone-chilling," repeated Ritchie.

Buddy said, "I sure could use some time in Hawaii right now like when I went to Australia with Jerry, Joe B., Norman and Vi. The weather has gotta be a lot nicer than here in Iowa, right Ritchie?"

"I'd love to be anywhere warm."

"Has anybody heard of anyone being hit by lightning while playing an electric guitar outside?" asked somebody on the bus.

Buddy was the one who answered. "I've never heard of that, but my mother told me about a farmer who was hit by hail near Lubbock when I was two years old. He's the only person in America that ever got killed by hail. Now that was fate."

The Big Bopper, who his friends called Jape, said, "I think I'd want to know when I'm gonna die so that I can plan for it. Not exactly when I die and, for sure, not how."

"Not me," disagreed Tommy Allsup, "I'd worry about it all the time. I just want a hailstone or airplane to fall on my head and kill me before I even realize what happened."

"Hey that's not funny," Ritchie snapped. "Two planes crashed over my school and lots of kids in the yard got killed. One was my best friend."

"Holy shit!" said Tommy. "I'm sorry. Were you okay?"

"I was lucky, I guess," Ritchie mumbled. "I was at my grandpa's funeral."

Buddy said, "You wonder if fate doesn't put a person in the right place at the right time. Or worse, put the person in the wrong place at the wrong time."

Waylon Jennings said, "If we survive this tour, I wonder what fate will have in store for each of us?"

"Waylon, I'm sure that you're gonna be a big star someday. When we get back to Lubbock, I have big plans for you," said Buddy.

Jape chimed in. "A rock 'n' roll or country singer." Jape was older and wiser than the others. "Maybe we can't control our future but if you want to succeed in life, nobody else is gonna do the work for you. To be a big success in anything you gotta work hard and be lucky too."

Buddy continued. "Talk about fate. My brothers fought in the War. Travis was at Iwo Jima."

"What hell he must have seen."

Buddy continued, "But he got through it somehow. I wasn't even ten years old when Travis came back after the war and taught me how to play guitar. If Travis was killed, maybe I would never have had a hit song and then I wouldn't be here on this bus with you guys freezing my ass off. That's fate."

"It sure makes you think, doesn't it?" said Jape.

Buddy went on. "We've all heard of Hiroshima. Have you heard of Nagasaki? It's where the second atomic bomb was dropped. Right after that Japan surrendered and the War was over. If the War hadn't ended then, my older brother Larry was going to be in the first group of Marines to land just south of Nagasaki. Larry told me that he heard that if his division had landed there before the War ended, they'd expected to have 95% casualties. Dropping the atomic bombs probably saved Larry's life. And maybe Travis's too. Oh Lord. My poor mother. It's awful to think how many more Americans would've died if the War had kept up even a little longer."

Everyone on the bus was paying attention and considering what Buddy was saying.

"Even my eye doctor fought in the Pacific and survived to look after my family. He was the one who found me these fancy glasses in Mexico. Dr. Armistead told me some cool stuff about his own family. He had a relative, General Armistead, who got killed at Gettysburg. Also another Armistead commanded Fort McHenry where the Star-Spangled Banner was written. Boy, do I feel lucky that I haven't had to fight in a war. Maybe World War II will really be the war to end all wars and the last time that America sends its boys to die."

CHAPTER 58

It was Groundhog Day, February 2, 1959, another frigid day in Clear Lake, Iowa. The Winter Dance Party was playing at The Surf Ballroom. As the crowd of 1,500 people swarmed in they could see the stage on their left. Straight ahead of them was the large wooden dance floor. The dance floor was encircled by booths, at some points seven rows deep. Half the attendees were unable to get seats and stood to watch the performances.

The show started with the relatively unknown Frankie Sardo. He appeared on the bottom of the Winter Dance Party poster below Dion and The Belmonts. Buddy and his Crickets topped the poster with the Big Bopper and Ritchie Valens sharing equal billing on either side. Rock 'n' roll filled the ballroom. The awestruck audience beheld their idols and danced along. Ritchie Valens, The Big Bopper, Dion and his Belmonts all performed their sets. The Surf was the place to be for a good time and warmth on this bitterly cold Iowa night. The young crowd was thrilled to be entertained by these top recording stars.

Then it was Buddy's turn. He was being backed by his alternate Crickets, Waylon Jennings and Tommy Allsup. Buddy had brought them for this tour as the original Crickets, Jerry Allison and Joe B. Mauldin, had split with Buddy several months before. The show would be ending soon and the throng was jamming closer to the stage. The kids adored him and his rock 'n' roll. Buddy was

Saving Buddy Holly Blue Days Black Nights

rightfully proud of his music: singing, playing and writing. He could not have imagined that decades later his fans would come from all over the world to dance on this same floor, in this same building and to the same music that Buddy was playing. He had no idea that some of the kids watching and listening to him right then would return here and meet Charlie Harding and Dolly years later. But the tragedy of February 3, 1959 had not yet occurred and if it had been up to Buddy's family, friends and fans, the airplane crash that was soon to occur would never have happened.

Buddy had been thinking about a better way to get around than on those darn buses. There had to be something warmer and more reliable. Earlier in the day Buddy had found the manager of the Surf Ballroom Carroll Anderson and asked him if it were possible to get a plane to the next show in Moorhead, Minnesota. Mr. Anderson had arranged it all for him. Buddy had always loved flying and had even taken a few lessons on a small plane back home in Lubbock.

Before the show, Buddy had told the others of his plan to skip the bus ride, get some of their clothes laundered and get some warm rest in a hotel room. The plan had been to have Buddy, Waylon and Tommy fly to the next show. Jape had the flu and Waylon kindly allowed Jape to take his place on the plane. Ritchie had been begging Tommy over and over to give him his spot on the plane. Tommy finally agreed to a coin toss for his seat. The momentous coin flip transpired. Ritchie called heads and then cried out, "I win! I never win anything." Ritchie had a seat on the plane.

Tommy told Buddy that he had flipped a half-dollar with Ritchie and that Ritchie would be taking his seat on the plane.

Buddy asked, "Was that a Kennedy half-dollar?"

Tommy asked quizzically, "Kennedy half-dollar? Who's Kennedy?"

Buddy was perplexed too. "I have no idea. I don't know where that came from."

Gerald I. Goldlist

♪♫♪♫

Buddy was happy after the show. He saw the Surf's Carroll Anderson.

"Thank you so much for driving us to the airport, Mr. Anderson. How far is it from here?"

"Just a couple of miles to Mason City Airport. It'll take no time at all. Everything is set there for takeoff. You'll be flying in Jerry Dwyer's airplane. There's a young fellow lined up to fly you up to Fargo. When you get there, it'll be nothing to grab a cab from the Fargo Airport and then across the river to Moorhead. You'll find a room there no problem."

"Thanks for everything, Mr. Anderson. We enjoyed playing here at The Surf. I'd love to come back some day. Maybe in the summer."

Just as Buddy was about to go outside into the cold, he said to Waylon, "You're a good fella to give up your spot to Jape. I hope your old bus freezes up."

Waylon laughed and then said something that he would regret for the rest of his life. "Well, I hope your old plane crashes."

CHAPTER 59

Jape, the Big Bopper, asked the pilot, "Whew. How cold is it?"
Roger Peterson responded, "At midnight it was eighteen."
"Eighteen! Oh man!"

Buddy stepped out of the office into the frigid night. He huddled up his coat's fur collar. He walked briskly toward the plane, wondering once more what a Texas boy was doing in Iowa in this February freeze. Suddenly he clutched his temples. His eyes squeezed shut. He shook his head as disturbing thoughts crept into his consciousness.

What is this? What's wrong? Something in my head is telling me not to get on the plane. Maria told me not to fly on small planes because of her dreams last month. That's ridiculous. Dreams are just dreams.

There was a struggle going on in Buddy's mind.

Something in my brain seems to know that I must not get on that plane.

The eerie conflict continued in his mind.

Am I going insane?

It was difficult to read the registration ID on the plane waiting on the runway. In his head Buddy heard, "No! No! 3794." As he pressed forward, the registration became clearer. He saw the wing number of the plane: N3794N.

Ritchie was walking ahead of Buddy and sneezed.

"I know it's cold," Buddy called out. "Just give me a second to catch my breath. I'll be with you guys directly."

He squatted on his haunches, looked down and closed his eyes. Buddy took three slow deep breaths. The plane was only twenty feet away, a red and white Beechcraft Bonanza with seats for four people: the pilot and three passengers.

What was going on in his head?

It's like a dream talking to me. It's like the time I was hypnotized, and it felt like someone else was trying to get control of my mind.

He had been told that even when you're hypnotized no one can make you do what you don't want to do. Something inside his mind was not forcing him but was trying to convince him not to get onto the plane. Buddy saw a misty indistinct image within his soul. It was the front page of a newspaper. He saw "Death" in the headline. "Death".

He opened his eyes and looked around at the flat expanse before him. Buddy did not want to make a fool of himself in front of his companions. He did not want them to think that he was acting crazy.

Tiny snowflakes were drifting down and landing on his glasses. Buddy started to get up and move toward the plane. His knees were straightening when the front page of a Clear Lake newspaper flashed into his head again. His knees buckled and he was deep in a crouch with his eyes closed again. He was seeing the front page of the Clear Lake Mirror-Reporter. "Death of... Shocks Nation" was the headline. Buddy had looked through the local newspaper late that afternoon before the show, but his tired mind and body must be playing tricks on him. The newspaper page he was seeing in his mind was not the one that he had read earlier that afternoon. It was not even today's headline that Buddy was seeing. His mind was whirling and confused. He was tired. He was cold and his brain was sending him strange messages. He felt sure that he had seen this headline before. He had never been to Clear Lake except for this Winter Dance Party tour, yet he felt certain that the front page was one that he had read before. Although it was very cold, he was perspiring.

I'm overtired, he thought.

He opened his eyes and closed them again. He was afraid of embarrassing himself and started to get up. He thought the sooner they got to Fargo, the sooner he would get some rest.

The image was clearing: "Death of Singers." It looked familiar. "He knew, did not remember, he knew what it said." There were two pictures on the front page. Buddy stopped fighting the invading mind and let the alien thoughts come to the fore. He had seen this newspaper before. He had read this many times. He knew what it said. But how? The tiny line above the headline was coming into focus now. The date line said, "CLEAR LAKE, IOWA, THURSDAY, FEBRUARY 5, 1959."

Thursday? Today is... What time is it? Today is the morning of February 3rd. Yesterday was Monday. We just played on Monday night. Today is Tuesday. The newspaper is dated two days from now.

"The Clear Lake Mirror-Reporter" was now clearly visible in his mind's eye. Under it Buddy could see in larger and bolder print, "DEATH OF SINGERS HERE SHOCKS NATION." The next line read, "Rock 'n' Rollers, Pilot Die in Tragic Plane Crash." He saw the gruesome photos of a crumpled crashed small plane and the bodies of three of the four victims. The dark lumps on the ground were identified as "Ritchie Valens, lower center; Buddy Holly, far left; and J.P.Richardson, across fence."

His whole body went numb and cold. It was not the cold of an Iowa winter night but the cold feeling of the blood draining from his body. It was the same coldness that Ebenezer Scrooge must have felt when he saw the vision of his own funeral. Buddy was seeing his own obituary, an obituary that was soon to be written. The front page of the Clear Lake newspaper was announcing the death of Buddy Holly and the young men with him right now.

His mind's eye envisioned a gravestone with a guitar engraved on it. He had visited this grave. It was the gravestone of Buddy

Holley, spelled with an "E". It was engraved with the date September 7, 1936 and February 3, 1959. Today is February 3, 1959.

Ritchie looked over. "Buddy, are you alright?"

"Maybe," came back a whisper. And then Buddy's strength and resolve began to grow. "Excuse me. Pilot Roger! Roger, do you know my wife's maiden name?

Roger replied, "I didn't even know you were married."

"My wife's maiden name is Santiago and your wife's maiden name is Lenz.

"That's right," said Roger. "We just got married a few months ago."

"Roger, I have two older brothers and a sister? Do you know their names?"

"Mr. Holly?" said Roger deferentially.

"Call me Buddy."

"How would I know their names?" Roger was puzzled.

Wondering what was going on, Jape and Ritchie came closer.

Jape sneezed. He was tired and cold. "Buddy, it's freezing. We need to get going. The sooner we leave, the sooner we'll be in a warm room in Fargo or Moorhead."

Buddy spoke slowly and evenly. His voice was calm. "Fellas, we've spent a lot of time together over the last ten days. Something weird just happened to me. I don't know exactly what to call it. It was a sign or a warning."

"Buddy, you sound really tired," Jape interrupted.

"Buddy, let's get on the plane and talk there," Ritchie pleaded.

"Fellas," Buddy continued, "we mustn't get on the plane."

"What?" said Ritchie.

"Ritchie, Jape, I know if we get on that airplane, we're never going to see our family and friends or anyone in this life ever again. I feel like something is warning me that the plane is going to crash. Tonight."

Jape said, "I don't want to quarrel with you at one in the morning in this freezing weather. Buddy you're just exhausted. Have you been reading horror stories lately?"

Buddy had already decided that he was not getting on the plane. Buddy Holly, once he had made up his mind, was like a huge ocean liner, hard to turn. He tried to convince the others.

"Roger," Buddy said in a calm steady voice, "Do you know the names of my brothers and sisters?"

The other two were quiet.

"Buddy, of course I don't know their names," answered Roger.

"Roger, your parents like the letter 'R' for the beginning of boys' names."

"Is he right?"

"Well, pretty much."

"Your sister's name is Janet."

"How did you know that?"

Buddy continued, "I don't know how, but I know. Ronald and Robert and Janet."

"Dammit! How did you know that?"

"Is he right, Roger?" asked Ritchie, his eyes growing wide.

"Yes, he's right. How can Buddy know that? We just met a few minutes ago."

"Listen," said Buddy, "Please trust me on this. I just know it. I won't go for sure. Fellas, don't get on that plane."

And so Charlie Harding had done it. Charlie had achieved his goal: he had warned Buddy Holly off the plane.

Jape said, "Buddy, I believe that you've got a spooky feeling about the plane. Let's compromise. Do you think you know when the plane is gonna crash?"

Buddy answered, "About 1:00 a.m. is the time. Around this time. Now. Any minute. If we leave, we will crash right after takeoff."

"So let's wait a few hours and leave after 2:30 or even 3:00. Then we can still get in early enough tomorrow to get a break before the show in Moorhead. What do you say, Buddy?"

"Jape, I don't want to argue about it. We shouldn't get on any plane tonight."

Ritchie agreed. "Okay, man. If some spirit is telling you to stay off of that plane, I'm not going either."

Then Jape said, "Buddy, you look like you've seen a ghost. Okay, I won't tempt fate on this. Let's get back inside and warm up. Then we can think of another way to get to Moorhead for the show tomorrow."

Tightened muscles began to relax all over Buddy's body. A tiny tense smile appeared on his face. Ritchie and Jape smiled and then laughed. At first there were little nervous laughs and then chuckles and finally they all broke into nervous guffaws. Peals of laughter rang out over the runway.

When the four of them walked into the warm office near the hangar, Jerry Dwyer, the owner of the plane, was still there.

"Is something wrong?"

Buddy answered, "I just had this fear of flying come over me. I can't explain it. It overcame me as we were about to get on the plane."

"You aren't pulling my leg, are you?"

"Keep the money we paid you. If you don't mind, we'd just like to sit here, warm up and think for a bit."

Jape spoke next, "Buddy, I feel better now about not flying tonight. The bus is gone though. We have to figure out how we're going to get to Moorhead."

Buddy said, "Jape, let's calm down and give it some thought. I'm sure we'll have a solution directly."

Jerry Dwyer started toward the door. "I'm on my way home, fellas. You are welcome to stay for as long as want. I'll get you a refund for the gas. Roger should get paid for his time though. Roger, will you give these guys a ride to a motel or something?"

"Sure thing, Mr. Dwyer. Goodnight. See you."

The door closed leaving the three singers and the pilot.

Buddy stood up. "I have it! Let's try and get a car and drive to Moorhead. It'll take longer but at least we'll get there in one piece."

Buddy turned to face Roger. "Roger, can you help us find a car to rent so we can drive to Moorhead for tomorrow's show?"

Roger thought for a moment. His small-town honesty and friendliness were enhanced even more by the awe of being with famous rock stars and so he said, "I can lend you mine. My car is here. You can drive me home then take off north."

"Maybe take off is not the right word," Jape said. "Does the heater in your car work?"

"Just fine," Roger replied.

"Sounds good to me. It's better than a freezing bus," said Ritchie with a smile.

"Listen, Roger, we'll be real careful with your car, the weather being real bad and all, but how will we get your car back to you?" Buddy asked.

Roger was thinking, not realizing what hung in the balance. Two identical snowflakes fell to earth. Fate, all the forces of the planets, the solar system, the galaxy and the cosmos were falling into place. Forces were being brought to bear on this tiny point in time. Somewhere an hourglass was tipping over about to shatter and spill its contents. Time lines converged as the words came out of Roger's mouth.

"I was planning to pick up some stuff in Fargo anyway." His answer was predestined and foreordained. "I'll drive."

About the Author

Gerry Goldlist is a retired Canadian physician, who practised ophthalmology in Toronto from 1976 to 2016. While researching this book he became an expert on Buddy Holly. In 2006, his article entitled "The Definitive Story of Buddy Holly's Glasses" was published in the "Canadian Journal of Ophthalmology". The article highlights the letter Gerry received from Buddy's optometrist, the man who prescribed those famous glasses.

Gerry met Buddy fans from all over the world in Clear Lake, Iowa at the Winter Dance Party and Buddy Holly Tribute that happens yearly at the Surf Ballroom where Buddy last played. He has also met family and friends of Buddy Holly in Lubbock, Texas, Buddy's hometown, including Peggy Sue herself, who is seen holding Gerry's guitar in the above photo.

Gerry continues to live with the love of his life, Leza, his wife of over 50 years. After a hectic schedule for his whole life, he now spends as much time as possible relaxing at his cottage, staring at the lake and fire. His current hobbies are: baseball's Blue Jays and watching the insanity of American politics.

Manufactured by Amazon.ca
Bolton, ON